D0445050

I AM THE
MISSION

I AM THE MISSION

THE UNKNOWN ASSASSIN
BOOK 2

ALLEN ZADOFF

LITTLE, BROWN AND COMPANY
NEW YORK   BOSTON

Little, Brown and Company

Hachette Book Group
237 Park Avenue, New York, NY 10017
Visit our website at lb-teens.com

Little, Brown and Company is a division of Hachette Book Group, Inc.
The Little, Brown name and logo are trademarks of Hachette Book Group, Inc.

The publisher is not responsible for websites (or their content) that are not owned by the publisher.

First Edition: June 2014

Library of Congress Cataloging-in-Publication Data

Zadoff, Allen.
  I am the mission : a novel / by Allen Zadoff. — First edition.
    pages cm. — (Boy Nobody ; [1])
  Summary: "Teen assassin Boy Nobody is sent on a mission to assassinate the head of a domestic terrorism cell, but his mission turns up more questions about his job than answers" — Provided by publisher.
  ISBN 978-0-316-19969-8 (hardcover) — ISBN 978-0-316-25504-2 (library edition ebook) — ISBN 978-0-316-25502-8 (ebook) [1. Assassins—Fiction. 2. Brainwashing—Fiction.] I. Title.
  PZ7.Z21Iam 2014
  [Fic]—dc23

                                                                        2013024561

10 9 8 7 6 5 4 3 2 1

RRD-C

Printed in the United States of America

I AM THE
MISSION

I STAND ON THE ROCKS HIGH ABOVE A LAKE.

The water below me is inky green, waves lapping gently against the banks of a shade-dappled cove. It's a warm summer's evening, but I know the water will be cool here under these trees.

Cool and deep.

We're not supposed to be here at all, much less climb the rocks and high-dive from the top. The camp counselors think it's dangerous, and they're right. If you angle it wrong, hit the shallow water, slip and tumble and smack the rocks, you could hurt yourself.

Or worse. You could break your neck. That's why this place is strictly off-limits.

Not that I care.

It is the evening of the third day since I've come here—a summer sports camp for boys located in southern Vermont near the New Hampshire border. I am a CIT, a counselor in training. Or so they think. There are campers and counselors who have met me, but they do not know who I am. My real identity.

They do not know there is a soldier among them.

I look at the water below me.

It's dangerous to jump from up here. That's what they say. Most kids are afraid to do it.

Not me.

I jump.

There's a thrilling sensation as I leap into space, open air around me, and then I am falling, falling, my speed increasing as I plunge headfirst into the lake. My angle is perfect and it sends me down through the water like a bullet. I kick to increase the depth of my dive, and the black bottom rushes up fast. For a second it looks like I misjudged, kicked too hard, and I'm going to smash into the lake floor and snap my neck. I stretch my arms out in front of me, brace for the sickening crunch of bone against rock.

It doesn't come.

The water resistance slows me down just in time for my fingertips to lightly touch the bottom.

I settle there. I pick up two heavy stones and hold them in my hands, using them to weigh me down.

I stay where it is quiet and dark, where no people or thoughts can disturb me. My last mission was only a week ago, but it seems far away now.

The girl seems far away. I can't see her face in the darkness.

I'm grateful for this.

My lungs are burning, the oxygen depleted in my system. I let them burn. The pain feels good.

I am trained to deal with pain, to absorb its intensity, spreading it across my body until it disperses through the entire neural network.

Physical pain is easy. It's the other kind that's new to me. The emotional kind.

My body is screaming for oxygen now, but I deny it, staying down an additional two minutes.

Pain control. It's good practice.

When I'm ready, I push off the bottom and hard-kick my way to the surface. That's when I see him. A boy standing on the riverbank, watching me.

How did I miss him? Even underwater, I should be able to detect this level of attention directed toward me.

The boy says, "You were down there so long I thought you were dead."

"You wish."

He smiles and so do I.

This boy's name is Peter. He is a CIT in the bunk next to mine. I met him three days ago, and he has become my friend. An instant and easy friend.

I am expert at making friends. It's what I've been taught to do.

Or at least pretend to do.

"I saw you jump from the cliff," Peter says, astonishment on his face.

"That's not a cliff," I say.

I climb out of the lake, shake water from my hair.

"It looks like a cliff to me," he says, looking up at the rocks. "A scary friggin' cliff."

"Everything is scary to you. You play soccer with a mouth guard."

"I like my teeth. You can't fault me for that."

"I like my teeth, too. But I'm not afraid to lose a couple for the cause."

"What cause? This isn't the army; it's a stupid sports camp."

The bell from the dining hall rings in the distance.

"Is it dinnertime already?" I say.

"Second bell. That's why I came to find you."

Two bells. We only get three. Then we miss dinner for being late.

They're trying to force some discipline onto the campers, and as CITs, we're supposed to lead by example.

"Let's get going," I say. "I'm starved."

I pick up my T-shirt from the bank where I left it earlier. I slip it on as we head to camp.

Peter turns his back to me, exposing himself to danger without knowing it. An attack from the blind spot is always the most effective. Before Peter realized what was happening, it would be too late.

"What are they serving tonight?" I say.

Peter looks back at me. I keep an appropriate distance, four feet. Nothing that will cause him to be alarmed.

"It's Fish Thursday," he says. "That means excessive stink factor."

I grin at him.

"You never laugh," he says.

"I laugh."

"You smile. You don't laugh."

"What's it to you?"

"Nothing. I'm just saying."

This is why I limit my connection with people. They start to pay attention and ask questions. I look at Peter, the flop of brown hair that falls onto his forehead every time he moves his head. He is not a danger to me now. He's just talking.

"You seem serious today," he says. "Something bothering you?"

My thoughts drift to my last mission, a girl's eyes looking up at me in a silent plea for mercy.

"Have you ever done anything you regret?" I say. The words slip out before I realize what I'm saying.

"That's some question," Peter says.

Peter is sixteen like me. But he is a normal kid from the suburbs, a kid in eleventh grade, a kid who thinks he knows what's going on in the world but who has seen nothing.

I'm sixteen, but I've already lived two lives. I've seen people die. I've done the killing myself.

"Forget I asked," I say.

He doesn't speak, just walks with me through the forest that leads back to camp.

"My brother," he says. "That's what I regret."

"I didn't know you had a brother."

"He doesn't talk to me anymore."

"You had a fight?"

"He was using drugs a couple years ago and I found out and told my parents. Now he's at boarding school on the other side of the country, and I'm the asshole brother who betrayed him."

"If he was using, you might have saved his life."

"Yeah, maybe. Or maybe it was just a phase and I ruined his life. Hard to know."

"I think you did the right thing."

"That's what the counselor at school told me. But I don't know. If I was loyal, maybe I would have kept my mouth shut."

I look at Peter. I detect no lies, no subterfuge. He's not trying to trick me or make me like him. He's just telling a story, as friends do.

"What about you?" Peter says. "What do you regret?"

I asked the question, but I can't answer it. I'm forbidden to give details about missions past or present.

I live a secret life. Nobody knows the things I do or why I do them.

"A girl." That's all I can say.

"A hot girl?"

I smile. "Very hot."

"Did you two sleep together?"

"I don't want to talk about it."

Peter is arm's length away, inside the kill zone.

"I just wonder what you regret about her," he says.

The dinner bell rings for the third time.

"Everything," I say.

HE APPEARS IN A DREAM THAT DOES NOT FEEL LIKE A DREAM.

My father.

I am twelve years old, the time before The Program changed my life forever. My father is next to me, his arm warm around my shoulders.

When I am awake, I don't think about my father's death. My feelings about it are buried far away, where they cannot distract me. But when I am asleep, the memories return, along with the incredible pain of losing him.

In the dream, my father has something important to tell me. It's something he needs me to understand, something critical to my survival.

I lean toward him. He opens his mouth to speak—

But instead of his voice, I hear a popping noise, something like the sound a can of soda makes when you pull the top.

The noise is familiar to me. It is the pop of a gas grenade, and in my mind's eye, I see the familiar oblong metal encasement, a top with a pull ring. Yank and throw, and the grenade hits the floor and rolls as it has been designed to do.

If this was a real noise, it will be followed by something else.

The hissing sound of escaping gas. That is what I hear now.

Move. Quickly.

By the time I know the grenade is real, my body is already in motion. I roll out of my bunk and hit the floor.

I stay low because gas rises. It's a warm summer's night, but I know from my training that the gas will be warmer than the air at initial release. It will rise until it hits the roof, then collapse on itself and fall toward the floor. I have time. Seconds. Perhaps as much as half a minute.

No more.

I know all this without thinking. I know it instinctually, and that is enough, because I have been trained to act on instinct. Not to weigh the options, do a pros-and-cons list, strategize. There is a time to do all of those things, and then there is a different time.

A time to survive.

I am on my belly in the dark now, moving past the sleeping campers around me, crawling toward the bathroom area in the rear of the cabin.

I listen to the gas releasing. A single canister.

It's a twelve-person cabin. I consider the size of the room, calculate the expansion and absorption rate. I consider the purpose of a gas grenade. There are three primary uses of gas attack:

Cloak.
Disable.
Kill.

Whatever the purpose of this attack, I suspect I am the target.

After my last assignment, I was told to wait somewhere for

further instructions. A certain hotel in a certain city. That is standard operating procedure for my employer, The Program. I carry out a mission, and then I wait for The Program to send me instructions.

But as I sat in an empty hotel room in a strange city, there was nothing but time to think about the things I had done. When the thinking got too loud, I went for a walk. The walk led me to a bus. The bus brought me to Vermont, where an ad posted on a local diner's wall led me to the camp and a CIT position.

I wanted to get away from the mission, the thoughts of the girl, and the dream of my father that comes when I wait.

But the thoughts and dreams followed me. Evidently so did someone else.

I have an idea who it might be, but I can't be sure. With a gas grenade releasing in the cabin, I have no recourse but to protect myself.

Defend first, ask questions later.

I consider all this in the fifteen seconds it takes to inch on my belly toward the bathroom area in the back of the cabin, feel my way up the drainpipe under the sink, and reach across cool porcelain to find someone's hand towel.

I wet the towel and wrap it around my face to make a temporary mask. It should buy me a few extra seconds.

There is a rear exit out of the cabin, but I'm sure it will be guarded.

I pause on the floor of the bathroom and I listen.

No footsteps. That means they are waiting for the gas to do its job.

That's how I would undertake an operation like this. Seal the cabin, slide the gas canister through the front door, and wait. Then I would complete my assignment.

What is *their* assignment right now? I don't intend to be here to find out.

With the wet towel on my face, I make my way, not toward the front or rear door, but to a removable wooden panel in the bathroom floor. My guess is that their recon has not uncovered its existence, because ours is the only cabin that has it. A secret Color Wars project from years past. That's the story I was told, and it's the reason I chose this cabin. I pop open the trapdoor and drop into the cool dirt below.

I do not know what's waiting for me in the darkness outside, so I must be ready for anything.

THERE ARE SOLDIERS HERE.

I make out a handful of them in the dark, an advance team, tactical aiming lasers playing across the wood of the cabin above me.

I roll along the ground, exposed for a few precious seconds until the motion carries me under the frame of a neighboring cabin.

Peter's cabin.

I do not owe him anything. I've only been here for three days. I have stayed nearly invisible, my personality softened, everything about me fuzzed down like a dimmer switch turned to its lowest setting. Only Peter knows me, or at least the me I want him to know.

Maybe he knows more. I've talked more than usual. I've needed to talk.

Still, I should not care about him. Instead I should roll from beneath this cabin to another, hopscotching from cover to cover until I am on the edge of the camp and I can disappear into the woods.

But I cannot let Peter suffer for befriending me. I have to warn him.

So I pull myself from under his cabin, run my fingers up the wooden slats, and find a ledge beneath the window. There is only one soldier nearby, his laser aiming away, so I dead-lift myself up by my fingertips, tilt up the window covering, and peer through the screen.

There is a gas canister here, too, releasing its contents in the center of the floor.

I gasp a lungful of clean air and thrust myself through the window screen. I stay low and move through the darkness, just under the layer of gas.

I quickly locate Peter lying in his bunk.

I shake him. "Wake up!"

He's nonrespondent. I lean down and listen to his chest. His heart's still beating, slow but steady. His breathing is shallow but regular.

The boy next to him is in the same condition. And the one next to him.

Knockout gas. That's what is in these grenades.

I know now that Peter will survive, so I fling myself back through the window to the outside.

The gas is everywhere now.

It rolls from the cabin doors and floats across the ground like fog in the moonlight.

I cannot help Peter. It's too late for that. So I will help myself.

I run.

I fling myself against the side of a cabin, keeping my body close to the wall for cover. I wait for a moment, then I dart out again, moving cabin to cabin toward the safety of the forest that surrounds the camp.

I make it to the farthermost cabin, but before I can make a break for the woods I see a mass of soldiers coming toward me, rising out of the darkness of the forest. There are at least two dozen of them, professional soldiers in tight formation following on the heels of the advance team. They are in Tychem Coveralls with breathers and night-vision goggles. Their guns are up and at the ready, lasers criss-crossing the area as they search for me.

The soldiers are well trained and highly equipped. Could they be working for The Program? The Program doesn't have military assets in the formal sense, but their reach is enormous, their resources nearly unlimited.

But if it's not The Program, who else could it be? I think about the many other groups I've brushed up against in previous missions. Rogue elements of the Mossad, Ministry of State Security agents from China, SZRU operatives from the Ukraine. None of them are likely to be able to track me, much less to the woods of Vermont, but now is not the time to take chances.

I must escape.

If I step away from the cover of the cabin wall, my heat signa-ture will give me away. My only hope is to stay where the gas is heaviest. It may disrupt their enhanced vision long enough for me to get away.

I dive for the nearest cloud of gas, but the soldiers are on me before I can do anything, a closing maneuver that overwhelms with sheer force.

I freeze, caught in the open.

The laser sights of their weapons play over my body. They sur-round me, circling, two dozen men with guns, with technological advantage, with overwhelming power.

I rapid-scan the area, looking for angles, routes of escape, any way to reduce their firing solutions, but I do not find any.

I am caught.

I note the feet of the soldiers around me shuffling back and forth. Nerves. Overwhelming numbers and power, yet they are nervous.

Which means they know who I am.

How is that possible?

Suddenly the circle parts, two of the soldiers stepping back to make space. A man comes out of the shadows and strides purposefully into the circle. He wears no protective suit, carries no weapons. Even before I see his face, I know who he is. I know from the certainty with which he moves. I have not seen him in more than two years, but we have spoken on the phone dozens of times as he guides me through my assignments.

This is the man who trained me.

The man I call Father.

He is not my real father. He is something else. My commander.

Now I know who has come for me. It is The Program. But why have they come like this, with dozens of soldiers?

I watch Father's face. It is impassive, unreadable.

Something contracts in my chest, my breathing suddenly shallow.

I give the feeling a name:

Fear.

But it fades almost as quickly as it arises.

That's how it's always been. Things that would make other people afraid don't seem to affect me.

I look at Father coming toward me.

Instead of being afraid, I recalculate the angles and odds. Father's presence inside the circle has reduced the firing solutions by as much as 20 percent. The soldiers cannot shoot through him, so he has unwittingly tilted the odds. Not yet in my favor. But better.

He comes closer until he is no more than eight steps away. Far enough to be out of range of a physical strike, close enough to be heard.

"They do not know your name, so I will not use it," he says quietly.

I look at the soldiers.

"These are not our people," he says. "They think they're backing a Homeland Security operation."

The Program is not a part of Homeland Security. We are something else. Something that does not officially exist.

"Why do you need them?" I say.

"A precaution," he says. "We didn't know your status."

I scan the area, judging the size of the operation.

"It's a lot of people for a status check," I say.

I note the tension in Father's jaw. There's something he's not telling me.

"What do the soldiers know?" I say.

"They know you are deadly. They know you are potentially an enemy to the United States."

An enemy?

But I am the opposite of an enemy. I am a soldier for The Program, which means I am a patriot defending the United States. This is the basis of my training, the entire reason for The Program's existence.

Why would they think differently?

Father does not provide me with any clues. He crosses his arms and examines me from a distance.

"It's been a long time since I put eyes on you," he says.

"True," I say.

I haven't seen Father since graduation day. I had fought dozens of people by that time, and I had an inch-deep knife wound in my chest. The knife belonged to Mike, my so-called brother in The Program. My brother who was ordered to kill me as a test.

I survived my first fight with Mike. So I completed my training.

"Graduation day," Father says. "That was the last time."

He remembers, the same as I do.

"That was two years ago," I say.

"Two years and a lifetime. You've done so many amazing things since then, grown in ways we could only dream of. Mother is very proud of you."

Mother. The woman who controls The Program.

"So am I," Father says. "Which is why I'm surprised to find us in this predicament."

He gestures to the soldiers around us.

Predicament. Now I understand why this is happening. At least a little of it.

"I've been off the grid for seventy-two hours," I say.

"Seventy-two hours or seventy-two minutes. You don't go off the grid. It's not a part of what you do."

My protocol is to complete the assignment, then wait for the next one. This is the perpetual cycle of my life. Work and wait. Work again.

Simple.

"Why would you come to a place like this?" Father says, looking around disdainfully.

"I needed to get away," I say.

"Away from what?"

My memories. But I don't tell him that.

"Just away," I say.

"You are a soldier," Father says, as if he understands the problem without my telling him. "You do work that has to be done. Sometimes it can be unpleasant, but that's not news to you."

"No."

"Then what happened?"

The truth is that I don't know. The old me would never be here at a camp, disobeying orders, even in the smallest way. The old me did not go off the grid. It wouldn't even enter my consciousness.

That was before my last mission.

Before the girl.

"Are you going to hurt an entire summer camp to punish me?" I say.

"Hurt? No. They're sleeping. About six hours, and they'll wake up with terrible headaches and diarrhea. They won't remember anything. Worst-case scenario, they'll examine last night's dinner in the trash. It will be filled with salmonella. We'll lace it before we go."

"That will explain their symptoms."

"An entire camp feels bad the morning after Fish Thursday. Life is cruel like that."

But maybe *I* am the cruel one. I came here, after all. And what did I think would happen to these boys? To Peter?

Father takes another step toward me. His voice softens.

"I know why you did what you did," he says.

The statement surprises me. I watch Father more closely.

"The thing with the mayor's daughter shook you up," he says.

His voice is uncharacteristically sympathetic, like he's talking to someone he cares about and wants to help. I feel my body relax the tiniest bit.

"You understand?" I say.

"You needed some time," he says. "You could have asked us for it. You could have made the call."

My special iPhone. Destroyed at the end of each mission. That's standard operating procedure. But I didn't pick up another one. That's where things got strange.

"It was wrong of me to cut off communication," I say.

I look at the two dozen soldiers around me standing at full readiness, fingers inside trigger guards.

These men are prepared to fire.

That's the first lesson of weapons training. Do not touch the trigger unless you're prepared to fire.

Father said the soldiers were here as a precaution, but they have not lowered their weapons. Which means Father does not trust me.

It's true that I went off the grid, but this reaction seems out of proportion. Father could have sent a car to pick me up or passed a message through channels. He could have made up some excuse and knocked on the door of my cabin. There are a thousand ways he could contact me if he wanted to do so, none of which involve weapons.

So what is going on here?

I calculate the angles, the danger to myself and Father, the bullet trajectories.

I look for an escape.

I might make it to one rifle, use it to take out the one opposite. But these men are not stupid and they have staggered their positions so as not to be directly in each other's lines of fire. Still, I might achieve something. I might take out one or two. Maybe even four. But two dozen men?

Perhaps if I got to Father first, the soldiers would not shoot—

No. Everyone is expendable. That's what I've been taught.

Father. Mother. All of these soldiers.

And, of course, me.

"I know what you're thinking," Father says.

"Do you?"

"Naturally. I taught you how to think."

"What am I thinking?"

"You're wondering the purpose of these soldiers and why they have not lowered their weapons. And you're calculating angles."

"How do you know?" I say.

"That's what I would do in your situation."

"Have you ever been in my situation?"

He doesn't answer, only smiles at me. A sly smile.

That's when I see it. The way out.

I've been thinking about it wrong. I don't need to use Father as a deterrent.

I need him as a shield.

Get to the first soldier, use his rifle to take out the two across, then grab Father and use his body to protect me against the inevitable fusillade of bullets.

If I sacrifice Father, I will live. I play it out in my head, and I know my chances are good.

My facial expression does not change, not in any way a normal person could detect, but Father is not a normal person.

He grins. "You see it, don't you?" he says.

"I do."

The calculus of bodies and angles in space. A human puzzle devised by Father as a test.

It's always a test—that's what I've come to understand.

"It's you or me," he says. "But not both."

I nod.

"You've been trained to protect The Program and survive at all costs," Father says. "That's your mission imperative."

I look from Father to the soldiers. I take a long, slow breath, preparing myself to leap at him.

"Would you sacrifice me to complete your mission?" Father says.

"I'd have to determine which of us was more valuable to The Program."

"And then?"

"And then I'd do what I had to do," I say. "I'm loyal to the mission. Not to you."

That's all it takes.

Father raises his hand, signaling to the soldiers. I brace myself for the pain of multiple bullets.

It doesn't come.

Instead fingers are removed from triggers. Guns are lowered. The circle disperses.

"I came to check on you," Father says. "But I see now that you are well."

I was right. It was a test.

And I passed.

The soldiers walk back into the forest. Father comes toward me now, a wide smile on his face.

"Well done," he says.

"You needed all these troops to make your point?" I say.

His face turns serious.

"There are some things you don't know."

"What kinds of things?"

He looks around the camp. "Not here," he says. He turns toward the forest. "I think we need some father-son time."

"What do you have in mind?"

"A driving lesson."

"I already know how to drive."

"A different kind of driving lesson," he says, and he heads into the woods.

I have no choice but to follow him into the darkness.

WE WALK FOR ABOUT A CLICK BEFORE WE COME TO A CLEARING.

Military trucks are parked in a convoy. This is the staging area for the operation in the camp.

"Are you ready for your lesson?" Father says.

He reaches into his pocket, removes a key chain, and tosses it to me.

"I know how to drive a Humvee," I say.

"I don't mean the trucks," he says with a smile.

He points to a clearing beyond the staging area. I note the blades of a helicopter rotor camouflaged in the forest.

"I'm not rated for a helicopter," I say.

"Not yet," he says.

DAWN IS BREAKING OVER THE VALLEY BELOW US.

I'm piloting the helicopter with Father next to me, watching the ground whip by beneath. Apple orchards, farmland, stretches of forest. The beauty of the Northeast spreads out for miles in all directions.

"How do you like her?" Father says over the roar of the wind.

"She's a beautiful machine," I say.

Helicopters are complex to fly, even more so than small planes. I did seven and a half hours in a trainer as part of my initial studies in The Program, but I didn't get my rating. It was deemed unnecessary. I received enough training to understand the flight dynamics along with the basic controls and avionics should I need to talk about helicopters in conversation, or more likely, if I intercepted information about them and had to interpret what I was seeing.

But now I'm actually flying a military helicopter under Father's tutelage.

"Pull the cyclic toward you," Father says. "Gently. That's it. Now give it some throttle."

I do as he says, and the craft adjusts, the angle steepening as we aggressively power forward.

"This is great!" I say.

"She's a beast," Father says. "This is a domestic variation, but you should see the real thing in combat."

"I'd like to," I say. A blur of speed, a flash of dark blue as a lake goes by, all of it accompanied by the whoop of rotors churning above us.

I can't help but smile. How many sixteen-year-olds get to fly a helicopter?

A small mountain looms several miles ahead, high enough that we won't clear it. I bank east, anticipating it with plenty of time to spare.

"You didn't think you could handle her, did you?"

"I wasn't sure."

"But you can," Father says. "You can do anything. You just have to remember your lessons."

Father is being kind, guiding and teaching me. This is how it was when I came to The Program. I lived and trained for two years at the house. I passed from normal life into this new life, a life most people only experience for a few hours when they're watching a movie.

"I brought you up here so we could talk man-to-man," Father says.

I glance over to find him looking at me. I don't like what I see. I grip the cyclic too hard, and the helicopter tilts left.

Father notes it with an eyebrow raise.

He reaches across my seat, puts his hand on top of mine, and adjusts the flight path. His touch surprises me, the sudden intimacy of his hand on mine in this small space. But his adjustment does the trick. The helicopter stabilizes.

"Are you off the reservation?" Father says, his voice serious.

"Why would you think that?"

"You went away."

"I took a break," I say.

The mountain has somehow returned to the center of my windscreen in the last adjustment. I bleed off power and angle the rotors to take us out of its path. But before I can complete the maneuver, Father reaches over and puts his hand on top of mine, clamping down and preventing a change of direction.

That puts the mountain in front of us on a collision course.

"I said a man-to-man talk. That means we tell each other the truth," Father says.

The test with the soldiers was not enough. I see now that there is another test.

There's always another test.

Do not fight power with power. Flow and redirect it.

That's a principle of many martial arts, and it's a lesson I have been taught over and over again by Mother.

So I don't argue with Father. Instead I tell him the truth. As much as I can.

"I went away because I needed time to think," I say.

"We give you time between assignments."

"I needed my own time. In my own way."

Father puts more pressure on my hand. The craft angles forward and down, the mountain threatening before us.

"We're in danger," I say.

"Exactly. It's a crisis of confidence," Father says. "You in us. And us in you."

The mountainside comes into focus. What looked like a beautiful mosaic of green and brown from a distance becomes jagged rock peaks and sharply angled trees.

"After the mission I was waiting in the hotel as instructed," I say. "But the thinking started."

I hesitate, not knowing how much I can risk telling him.

"The thinking?" Father says. "What is that?"

I glance through the windscreen. Forty-five seconds until impact.

"Sometimes it gets difficult for me between missions," I say. "I start thinking about the past and the things I've done. I came here because I needed to clear my head."

"You weren't hiding from us?"

"No."

Collision sirens blare. Lights flash red across my instrument panel.

"What can we do to help you?" Father says.

"Get me back to work," I say.

Father watches me carefully, his hand never moving from the cyclic.

Fifteen seconds before impact. My eyes scan the mountainside ahead. The density of the trees, the lack of a landing zone.

"I need to know where your loyalties lie," Father says. "Are you still with us?"

Why is he asking me these questions?

"Who else would I be loyal to?" I say.

I note the square set of Father's jaw as he searches my face for the truth.

Then, suddenly, he removes his hand from the controls.

But it's too late.

"Prepare for impact," I say, bracing my back against the seat to protect my spine.

"Listen and do exactly what I tell you," Father says. "Pull the cyclic aft, reduce the collective, and give it hard right pedal."

I do it. I don't ask questions.

G-force pushes me forward as the helicopter rapidly decelerates.

"Now gain altitude. Faster."

We rise and bank tightly, wind whipping by outside, the mountain coming up fast—

And then, as if by magic, the aircraft shudders and lightens, the angle increasing as we clear the mountain by no more than ten feet. I wait for the crunch of metal on stone, for the skids to catch on a tree branch and yank us down, for any one of a dozen things that could propel us into a fiery impact.

But they don't come.

We are clear. We are safe.

"What's happening here?" I say. "The raid at camp, this flight, all your questions—this is not about me going away for a few days."

Father pauses, taking time to choose his words carefully.

"Someone went missing," he says.

"Someone?"

"A soldier. Like you."

"Was it Mike?"

Mike is the only Program soldier I know other than me.

"It's not Mike," Father says. "Something like this would never happen to Mike."

"Who, then?"

"Someone else."

There are others.

That's what Father's telling me without saying it directly. There are other operatives in The Program besides Mike and me. I thought there might be, but I've never known for sure.

"So you lost a man?" I say.

"A boy," Father says. "He was just a boy. He disappeared a few weeks ago, then you cut off communication. You can understand why we needed to be cautious in finding you."

This explains Father's behavior, his testing me.

"The soldier," I say. "What happened to him?"

"He's dead," Father says.

Father's voice is matter-of-fact, but his face is tense. When I glance at him, he's looking forward through the windscreen, refusing to make eye contact with me.

"It's happened before?" I ask.

"Never."

I search his face for any sign of an emotional response to losing one of his soldiers, but I don't detect any.

"You're wondering what I'm feeling," Father says.

"I am."

"My feelings are separate from the assignment. I don't bring them to work."

Now it's my turn to avoid Father's look. There is an implied criticism here. I had feelings about my last mission, and it affected my behavior afterward. That was unprofessional of me.

"We are at war," Father says. "There are casualties. I mourn privately, then I move on."

I think of the girl from my last mission whose face I still see.

She had a name.

Samara.

Father is right. It's time for me to move on.

"Tell me more about the soldier," I say.

"He was on a critical assignment when communication was severed," Father says.

"Do you know for sure he's dead?"

"We haven't recovered a body. But he was inside for three months without a problem, and then he dropped off the map. It's been over a month since we've heard from him. There's no other reason he could disappear for that length of time."

I try to think of a scenario where I would not be able to communicate on a mission. Not just for a few hours, but for weeks in a row.

"Maybe he's imprisoned?" I say.

Father shakes his head. "We have protocols for that."

Father is referring to the prime objectives that govern my operations.

    1. Protect The Program.

    2. Survive.

The issue is that the first objective can negate the second, because in the highly unlikely scenario where I am imprisoned and my identity is revealed, I must protect The Program first and foremost. If it is not possible to both survive and protect The Program, the organization comes first.

I would have to sacrifice myself.

I've never been put in that position, but I believe I have the courage to do it if the time ever comes.

"Do you understand?" Father says.

I nod. "There's no way he could be alive."

"That's right," Father says.

Whether the soldier was revealed, caught, or captured, he must be dead now.

I think about what he might have faced on assignment, a situation grave enough to overcome both his training and the resources of The Program. I try to imagine what that might have been, but I cannot.

"I'm sorry your soldier was killed," I say, "but I don't understand what it has to do with me."

"We lost the mission," Father says.

A lost mission. That's Program parlance for a failed operation. It's an expression I've never had to use before, one I've never even heard spoken out loud.

"You're saying the soldier was killed *before* he completed his assignment?"

"Yes," Father says. "And we need you to go in and finish the job."

FATHER INSTRUCTS ME TO HEAD DUE EAST IN THE HELICOPTER.

We fly for a while, long enough that we eventually cross the Vermont–New Hampshire border and continue on a nearly straight line east.

"Have you heard the name Eugene Moore?" Father asks.

Something about the name disturbs me. I must have come across it at some point in the past. My memory works like that, memorizing salient facts and sorting them into rough categories so that I can access them later if need be.

Eugene Moore equals violence/danger. That's what comes up.

"Eugene Moore runs a military camp for teens in rural New Hampshire," Father says.

That's when I remember where I've heard the name. "It's not a typical military camp," I say. "It's like a training facility for the children of right-wingers."

"Correct," Father says. "It's called Camp Liberty, and he refers to it as training for the 'other' army, the army of the people. Say your politics run to the far right—so far right you don't trust the

31

government—but you want your kid to know how to shoot a gun and run around in the woods. You don't send him to a standard military academy. You send him to Eugene Moore."

Father points, suggesting a course correction to the south.

"Wasn't Moore in the army himself?" I ask.

"He rose to lieutenant colonel before he was court-martialed for disobeying orders."

"Something political, right?"

"He was attending political rallies in uniform during active duty. They began court-martial proceedings, but he sued and ended up with an administrative discharge. It's a big point of pride for him. He considers himself a conscientious objector. You take his radical political beliefs, add them to a pile of money from wealthy supporters along with serious tech know-how, and you have a dangerous formula."

"This camp. Where is it?"

"It's set in a valley in the mountains north of Manchester, New Hampshire. This is no cabin in the woods. It's a sophisticated, high-tech operation, nearly impenetrable by ground or air."

"You said the camp is made up of kids."

"That's right."

"Why does The Program care if kids want to play soldier in the woods?"

Father pauses. "That's an unusual question."

"It's an unusual situation."

Normally I don't ask the reason behind a mission. It's unnecessary, even distracting. My job involves target acquisition, pure and simple. I concern myself with who, not why.

But this time things are different.

I say, "I'm being brought in to complete a lost mission, and that's never happened before. I need as much information as I can get."

"I don't disagree with you," Father says. "That's one of the reasons I'm here in person."

I usually receive my briefings remotely via social media, the assignment dossiers hidden in plain sight behind ever-changing Facebook profiles.

"I'm going to answer your question," Father says. "I just don't want there to be any misunderstandings in the future. This is a one-time deal."

"I understand," I say.

Father nods. "We care about Camp Liberty because our assets have picked up indications of troubling activity online, emanating from the camp. They are probing infrastructure in the Northeast. Electrical plants, Department of Transportation computers, and the like. Individually, they've been mostly benign computer breeches, but taken as a whole, the portrait is troubling. Our algorithms suggest there's something big coming, and we can't wait for it to happen. We have to act now."

"When are you sending me in?"

Father studies my face, trying to determine something. After a moment he says:

"We've got to take care of a few things first."

Father points out the window to the right.

"That's Manchester up ahead," Father says. "We're going to that set of buildings just outside town."

He indicates a sprawling structure set off from the highway, one roof marked with a large white cross with an *H* painted in the center.

"A hospital?" I say.

"When's the last time you had a physical?"

Father knows when it was. Two years ago, when Mike stuck a knife in my chest during my final exam.

I don't bring that up. Instead I say, "It's been a long time."

"We need you at full operating capacity before your mission."

On the rooftop, a man in an orange jumpsuit waves his arms at me.

I say, "We're not a hospital chopper. We'll attract attention."

"We initiated a CDC emergency protocol. The hospital has prepped and cleared an entire floor for us. They won't know who we really are."

The Program is invisible in the world. Like me, it can appear to be whatever it wants to be, but I have not seen it use resources to this degree—Homeland Security troops to find me, Centers for Disease Control and Prevention regulations to take over hospital facilities. The fact that they're using so many resources indicates how important this is to them.

"We'll get you looked at, then I'll finish your briefing," Father says.

I note that Father didn't answer my question about when I will go after Moore, but now is not the time to probe further.

The man in orange is guiding me in using red flashlights. The way he waves his arms, it almost looks like he's warning me to stay away.

FATHER REMAINS BEHIND WHILE THE MAN LEADS ME DOWN A STAIRWAY INTO THE HOSPITAL.

The floor is completely deserted, gurneys at the ready, machinery hooked up but unused. The man stops in front of a doorway, then without a word, he walks away.

As I reach for the door, it opens.

A beautiful young woman in a white lab coat is looking at me. She has long dark hair and intense eyes.

"I'm Dr. Acosta. Father and Mother assigned me to take care of you today."

I examine her face, note the subtle hint of makeup around her eyes.

"Lucky me," I say.

"You haven't heard what I'm going to do to you yet."

"Should I be worried?"

"You don't look like a guy who worries much," she says.

"I'm more sensitive than I look."

"Maybe we should send you to the shrink instead of me."

"You're not the shrink?"

"I deal with the body only," she says.

"I knew there was a reason I liked you."

I note the smile at her lips. It's quickly wiped away and replaced with a physician's countenance.

"Let's get started," she says. "Take off your shirt."

She begins a lengthy physical exam followed by a stress test, lung and heart capacity measurements, ECG and EKG, and a full blood workup. Dr. Acosta guides me through the process quickly and professionally with a minimum of conversation. She's young, but she's obviously very good at what she does.

With the preliminaries completed, she guides me down the hall to an imaging laboratory. In the center of the room sits a high-tech diagnostic machine. It appears to be something like a CT scanner, but I don't recognize much of the technology employed there.

"What am I looking at?" I ask.

"It's a state-of-the-art sixty-four-slice SabreLight PET/CT scanner with advanced assessment protocols. Any more questions?"

"Will you hold my hand during the scan?"

"No, but I'll give you a lollipop after," she says.

"Deal."

"Okay, then. Lie back and enjoy the ride."

I lie down on the table. Dr. Acosta adjusts a few dials on the side of the device, makes sure I'm positioned correctly, then steps into the safety of an adjoining room, where she can watch me through the glass. It's dark in her room, and I can just make out her outline hunched over a control panel.

"Are you ready?" she says, her voice coming through a speaker on the side of the machine.

I give her the thumbs-up.

The machine starts to move over me.

I glance toward Dr. Acosta behind the glass. I notice a taller fig-ure has joined her now. I recognize the stiffness in his posture.

It's Father.

"Take a deep breath and relax," Dr. Acosta says over the speaker. "Don't move for a little bit."

The machine clicks and whirs as the scanner passes over me from head to toe, one full scan. I prepare to get up, when Dr. Acosta says, "Just another minute, please."

The scanner passes up my body again, this time stopping at chest level.

I feel a surge of warmth in the area beneath the scar on my chest. It's followed by a wave of dizziness.

"I'm feeling a little light-headed," I say.

"We took a lot of blood earlier," Dr. Acosta says. "It's not out of the ordinary."

The sensation of heat beneath my scar increases almost to the point of being painful, and then suddenly it's gone.

"Better now?" Dr. Acosta says through the speaker.

"Much," I say.

"A few more seconds—"

The machine whirs to a stop, the assembly moving up over my head and away from my body.

I take a deep breath and glance through the window.

Father is gone.

"We're done," Dr. Acosta says.

I rub the area over my scar.

"Can I get my lollipop now?" I say.

"Darn, we ran out," Dr. Acosta says. "I promise I'll get you one next time."

"I'm very disappointed, Doc."

"Life is filled with disappointment," she says. "Rest there for a few moments and someone will be in to get you."

I WAIT FOR THE RESULTS IN A NEARBY EXAMINATION ROOM.

Twenty minutes go by before Dr. Acosta comes in. She seems more energetic than before, her hair freshly combed, her cheeks ruddy with blush.

"Excellent news," she says. "You're approved for assignment."

"Anything I need to be concerned about?"

"Father will tell you everything you need to know."

"Father's not a doctor," I say.

I turn on the charm, giving her a warm smile. My intuition is telling me I need to see the results of the scan. My hand unconsciously rises to my chest, my finger probing the scar there. I purposefully put my hand back by my side.

"He's not a doctor," Acosta says, "but rest assured he understands the information I share with him."

"I have no doubt," I say. "But I'm thinking a peek at the results would be helpful. I'm a raw-data man."

She studies me for a long moment.

"A peek at the results isn't possible," she says. "But there's something else we should do before you go."

She begins to unbutton her lab coat. It takes a moment to understand what I'm seeing. Then she unbuttons the top button of her blouse and there's no doubt of what I'm seeing.

"Is this part of the physical?" I say.

"In a manner of speaking. Let's just say it's a component of my professional duties."

"Father's idea?"

She shakes her head. "Mother thought you needed some R-and-R."

She undoes the remaining buttons of her blouse, revealing a pink lace push-up bra beneath.

"Nice of Mother to think of me."

"Forget about Mother," she says. "You've got more interesting things to focus on."

A hint of perfume rises from her cleavage as she reaches for me.

We kiss. Her lips are soft and warm, wet with some gloss she must have applied before she came back into the room. I think about what's going to happen, the pleasure and possibility of it.

Then I think of something else.

I put a hand on her shoulder to stop her.

"What's wrong?" she says.

My last mission is in my head. The things that happened in New York.

"I can't," I say.

"Can't?"

"I don't want to. Not now."

She searches my eyes for meaning, but I don't show her any. After a moment she steps back. I suspect this will be included in her report. Mother and Father will wonder about it, but I'll deal with that when the time comes.

"It's not that I don't appreciate the sentiment," I say.

"There's no sentiment here. This is strictly professional, which incidentally doesn't mean I wouldn't have enjoyed it."

She hesitates for a moment, perhaps giving me another chance. I don't take it.

She sighs, tucking in her blouse as she walks to the door.

"Maybe another time," she says.

"I wouldn't rule it out," I say.

She smiles at me and I smile back. I consider changing my mind, but I don't. Better to focus on the mission at hand. Everything is easier when I'm on assignment.

She turns before going out. "Good luck with everything," she says.

"I don't need luck."

"I know you don't," she says. "But it's what normal people say to each other."

I'm not a normal person.

That's what I think, but I don't say it.

She opens the door to find Father waiting. She nods once, hands him my medical chart, and continues on her way. Father comes into the room and closes the door behind him.

"Did you enjoy your visit to the doctor?" he says.

"I was too distracted to enjoy it."

He looks at me, concerned.

"The assignment," I say. "I'd like to get started as soon as possible."

"I can understand that," he says.

"You saw my test results?"

"All positive. Dr. Acosta has cleared you for assignment."

I pick up my shirt, but before I can put it on, Father steps forward to examine the knife scar on my pec. "This has healed nicely," he says.

I glance at the scar. I think of Samara asking about it before we made love in New York.

"It's an identifier," I say to Father. "A vulnerability."

"We've thought about that."

"I'd like it gone."

Father nods. "We'll schedule a plastic surgery in the near future. We'll cover it up forever."

"Good."

"But not now. Now we need you back in the field."

"That's what I need, too," I say.

"Then it's time to begin," he says.

Father walks over to an IV infusion pump, the kind commonly found in any hospital. What happens next is not common. He opens a camouflaged plastic port on the side of the device, and out telescopes a small antenna. He then programs a code into the pump. I hear an electronic click, and a blue light begins pulsing in the center of the device.

"What's it doing?" I ask.

"We call it an MSRR—mobile safe room relay. Mobile because we can camouflage it inside other devices and move it as needed. A safe room because all signals into or out of this room are now blocked. It uses active noise control technology to feedback on whatever sound is generated in the room, effectively canceling it out. We are, for all intents and purposes, in a comms black hole."

No comms means no communications of any kind.

"This would be great for the bathroom," I say. "Total privacy."

"Haven't used it for that," Father says with a smile, "but thanks for the suggestion."

He takes an iPad from his bag and puts it on the counter in front of us.

He says, "While the MSRR blocks all external signals, it also provides us with secure digital-satellite uplink."

"Why do we need all this?" I say.

"Because we're going to finish your briefing now," Father says.

"We?"

Father performs a special finger gesture on the surface of the iPad, a version of the secure gesture I use on my iPhones. All of our digital devices in The Program have covert operating systems that run parallel to the system on the surface.

A moment later a window opens on the iPad screen.

It's Mother.

She's sitting in an office somewhere. She looks at me, a digital earpiece glowing on the side of her head.

My back stiffens, my body automatically shifting to attention, the posture of a soldier in front of his superior.

"Your father tells me you are well," Mother says.

"I am," I say.

"I was worried when we didn't hear from you."

"I'm sorry," I say. "It won't happen again."

"You are so valuable to us," Mother says. "To me."

Valuable. Possessions are valuable, not people. But I understand what Mother means. I am a soldier, an asset to The Program. And in her own way, I believe Mother cares about me. After all, she took me under her wing and trained me to become the person I am today. She gave my life a new purpose after my real father was killed.

The part we have never discussed: It was likely she who ordered the killing in the first place.

"Father brought you up to speed?" Mother says.

"In part," I say.

Mother's image is replaced by a series of photos on the screen. I see a tall, intense man with a shaved head, first in military service photos, later as an older man in what appear to be surveillance photos taken from a distance with a telephoto lens.

"This is Eugene Moore," Mother says.

"We don't have many recent photos," Father adds. "Moore has become increasingly paranoid and isolationist over time. He rarely leaves Camp Liberty."

Next I see photos of a young man and woman. The boy has closely cropped brown hair, the girl long red hair and freckles with a beautiful tomboy quality. I note familiar facial characteristics in both of them.

"Moore has two children," Father says. "A son named Lee who is your age, and a girl named Miranda. She's a year younger."

Mother's image returns to the screen.

"Moore is the target, correct?" I say.

"That's right," Father says.

"And which of his kids is the mark?" I say.

My assignments have two components. First there is the mark, someone my own age who I get close to and who leads me inside. Then there is the target, the one I am assigned to terminate.

"There is no mark," Mother says.

"I don't understand."

"We're sending you at him directly," Father says.

The images of Moore and his family disappear from the iPad screen, replaced by shots of a large brick building surrounded by a parking lot.

Mother says, "Moore holds a recruiting event several times a year in different towns throughout New Hampshire. Parents and kids apply from all over the United States to get an audience with him. You'll be at his next event."

"Am I going to fill out an application?" I say.

"You already have," Mother says. "We took care of it. But unfortunately it's not that easy. Moore selects candidates from the crowd who he wants to meet after the event. Just because you're there doesn't mean you get an audience with him."

"How does he decide who to meet?" I say.

"He claims to have a sixth sense," Father says. "He believes he can feel whether a young person is a proper candidate or not."

"How can I make myself feel like a candidate if I don't know what he's looking for?"

Mother's image appears on the iPad. "We think you already feel like a candidate," she says.

"What does that mean?" I say, willing my voice to remain steady.

Father steps toward me. "She's talking about your recent issues. The things that caused you to drop off the grid."

I had issues during my last mission that caused me to question my orders for the first time. I deviated from my assignment, thinking I knew better than Mother and Father. Only later did I find out that The Program had been right all along, and I had been wrong.

I meet Mother's eyes on the iPad screen. "Those issues have been dealt with. I told Father that I just need to keep working."

"He told me about your conversation," Mother says. "But the fact remains you know what it feels like to have doubts now. We need you to access that part of yourself."

I sit very still and take slow breaths.

For a moment, I wonder if this is another test, the entire scenario constructed as a way of gauging my loyalty.

"You *want* me to have doubts again?" I say.

"Not exactly," Mother says. "We want Daniel Martin to have doubts."

45

"Who is Daniel Martin?"

"That's your identity for this mission," Father says.

A different mission, a different name. That's how it always is.

Mother continues, "Moore will be looking for young people who are confused and questioning the status quo. Disorganized minds he can mold to his purpose. You need to appear to be one of those kids."

I think about what this means, the mental confusion I have to embody to seem like a viable candidate to Moore.

"You want me to get recruited," I say. "That's the mission."

Father nods.

"So I'll get into camp and take him down from the inside."

"Absolutely not," Father says. "We can't have you at Camp Liberty. It's too dangerous."

"There's a total communications blackout at the camp," Mother says. "It's in a valley surrounded by mountains. They have high-tech electronic signal blocking. Nothing gets in or out, person or communication, unless Moore allows it. If you were to go in, we would have no way to help you."

"You can't send a drone over?"

"Homeland Security tried. Two drones fell out of the sky. Moore has the technical sophistication to counter them."

That's when I understand what happened before me, the reason I'm receiving this assignment.

"The soldier—" I say. "He got inside."

Mother's face hardens into a mask of anger and disappointment.

Father looks away from the iPad.

I don't blame him. I hope I never see a look like that directed at me.

I watch the blue light pulsing on the MSRR. I think of the dead soldier, the things that might have happened to him alone and unable to communicate with The Program.

"This is a mission brief," Mother says. "Not a memorial."

Father snaps back to attention, and so do I.

Mother says, "We need you to get an audience with Moore so you can take him out at the event."

"In public?"

"In public but invisible," Father says. "Your specialty."

I consider the variables. The amount of time to learn Moore's world, to get into character, to acquaint myself with the facility where he will be appearing and run multiple entry and exit scenarios, escape plans, and contingencies.

"When is the next recruiting event?" I ask Father.

He looks from Mother to me but doesn't answer.

"When am I going in?" I say.

"Tonight," Mother says.

I'M LEFT ALONE TO CHANGE INTO A FRESH SET OF CLOTHES.

I'm given a surgical mask, then I'm taken down through the hospital like a regular patient and wheeled out through discharge by an orderly. After that I'm transported by ambulance to a residential neighborhood in a suburb of Manchester.

The driver stops across the street from a Cumberland Farms convenience store and without a word hands me a slip of paper. I get out of the ambulance, and he drives away.

On the piece of paper is a number: 578.

I look at the house nearest me. It's number 62.

An ambulance in a residential neighborhood invites attention, so I'm guessing they dropped me off a ways from my location.

I start walking. I make my posture casual like that of a kid in the neighborhood coming home late from school on a Friday night.

After several blocks, the houses become sparse and the road dead-ends in a cul-de-sac with only a few homes, each hidden behind tall bushes. The mailbox identifies the house at the very end as number 578.

I walk down a pathway and come to a white-and-yellow house set back from the road with a silver Ford Escape in the driveway. I try the front door and find it unlocked. I go inside.

"How was school?" Father calls from the kitchen as if we've shared this moment together a thousand times.

"Great," I say as if I'm not surprised to find Father here, and I shut the door behind me.

I hear an unusual sound from the door, something like an air lock being sealed.

"We can talk for real now," Father says, his head popping through the door of the kitchen briefly before disappearing again.

I look around the living room. Small details of family life are everywhere, from portraits on the mantel above the fireplace to a green blanket thrown casually across the back of the sofa.

I hear the clatter of dishes from the kitchen. I walk in to find the table is filled with good food: chicken, burgers, salad, fresh bread. Father is pouring a glass of juice.

"It's a surprise to see you in the field," I say.

Father never comes on assignment with me. He's always there, monitoring the situation from afar, sending in cleaning teams or accessing digital resources on my behalf.

"We've got a different setup this time out," Father says. "For expediency's sake, I'm driving you in and picking you up after."

Father on an assignment with me. I think about what that might mean. It could represent a lack of trust, a belief that I need to be monitored more closely. It could be the opposite, a sense that I am trustworthy, so much so that Father is willing to put his life in my hands.

Or perhaps there's a simpler explanation. I am a valuable asset that needs protecting.

I look at the table covered with food. "You're so involved on this mission you made me dinner?"

"Are you kidding? Whole Foods."

He puts down an empty plate.

"Sit and eat," he says. He glances at his watch. "We have three hours before we go mission ready. There's a lot to do before then."

I CONSUME ENOUGH CALORIES FOR TWELVE HOURS OF HIGH-ENERGY WORK.

I won't need more than that.

When I'm done eating, I meet Father in the living room. I note a slight color deviation in the light coming through the windows. I suspect it's caused by a security laminate, a nearly invisible film that covers the inside of the window, allowing us to see out but preventing people from seeing in, as well as blocking laser microphones and other surveillance devices.

It also renders the glass bulletproof, at least up to the level of .50-caliber rounds.

"This is a safe house," I say.

"A temporary one," he says.

"The Program owns this house?"

He shakes his head. "The family is out of town for a few days. We're here for now, and we'll be gone before anyone knows the difference. In the unlikely event we cannot rendezvous immediately after the event tonight, you will make your way back here and await instructions."

Father takes out a manila envelope and passes it to me.

I open it and a new iPhone slides out.

I swipe with a finger gesture. I check SETTINGS:GENERAL:ABOUT and find the phone set as:

Daniel Martin's iPhone

Father says, "You'll find your background profile on Facebook. You'll have time to study it, and then it will be erased. We'll also go over plans for the community center and our protocols for ingress and egress. But now I want you to spend some time with this."

He reaches into his pocket and removes a small eyeglass case.

"Did Dr. Acosta say I had vision problems?"

Father takes out the glasses and looks through the lenses. "Your vision's fine. There's a very minor correction for reading in your nondominant eye. Enough to pass as an actual prescription if anyone examines them, but not enough to inhibit your vision in any significant way."

"Why do you want me to wear glasses?"

"The right temple arm. It's detachable."

He hands the glasses to me.

They're light gray, an average brand but a nice design. They're the kind of glasses a stylish kid might buy from a mall in the Northeast. I play with the right temple arm, the part that goes above the ear. I twist counterclockwise, and it detaches from the hinge.

"Careful," Father says.

I note a spring action down one end. I press it once and watch a weaponized injector needle slide out from the opposite end.

I know this needle will be filled with three doses of nerve toxin, a poison I have used many times before. I've never needed more than one dose. Tap a victim and they are a few breaths away from a quiet death.

The toxin is familiar, but the tool is new to me. I must master it.

"Can you visualize the scenario?" Father says.

I've been taught to visualize, to project myself forward in time and space and see the successful conclusion of my mission.

I do that now, even without knowing the details for tonight or the layout, without knowing much of anything except the tool I will use and the target I will attain.

I imagine myself at the event meeting Eugene Moore. Maybe it happens in a private room where he interviews candidates. We will be sitting across the table from each other and I will reach across and tap his arm with the needle.

Or maybe it will happen in public, and I will use the confusion of bodies to remove my glasses, touch Moore with the needle, and step away. He will fall a few seconds later as if from a stroke or heart attack. I imagine myself slipping through the crush of panicked people to safety.

It's a high-risk gambit, but it is achievable.

I look up to find Father watching me.

"You can see it," he says.

"In general terms. Yes."

"It won't be easy."

"No. But that doesn't worry me."

He reaches toward me, puts a hand on my shoulder, and squeezes gently. It's a gesture a father might make.

A concerned father.

I step away from his touch. "I've got a lot of work to do to prepare," I say.

"Of course you do," he says. "I want to show you one more thing, and then I'll leave you alone to study."

I follow him outside to a backyard surrounded by high fencing. There is a small metal toolshed set back from the house with a padlock on the door. Father presses the center of the lock, and the top of the padlock opens up to reveal a digital thumbprint reader below.

"Your thumb only," Father says.

I press my thumb on the digi-reader, and the door opens with a hiss of hydraulics. The shed is empty except for two things:

The first is a glossy black object about the size of a shoe box.

The second is an S-59 high-tech recoilless rifle mounted on the wall.

Father says, "The black rectangle is a secure digital communications pack. It's here if you need to call home."

"What's the rifle for?" I say.

"Emergencies," Father says.

"I don't use guns."

"You don't, but they do. If you need it, you know where it is."

I shake my head.

"I understand that we've never been in the field together before," Father says. "Not in this way at least. But a safe house like this always exists for you."

"I know, but I've never needed one before."

"And I don't anticipate you needing one now. But this is an accelerated mission launch, and we haven't had time to put our normal protocols in place. We should be prepared for any eventuality."

"What about a weapon for you?" I say. "You said only my thumb opens the shed."

"Don't worry about me," Father says. "I've got resources at my disposal."

I think about the soldiers storming the camp early this morning. I have no doubt about Father's resources.

Father closes the shed door, and the lock seals shut.

"All right, then," Father says. "I'm going to leave you alone for ninety minutes, then you and I will run mission scenarios."

"Will do."

That gives me ninety minutes to learn about Daniel Martin, memorize the details of his life, formulate his worldview, and reorganize my thinking to reflect his experience rather than my own.

Father heads into the house, and I sit on the back patio. I take out my new iPhone and open the Facebook app.

I need to know enough about Daniel Martin to transform myself into him for at least an hour tonight. Then I can do what I've been sent to do.

Get close to Moore. Get done.

IT'S A CLEAR SHOT NORTH ON 93 TO THE PENACOOK COMMUNITY CENTER.

We drive in silence for a while, Father effortlessly maneuvering the Ford through light evening traffic.

"Are you happy?" Father says out of the blue.

"With your driving?"

He smiles. "In general. With your life."

"That's a strange question."

"It's been a strange day," Father says.

"Sometimes I'm happy," I say with a shrug.

"What's keeping you from being happy?"

He says it as if I'm supposed to be happy, as if happiness were a normal state of being for someone like me.

Am I happy? I know there are times when I feel good. When I'm in motion, when I'm on assignment, when I finish a mission and I'm heading away, sending a ping to Father to let him know my work is done.

Is that happiness?

"Maybe I am," I say. "I'm not sure what happiness is."

"I'll give you a hint," he says. "If you have to think about it that long, it's not happiness."

I'm confused by the conversation, but I sense Father is assessing me in some way and I need to be cautious.

"I'm happy when I'm working," I tell him.

"That's good," he says. "Any other times?"

"I'm happy now."

He looks at me, his face softer than I remember it. For a moment I imagine what it would be like if he were my actual father. Where would a real father take his son on a Friday evening?

Maybe to dinner. Maybe home from a baseball game.

I shouldn't be thinking about this now. I have a real father, and he's gone. It's as simple as that.

"Why did you ask me that question?" I say.

"Maybe when this is over, we'll try to get you some time off."

"Like a vacation?" I say.

"Would you like that?"

I think about free time and the things that could happen during it.

"No," I say.

He seems satisfied with that answer, so I drop it.

We're about half a mile away from the community center when I see a roadblock up ahead. Several dozen protesters line the road ahead of the police stop. They are angry, peering into cars and shouting at the drivers to turn back. Moore's anti-authoritarian philosophy is a lightning rod for controversy, even in the live-and-let-live atmosphere of New Hampshire.

State troopers stand in front of the protesters, keeping them restricted to the side of the road. I see that the troopers are on friendly terms with the protesters, speaking with them, politely urging them to step back.

We wait in a short line of vehicles for our turn at the roadblock. Up ahead, two troopers are helping an SUV make a U-turn. I note the license plate of the SUV printed with the familiar state motto of New Hampshire:

LIVE FREE OR DIE

When our turn comes, Father eases forward, and the trooper motions for him to roll his window down.

"Where are you folks headed?"

"I'm taking my son to the Camp Liberty event."

"Liberty," the trooper says derisively.

"Do you have a problem with that, Officer?" Father says.

His voice rises on the last syllable of *officer*, turning the word into a question about the trooper's authority rather than a question about our destination.

"I have a problem with children running around these hills with weapons," the trooper says.

"You may have a problem," Father says, "but the Constitution does not. It's called the Second Amendment."

The trooper's eyes register the insult, and I can see him briefly contemplate making this stop difficult for us. But Father's demeanor has completely shifted. He appears taller in his seat, a wealthy man of status, not used to being questioned by anyone.

"I'm all for the Second Amendment," the trooper says. "It's kids with guns that worries me."

"I'm not a kid," I say, like I'm insulted.

The trooper sighs.

"I can't tell you how to spend your free time," he says, looking from Father to me. "That's your own business. But I want to warn you to think carefully about your choices."

"This is just an informational event," I say. "I haven't made a choice yet."

The trooper steps back slightly. I can see he wants to get into this further, but he stops himself.

"All right, then, folks. We've got free speech, or so the big court tells us. It's up to you who you want to get involved with and why. I'm only suggesting you exercise caution."

"Thank you for sharing your concerns, Trooper," Father says, letting him know he's been heard and understood.

A flash of light reflects in the rearview mirror. A second trooper is behind the Ford, photographing our license plate with a flash camera.

"Very good, then. We'll get you on your way," the trooper says.

He walks in front of the truck and says something to his partner. They pull the roadblock out of the way, and the trooper waves us forward, watching closely as we drive by and head out on the empty road ahead.

"Are you ready?" Father says.

I press my glasses up on the bridge of my nose. I've been wearing them for hours now, getting used to the feel of them on my face, practicing taking them on and off with each of my hands until the gesture is ambidextrous and automatic.

"More than ready," I say.

"I'll drop you in front and then I'll be waiting half a mile north on the utility road as we discussed. There will be a few parents there, but we've deemed it better for you to go in alone. Let them believe I want you there, but there is some rift between us that Moore might take advantage of."

"Got it," I say.

"Don't use your phone in secure mode. These guys are technically adept, and they're sure to be monitoring all signals in the area. If you need me, use the public number I gave you."

We head down the road for another half mile until the community center comes into view. Orange cones are set up to form a single lane. Young men and women in pants and polo shirts wait at the entrance to the driveway, greeting people who are going in. There's even a guy with a mirror on a pole checking beneath cars.

Looking at the young men, I think of the dead soldier who was sent in before me. I wonder if he began his assignment driving into an event like this.

A young man in a blue polo gestures for Father to lower his window.

"How are you tonight?" he says, overly friendly.

"Very well," Father says.

"Me, too," I say, letting excitement cause my voice to rise.

"Invitation?" Polo says.

I take the printout of the acceptance e-mail from my pocket, the one Father received after sending in an application in my name.

"Daniel?" Polo says.

"That's me," I say.

"Welcome," Polo says. "And just so you know, there won't be any cell reception until after the event is over."

"Is that right?" Father says.

"There's a jammer set up in the parking lot. What's said in the room stays in the room," Polo says with a smile. "We turn off the jamming after the event."

"That's fine," Father says. "He can call us when it's all over, and my wife or I will pick him up."

"You won't be joining us, sir?" Polo says.

His tone is friendly, but the judgment is obvious on his face.

"I'm afraid not," Father says.

"Are you sure?" Polo says, pushing a bit. "You're welcome to stay if you choose. Parents are always welcome. You might find it interesting."

"Are you questioning my patriotism?" Father says, suddenly turning on him.

Polo stiffens. "Of course not, sir. I was just—"

"I've done more for this country in the last six months than you've done your entire life," Father says angrily.

Polo stammers: "I—I have no doubt."

"You're damn right," Father says. "My son will fill me in on the details later."

"There will be a thorough debriefing," I say, rolling my eyes like I'm a little embarrassed by my angry father.

Polo nods, obviously nervous. He points to an area set off to the side of the building.

"There's a drop-off zone over there if you don't mind pulling forward, sir," he says. "And I'm sorry again. I didn't mean—"

"Thank you," Father says, rolling up his window and putting the truck in gear before Polo can speak again.

I look at Father, impressed by what I've just seen.

"You're pretty good in the field," I say.

"*Pretty* good?" he says with a grin.

We pass a van parked in the front with several antennas and a satellite dish on top. Father notes me looking at it.

"Signal-jamming tech," he says. "Just like the kid said."

I slip out my iPhone, and I see there's no cellular service available. No connection of any kind.

"I won't be able to call you," I say.

"If everything goes right, you won't need to call me. I'll see you in an hour at our rendezvous point."

He looks at me for a long moment.

I slow my breathing, forcing my heart rate down into a zone that will allow my muscles to maintain optimal oxygenation.

"You're not to go into Camp Liberty. You understand that."

"Perfectly."

"You're ready, then," Father says. "Do it fast, do it right."

"See you soon," I say.

And I get out of the truck.

I'M SEARCHED AT THE DOOR BY A YOUNG SECURITY GUARD.

She is efficient and well trained like the rest of the young people I've seen here so far.

I make it easy on her because I'm carrying nothing except a wallet, a phone, and my eyeglass case. She quickly clears me and gives me a ticket for an assigned seat.

When I step inside, it's standing room only, seventy or so young people sitting in folding chairs, some of them with parents next to them. It's obvious that they're the candidates, while along the back wall stands a group of young men and women like the ones I saw at security outside, all dressed similarly in khakis and short-sleeved polo shirts. The boys have close-cropped hair or crew cuts, while the women's hair is pulled back in tight buns. If I didn't know what this was, I'd think I was at a Friday evening dance at the local military academy.

I find my assigned chair located toward the side of the room where I have a good view of both the front and the back. I search the room for faces from my briefing. I note a pretty girl with red hair standing in the front of the room laughing at something someone has said to her.

Miranda, Moore's daughter.

She has a gorgeous face with big, intense eyes surrounded by freckles and framed in wisps of red hair. Unlike the other girls, her hair is down and flowing around her shoulders. There's something strong in her presence, a no-nonsense quality that is unmistakable.

Near her is a tall, thin boy with an intense face.

Lee Moore.

He's nervous as he looks from his sister to the crowd and back.

I do my own scan of the space, matching the actual room to the schematics I went over with Father this afternoon. I note entrances and exits, a door next to the stage, which I'm guessing leads to the anteroom that exits to the back of the building. I imagine that's where Moore is now, and where he will be again after the event.

I use my time to adjust the map of the building in my head, working again through the dozen or so escape scenarios I developed this afternoon, rating them in order of preference.

As I complete my prep, the room starts to buzz with excitement. I sense movement from the anteroom.

Suddenly Eugene Moore strides onto the stage flanked by two young security men. I recognize him from his pictures. He is tall and well built with the military bearing of an ex-soldier. He places an iPad on a lectern, then begins pacing back and forth in front of it.

He says nothing, only walks the same pattern, the energy building inside him.

Finally he speaks:

"You've no doubt heard a lot about me," he says, "about my beliefs, about Camp Liberty and the things we do there."

He looks across the crowd, making sure he has our attention.

"Everything you've heard is a load of crap," he says.

Most of the people in the room lean forward, fascinated.

"Forgive my language, but I'm a plain-spoken man. I say it like it is. And what it is, my friends, is a fabrication. They say I'm building robots here, children who can't think for themselves, who follow authority blindly. Is that why you're here tonight, to follow blindly?"

"No!" a bunch of kids shout.

"I didn't think so," Moore says with a smile. "Let me tell you what it is I *really* do. I support young people in becoming strong, independent thinkers who are empowered to take action in the world. The powers that be have a problem with that. They don't want you thinking independently, because what if you disagree with them? And what if you decide to do something about it?"

Half the room applauds, while half are more cautious, sitting back in their seats, listening carefully.

"People have accused me of being a radical for starting Camp Liberty. Some have even called me a traitor to our country," he says.

There's a hush across the room.

"But I say if they can't tell the difference between a traitor and a patriot, I pity them."

Laughter and cheers from the khaki crowd in the back of the room. Goaded by their approval, Moore spreads out across the stage, relaxed and in his element now.

"If you've come here tonight, it's because you know something is broken in America. And maybe, just maybe, if we all start by admitting that, we can get on with the more important business of figuring out how to fix it."

Heads nod around the room.

"Out there," he says, gesturing to the world beyond the community center, "they are not ready. They are in denial. But in here?" He smiles. "It's a different story."

He looks across the audience.

"You are ready to hear the truth. Your parents want you to hear it because they brought you here tonight. Some are in the room with us now. I'll tell you what, parents. Why don't we send you away for a bit while I have a talk with the young people?"

The parents stay seated, slightly confused. Moore urges them to stand, and a group of kids from Camp Liberty gather them up and guide them toward a side door.

A small, powerful man in his early forties with a shaved head appears in the doorway waiting for them. He's somewhat incongruous among the young people from the camp, but he obviously commands their respect.

Moore trades nods with the man. "Sergeant Burch will take good care of you," he says, reassuring the parents. "You'll rejoin us in a little while."

With the adults gone, it's easier to see how many recruits are in the room. Maybe three dozen of us in numbered folding chairs, while an equal number of kids from Camp Liberty are lined up on the sides of the room and behind us.

I think about the logistics of my mission tonight.

Seventy-five people in the room, including two young security guards flanking Moore. Maybe twenty parents now in another room somewhere in the center.

That's a lot of eyes that might see me, and a lot of bodies that could try to stop me.

"Now it's just us," Moore says softly, drawing our attention back to the stage. The room instantly quiets down.

The two security guys spread out on either side of him like Secret Service agents. The boy on the left is in his early twenties with a tight, wiry build, his head on constant swivel, more security theater than security assessment.

Not so with the other boy. There is a stillness about him as he looks into the crowd, his head barely moving. He has thick hair and a beard, and he's wearing a long-sleeved flannel shirt despite the summer evening's heat. At first glance Flannel looks crazed, like a New Hampshire mountain man who stumbled out of the woods. His gaze drifts left and settles on me for a moment. I match the energy of the other young people in the room, mimicking their excitement and anticipation, but I add a deeper layer. A layer of doubt.

It's the layer that I think will interest Moore. It's easy to recruit people who already believe in you. But to convince someone who is skeptical requires greater skill.

Flannel studies me for a moment, then moves on to the next person.

Moore begins again: "I come into Manchester from time to time and walk around. I see good people like your parents who are trying to do the right thing, trying to be good citizens, working hard to take care of themselves and their families. They live their lives as best they know how—go to work, raise children, vote, save for retirement. So what's the problem?"

"It's boring!" one kid shouts from the middle row.

Gentle laughter all around.

"Boring it may be," Moore says with a grin, "but it's something else, too. Something more dangerous."

He pauses, waiting until all eyes are on him.

"It's expected," he says.

A few heads nod around the room.

"People do what's expected of them, and nothing changes. The system stays broken. Meanwhile everyone goes about their business, never asking the bigger questions."

Moore strolls around the stage now, his shoulders relaxed, his demeanor softer.

"And you know what? I don't blame them. It's difficult to question the status quo. It takes effort. It takes courage. And most of us, nearly all of us, do not have that courage, so we follow the rules and play the game. That's what I did. I went to school and got decent grades. When I got out I joined the military so I could make myself and my parents proud. I wanted to fit in. I wanted to find my place in the world. Mostly, I wanted to support our government as a member of the military because I believed what they told me—that they were a government of the people, by the people, for the people. Who wouldn't want to be part of a government like that?"

An uncomfortable chuckle passes through the crowd.

"Sadly," he says, "that's not the government we have. We have a government of the money, by the money, and for the money. Big government, big money. Reformers appear from time to time, many of them our friends in the Republican Party, well-meaning folks who try to bring about change from the inside, but the system resists. We end up with bigger government, bigger budgets, higher taxes."

He looks at the ground, his head seemingly weighed down with sadness.

"When you go inside, you become an insider. It's inevitable. There's a belief that change can only happen from the inside, but it's a myth. Your parents know this because they've tried it and it hasn't worked. That's why they brought you here tonight."

He walks forward, standing on the lip of the stage.

"They brought you to me."

He looks across the faces in the crowd.

"I am the outside. I am the place where change begins."

A roar of approval goes up from Moore's people around the room. They gaze at him with admiration in their eyes. I try to see what they see when they look at him, but I cannot. Not yet, at least.

"Your parents want you to be a part of that change. They need you to do what they could not do, not with all their money and power. But let me tell you a secret: *You* can do it."

A boy next to me nods in agreement.

"You may have come here today because you're afraid for your future. You worry things are only going to get worse, that we adults are making it worse, and you're the ones who are going to have to live with that."

He pauses, letting the idea sink in.

"You're right about that. But if that's not the future you want—you can do something about it."

The audience leans forward.

"Today. Right now. I have some ideas about how we can change things. Together. What do you think?"

"Yes!" the crowd shouts in unison.

"Do you trust me?"

"Yes!"

"Are you ready?"

"Yes!"

"If you trust me and if you're ready"—Moore looks into my eyes—"I can show you how to change."

Something leaps in my chest, a powerful sensation of hope and excitement.

Then Moore looks away, and the sensation is gone.

I see the smiles around me in the room, young people glowing, caught up in the same magnetism I felt a moment ago.

"Who wants to join me at Camp Liberty?" Moore says.

I look at the kids looking back at him, admiration on their faces. I feel it, too.

Doubts about my life. My choices up until now. The person I think I am versus the person I want to be someday.

The person I could be with Moore.

You know what it feels like to have doubts, Mother said.

Is this what Mother meant, the reason she sent me on this mission?

Suddenly I feel a rift opening up inside me. I try to stay in the room, but memories rush up, pulling me with them to another place and time.

MY FATHER IS IN FRONT OF ME.

My real father. He is tied to a chair, drugged, his head sagging, a drop of blood trickling from the corner of his lip.

I am twelve years old. Mike is next to me. He did this to my father—I know that now. I knew it then, too, in the terrible moment when I came home from my father's office to find Mike at the house waiting for me.

I think about what happened after that. Another house.

The training house for The Program.

Mike took me there the day he killed my parents. He put me in a room and left me to scream, left me to cry. And then he left me to my silence.

Only later did a man appear and ask if I was ready.

Ready for what?

I did not have the courage to ask the question.

This man was Father, but I did not know it at the time.

He gave me a towel and supplies and let me clean myself up. When I was ready, he led me through the house.

He brought me to the office where I would come to know the

woman who I call Mother. She asked me what I wanted. Now that my father was dead. Now that my old life was gone and everything was permanently and irrevocably different.

She told me I had a choice to make, a choice that would change the rest of my life.

THE RIFT CLOSES.

I am back in the community center, back in the moment with Moore.

Another time. Another choice.

Who wants to join me? Moore said.

I allow myself to get excited. About the greatness Moore sees in us. About the secrets he promises to show us if we follow him.

Moore continues a slow scan of the room, making marks on his iPad with a stylus as he goes. I now understand the reason for the assigned seats. Moore must have a seating chart on his screen. He's selecting the kids he wants to meet.

I wait for his gaze to come across me again. Our eyes lock for the second time.

I show him what I want him to see, the confusion and excitement I've allowed inside my mind just for him. I maintain eye contact, so I do not see whether he makes a mark with the stylus. Instead I make myself unconcerned with the results, focusing instead on the moment.

And then it passes.

Moore continues his survey of the room, finishing quickly and walking from the stage in silence. His security team reacts, forming up at his sides. They move him toward the anteroom next to the stage.

Kids from Camp Liberty are walking around the room now, searching out various recruits, chatting with them briefly before bringing the excited teens to meet Moore.

I adjust my glasses on my head. I wait.

A moment later I feel a tap on my shoulder.

IT'S LEE.

"My father wants to meet you," he says.

"Your father?"

"I'm Lee Moore," he says. "How's it going?"

I note pride in the statement, along with something else. He emphasizes his first name rather than his last, subtly setting himself apart from his father.

"Daniel Martin," I say, extending a hand.

"Daniel. That's right. I read your application. Your family lives in Manchester, don't they? I'm surprised you haven't been here before."

"We just moved six months ago from Boston. I'm an Exeter guy now," I say, reciting my backstory.

"You're a prep," he says with a smirk.

"Something wrong with that?" I say.

I'm showing him the Daniel Martin I've readied for tonight, a kid from a wealthy family, arrogant on the surface but with serious doubts about himself and his family lurking at his core.

"Nothing wrong with it," Lee says, backing off. "I just forgot that part of the story. To be honest, there are a lot of applications.

Sometimes I have to skim through the pile when the committee gives them to me."

It's an insult and an admission at the same time. On one hand, he's letting me know I'm not important enough for a serious read. On the other, he's admitting he's fallible, perhaps so I'll let my guard down.

"The committee," I say. "You don't handle recruiting yourself?"

"Not my thing. I just consult."

"What *is* your thing?"

I note a tightening in his jaw. The question irks him. Which tells me he doesn't know what his thing is yet.

The expression disappears in a split second, replaced by something else.

"I'm the son," he says, his voice certain. "That's my thing."

I take a breath, pulling my energy down to a lower level. Lower energy, lower status.

"To be honest, I don't know what my thing is," I say.

I see him relax, disarmed by my vulnerability.

He says, "Your application mentioned your dad was a big deal in the energy sector. You don't want to follow in his footsteps?"

I guess he read my application more closely than he admitted.

I shrug. "It's true he's successful, but at what cost? Sometimes I think I'm less of a son and more of a tax write-off. Know what I mean?"

He looks at me, his interest piqued.

"I noticed your father didn't come with you," he says.

"He dropped me off, but he couldn't stay. Just so you know, he wants me here more than anything. It was his idea in the first place."

"Not yours?" he says, paying close attention.

"Not mine," I say, "but I'm coming around to his point of view."

Lee smiles. "It's tough to admit that your dad is right about something, even when you know he is."

"No kidding," I say. "Anyway, my dad is totally supportive, especially if it means writing a check. That's one thing he's very good at."

"Nothing to write a check for. You didn't get in yet," he says.

It's a reminder of my status in the conversation. Lee has a strange way of opening up and then closing down again.

I decide to let him pull rank for now. Play on his arrogance to try to get him on my side.

"I'm not in yet," I say, "but I'm hopeful."

I look at him like I need his help. I feel his energy soften.

"Let's see what we can do," he says, looking toward the anteroom. "I'd better bring you over now."

He walks me across the back of the room, where we pass a table filled with snacks. It's split down the middle between healthy and unhealthy, one side packed with vegetables, cheeses, and protein bars, the other with cupcakes, brownies, cookies, and various forms of chocolate. He glances at the table as we pass, then looks back again.

"Hold up for half a second," he says.

He doubles back to the table, looking around the room with great care before turning his attention to the desserts.

"I've got a sweet tooth," he says.

He studies a plate of chocolate chip cookies like he's contemplating the secrets of the universe.

His hand moves toward the cookies, then over to the brownies, then back to the cookies.

"I can't decide," he says.

"Why don't you have both?" I say.

"I shouldn't be having any."

"Why not?"

"My father says sugar is bad for the body and soul."

"What do you say?"

He doesn't respond, just stays focused on the desserts. Eventually he selects a chocolate brownie with great care, then turns his back to the anteroom doorway before starting to eat it.

"I love chocolate," he says.

"Everybody does," I say. "So why do you have to hide it?"

Lee lowers his voice. "My father puts this stuff out on the table so he can see who eats it."

"He watches?"

"Everything," Lee says. "Nothing gets by him. Kids who eat the wrong snacks don't get the invite. He considers it an indication of weakness."

"That's a little weird," I say.

"Never let him hear you say that," Lee says.

It tells me a lot about Moore. It tells me how careful I'll need to be in the next ten minutes.

"Do you want something from the table?" he says.

"After what you just said?"

"It's between you and me," he says.

I look at the snacks on the table. Do I throw myself in with Lee, or do I set myself apart from him?

I turn my back to the anteroom like Lee did, and I select a chocolate chip cookie.

When in doubt, emulate. That's what I've learned.

"Nice," he says.

Lee finishes his brownie as I gobble down the cookie. When we're done, he wipes his chin and checks his shirt for evidence of crumbs.

"You ready?" he says.

"Hold up," I say.

I brush a couple of crumbs off his sleeve.

"You're good to go," I say, giving him the thumbs-up.

"Thanks," he says. "You're an okay guy, Daniel."

"I hope your father thinks so."

"Me, too," he says. "Let's see what happens."

"Let's," I say.

A DOZEN KIDS HAVE BEEN SELECTED.

They form up outside the anteroom, each with a minder from Liberty next to them.

Lee motions me forward. I reach up to my glasses, refamiliarizing myself with the invisible latch that detaches the temple arm from the frame.

We move past a woman in her midforties, wild black hair with blond dyed streaks, sweating in the air-conditioned room. She hangs around the side of the room, not in line but not far from it. Something about her energy doesn't seem right.

Lee nods to her as we pass by.

"Who is that woman?" I say.

"She's a troublemaker," Lee says, shaking his head.

"What's she doing here?"

"Her daughter is at Liberty, and she subs as an English teacher for us sometimes."

"So what's the trouble?"

"It's a long story," Lee says, unwilling to share more.

I shrug. "Interesting hairstyle."

"You know English teachers," he says. "They're creative."

To my surprise, Lee bypasses the line of candidates waiting for Moore, taking us right up to the front.

"No waiting?" I say.

"You've got VIP status because you're with me," Lee says.

"It's good to be the heir apparent," I say with a smile.

"Some days yes, some days no," Lee says.

I look through the door into the anteroom. Eugene Moore is sitting behind a table in the back of the room.

He is not alone.

Flannel is standing next to him but slightly away from the table, a defensive position that gives him a clear line of sight and movement. Moore's daughter, Miranda, comes in and sits next to her father. By her side is the wiry bodyguard with the swivel neck.

Moore, Miranda, Flannel, and Swivel Neck.

That makes four people in the room. When Lee takes me in, there will be five.

I'm going to have to create enough of a distraction to allow me to inject Moore without anyone noticing. I project myself through the process. I imagine taking off my glasses, dropping them at Moore's feet, arming the weapon at the same time. Maybe Moore leans down to help me pick them up, and a forearm is exposed. Or maybe I get them myself, and I press the needle into his calf.

It will be tricky, but not impossible.

Twenty feet away now, moving through the last line of security. Lee puts his arm on my shoulders, an indication to all that we're together. He's personally bringing me through to meet his father.

All my senses are firing. I will my body to relax and I steady my breathing.

I'm ten feet away when Flannel looks up. Our eyes meet.

His expression changes the instant he sees me.

Something is wrong.

Flannel touches Moore's shoulder. Moore stops what he's doing and leans toward him.

Flannel whispers something in Moore's ear.

Six feet away now. I slip the glasses from my head, rock them back and forth in my hand, establishing a natural pattern of motion.

Flannel finishes whispering. Moore nods once, then he looks over at us, first at his son, then at me.

His look is intense, not at all friendly.

I counter his energy, allowing my face to slip into an easy smile, relaxing my body posture, placing my shoulders at their lowest, least-threatening position. I tap the glasses against my thigh, my hand moving into position to detach them.

I take the final few steps toward Moore.

Lee begins to speak. "Dad, I want to introduce you to Daniel Martin—"

Moore cuts him off, shaking his head in a *no* gesture.

Things happen quickly after that.

Flannel steps in front of Moore, obscuring my view. Swivel Neck joins him, his hand rising in a blocking gesture.

Lee's arm slips from around my shoulder and grips my bicep.

"Hold up," he says.

Swivel Neck comes toward us.

"What's going on?" I say, tension in my voice.

"He doesn't want to meet you," Lee says.

"What do you mean? He chose me."

"He changed his mind. I'm sorry. It happens sometimes."

Lee is pulling me away from Moore now, and Swivel Neck has slipped his arm low around my waist, making sure I keep moving.

I could get away from both of them in a second, but it would bring more attention toward me.

"What about camp?" I say.

"Camp is not an option," Lee says.

"Maybe another session? Next summer or something?"

"When my father says no, the decision is made. I'm sorry you came all the way out here. I didn't know it would go like this."

Additional security people are moving toward us, tightening the circle around me. People around the room are craning their necks to see what's going on.

Something off to the side catches my eye. The English teacher with wild hair is moving behind the security people. She's using my distraction to move closer to Moore.

She fumbles in her purse, trying to get ahold of something.

"You're going to have to leave," Swivel Neck says, and he clamps down on my arm.

I look to Lee for help, but he's moving away, no longer willing to engage with me.

I resist Swivel Neck, and his grip tightens on my arm. He's strong, obviously a guy who works out, but he's not an expert. His grip is too low. Grab higher up on someone's arm and you lock out the shoulder joint. Even more effective would be to bear-hug me out of the space. That's how bouncers are trained to deal with drunks. Come up behind and clamp them around the middle, pinning their arms against their bodies.

Swivel Neck doesn't do that. He grips me low and by the elbow, and while it's painful, it allows the rest of my body full range of motion.

Just then the wild-haired woman pulls an object from her purse.

It's a small pistol, matte-black metal clutched in her hand.

I'm watching an assassination attempt unfolding. An inexpert one. The way she holds the gun, I can see she is not a trained assassin.

She's rushing toward Moore, trying to swing the pistol free from her purse when her wrist snags in the purse handle. She fights to free it, losing a precious two seconds.

Her loss is my gain.

I calculate the distance, the time it will take for me to get to her.

And I calculate something else—the chance of her success. Because if she shoots and kills Moore, I can walk away, my mission accomplished without my having to be involved at all.

But one look at her tells me the odds are bad. She's sweating and terrified, stumbling as she rushes toward him.

If she shoots at Moore and misses, the security cordon will close down around him. He will retreat to his encampment, and I will not get another chance.

So I make a choice.

I tense my shoulder, lift, and then snap my elbow down quickly, breaking Swivel Neck's grip.

I leap away, dodging another security guy in the process.

The security guards are reaching for me and shouting. Lee turns toward us, surprised to see me still there.

All attention on me now, none on the woman with the gun.

She raises the pistol, her face a mask of anger.

That's when I leap, propelling my entire body toward the woman.

I shout *"Gun!"* at the same time, hoping the word will be enough to set off a well-practiced response from Moore's bodyguards.

I hit the woman from the side and the gun goes off high, shattering a light fixture above us. Someone screams in the room behind me. The woman fires twice more as she goes down, but by then I've got her arm extended away from her body and toward the wall, where the rounds can do no harm.

The woman is shouting beneath me.

"Let me go! My daughter, he can't take her!"

I clamp her wrist hard, forcing her to release the pistol.

As soon as it's out of her grip, she cries in rage and frustration, collapsing into a heap under me.

Young people from the camp are on us by then, one pinning the woman's arms, another sitting on her chest so she won't be able to get away.

"You can't have her, Moore!" she shouts. "Not my baby!"

One of the boys is covering her mouth, her screams muffled beneath his hand.

I glance behind me, and a group of young people have surrounded Moore. They're rushing him out of the room.

"Call the police!" one of the recruits says.

"No," his camp minder says. "There's no need for that."

I look to the back of the room to see where Moore exited, and I'm surprised to find him still in the room, arguing with a group of campers.

They're trying to get him to go, and he's refusing to leave.

The English teacher is still pinned on the ground crying. Suddenly she gets a second wind, fighting her way out from the grip of several boys.

"Mooooore!" she shrieks. "You can't do this!"

That's when Moore comes striding forward through the crowd.

He touches the shoulder of one of the boys sitting on the woman's legs, and the boy stands up. He nods to the other boys holding her, and they, too, let go.

The woman doesn't know what to do. She lies on the ground like a baby. She looks up at Moore helplessly.

He comes closer to her and kneels down.

It's possible I could get to Moore, approaching in the confusion until I am close enough to inject him. But it's too risky.

I'm going to have to find a different way.

Moore whispers to the woman too quietly for me to hear it. Her face goes from hatred, to surprise, to something else, something almost peaceful.

After a moment he extends a hand to help her up. She takes it without a word, brushing herself off as she stands.

The two of them face each other—

Then Moore holds out his arms, and the woman steps into them, embracing him.

Several people in the room gasp. Next to me, a girl wipes tears from her eyes.

Moore hugs the woman, and a moment later he is on the move again, walking away, surrounded by his people. He looks at me as he passes by but doesn't speak. He quickly disappears through the back door.

A number of girls cluster around the distraught woman. They seem to know her, stroking her shoulders and back and leading her away.

A moment later Lee is by my side.

"Are you okay?" he says.

"I don't know," I say, like I'm shaken up, even though I'm quite sure I'm fine.

Lee checks me from head to toe, performing a quick injury assessment like someone with advanced first aid training would know to do.

"You weren't hit," he says.

"Thank god," I say. "Are the police here yet?"

"No police," Lee says. "We'll deal with this internally."

"Earlier you said that woman was a troublemaker."

Lee looks toward the ground. "She thinks her daughter is in danger, that something bad is going to happen at camp."

"Is it?"

"On the contrary," Lee says. "It's something good."

There's a joyful light in his eyes that troubles me.

I look around the room, gauging the reaction among the other campers. They are strangely quiet, going about their business cleaning up and organizing the room as if nothing happened.

They may be quiet, but I react like a normal boy would after the shock of an intense experience wears off. I start to shiver, let my breathing get shallow and rapid.

"I think I need to sit down," I say.

Lee looks worried. "Try to relax," he says. "It's totally normal to feel like this after your body gets a surge of adrenaline."

"I can't believe what just happened," I say. "She tried to kill your father."

"She tried," Lee says. "But you stopped her."

He backs away a little, his demeanor shifting.

"How did you stop her, Daniel?"

"I don't know exactly. I just grabbed her."

"You didn't just grab her. You tackled her and held her gun arm so she wouldn't have a firing solution."

He's much more perceptive than I realized. I have to be careful now.

"I was acting on instinct."

He shakes his head. "You looked like a pro out there," he says.

"A pro what?"

"A security pro."

"I have some training," I say.

"What kind of training?"

"Martial arts. My father thinks it's important that a person knows how to defend himself."

He glances over my shoulder toward the back door.

"You'll need to tell my father about that," he says.

"Your father?"

"He wants to talk to you now."

MOORE STANDS IN THE GLARE OF TRUCK HEADLIGHTS BEHIND THE COMMUNITY CENTER.

I cannot see his face, only his profile intermingled with those of the young men who protect him.

Lee guides me in. We pass Miranda, one side of her face lit by headlights.

Lee stops suddenly and gestures for me to continue forward on my own. The security people stand in a line on both sides, watching as I pass by.

Moore waits for me to come closer.

Four steps away now. The air seems to vibrate around him. He stands with one hand on the truck hood, his lower half lit by the headlights, but his face in darkness.

I stop when I am two feet away. It's known as the privacy zone. In America strangers naturally stand about twenty-four inches from one another. Closer in Asian countries. Farther away in Britain.

But it's twenty-four inches in the United States. Farther than that and you send the message that you are afraid. Closer and it feels rude, antisocial. Or dangerous.

I stop at twenty-four inches, communicating to Moore that I am neither afraid nor a threat.

I can't see his eyes, but I can sense him looking at me. There are people all around us, just outside the range of the headlights, watching my every move.

I consider reaching for my glasses, a seemingly innocuous gesture that would put a weapon in my hands, but when I glance left, I note a trace of red-and-gray plaid in the shadows.

Flannel.

He is here on the periphery, circling like a shark. I choose to keep my hands by my sides.

"Are you a hero?" Moore asks.

His voice is more powerful up close, clear and confident.

"I don't think so," I say, my own voice uncertain.

"You acted in a heroic way."

"It happened so fast. I'm not even sure what I did."

"You stopped an assassination attempt."

"I just reacted," I say.

"People who react are heroes."

"Really?"

"Really," Moore says, and he reaches out and puts his hand on my shoulder as if to steady me.

Physical contact. Moore is inside my kill zone, but I'm pinned in the light. I can't move in any way that might appear threatening.

"So you think I'm a hero?" I say, like I can't believe it.

Moore's grip suddenly tightens on my shoulder. I squirm beneath it, acting as if I'm surprised and in pain because of the pressure he's exerting there.

A normal person would be both.

I am neither. I am curious.

"You're hurting me," I say.

"You know what bothers me about what you did?" Moore says.

I try to get out from his grip, but I cannot, not without taking overt defensive action.

"The difference between a hero and a villain is a very thin line," Moore says.

I look up at him like I'm confused.

"I don't think I'm either of those things."

He bears down even more on my shoulder. I let my face wince in pain.

"You're wrong," Moore says. "I think you're one of those things."

I sense Flannel moving closer just outside my view. I crane my neck like a kid who is scared and trying to see what's going on around him. I use the gesture to inventory the bodies just outside the headlights. I might have to defend myself in a moment, and if I do, I want to know what I'm up against.

Moore's intensity grows as he stares at me.

"Which are you?" Moore says. "A hero or a villain?"

He waits for me to respond.

I exhale slowly. I'm trying to get a line on Moore so I know the right thing to say, but it's nearly impossible. His energy fluctuates in a way that makes it hard to follow him.

Still, I have to respond. He's on the cusp of deciding something about me.

Suddenly I have an intuition about him. He's a gruff ex-military man. I should appeal to that energy in a way that will feel familiar to him.

"I didn't come here for this shit," I say, and I wrench my shoulder hard enough to surprise him and break his grip.

Bodies leap toward us from outside the light, but Moore puts up a hand to stop them.

"I thought you were a great man," I say, talking fast. "At least that's what my father said, and I wanted to see if it was true. But I didn't come here to get shot or be interrogated. Seriously, to hell with this."

I stiffen my back and raise my face to him, challenging his power.

"You're not being interrogated," Moore says, momentarily on the defensive.

"I risked my ass to protect you from some crazy woman. And you don't even thank me. You accuse me of—I don't even know what. I just know I'm out of here."

I slump my shoulders and look at the ground, spent from my outburst.

"You misunderstand," Moore says. "We're simply having a dialogue."

"I want to go home and take a shower and forget I came here."

Then I do something Moore probably hasn't seen in a long time.

I turn my back to him and start to walk away.

"Just a minute," he says forcefully.

I stop, but I don't turn around.

"Maybe I was wrong about you," he says.

Moore comes forward, breaking the two-foot rule.

He is close. Close enough for me to finish my mission.

My assignment is always to assassinate in a way that will appear to be from natural causes. I must complete the assignment without revealing myself or threatening The Program.

In a situation like this with a high likelihood of being detected, protocol dictates that I back away until another opportunity presents itself. On every other mission, I've had the time to properly acquire my target, and multiple opportunities to act. My job is simply to set the stage and choose one.

It's never been like tonight.

One event. One shot. One moment with Moore.

I may not get another.

"Can I trust you, Daniel?" Moore asks.

"I guess saving your life wasn't enough to earn your trust?"

Moore looks toward the sky, subtly craning his neck. Crickets sing in the tall grass around us.

"You're a wiseass," Moore says.

"A little bit," I say.

Moore smiles.

"You remind me of myself," he says.

He nods once, and then he's gone, backing away from me quickly and disappearing into the night.

I stand alone, pinned in the headlights.

I've lost the mission.

I think about Father waiting for me half a mile away. I imagine going to him and telling him what happened here tonight.

The mission was lost once before. What will it mean that I can't complete it now? This on top of the concerns The Program already has about me, my disappearing to Vermont, the issues with my last assignment—

Brakes squeal behind me. I turn to find Moore standing next to an SUV, leaning over and whispering to Lee. A moment later Moore climbs into the SUV and it immediately peels out, one truck in front and one behind in a motorcade formation.

Moore is gone, and with him, my mission.

Lee comes over to me, an expression of surprise on his face.

"Unbelievable," he says.

"What?"

"My father invited you to tour Liberty."

"Really?" I say.

This is the moment I've been trained for, the junction of fate and opportunity that separates the experienced operative from the amateur. The amateur hesitates, while the experienced soldier acts.

The problem is Camp Liberty. I've been forbidden to go there.

"What do you think?" Lee says.

"A tour? That's great news," I tell him.

I can go back to Father now, not with a lost mission, but with an alternative. I will go into Camp Liberty and get Moore. It's not the mission I prepped for—it's more complex and difficult—but it can be planned, mapped out, then executed.

I will finish my mission. I'll just have to persuade Father to let me do it from the inside.

"When can I come for the tour?" I ask Lee.

"Right now," he says.

"That's not possible," I say.

"Why not?"

I can't go in now. I've got no backup and no contingency plan. Father doesn't have any information about what's gone on tonight.

"It's late," I say, struggling for a viable excuse that will keep me out of the camp.

"You can stay over tonight," Lee says. "There's plenty of room. We'll show you around in the morning."

We can't have you at Camp Liberty. That's what Father said.

"My dad is coming to pick me up in a bit," I say.

"You can call him from the road," Lee says.

A black truck pulls up next to us, the engine idling. Flannel is in the driver's seat looking straight ahead.

"We have to go now," Lee says. "If you're coming with us, that is."

Lee opens the back door.

I glance at my iPhone. The signal is still blocked from the jamming vehicle in front of the community center.

I imagine Father out on the utility road waiting for me. I can be there in ten minutes, safe and warm in the front seat, discussing what went wrong tonight and what we might do about it.

But if I don't go now, what chance do I have of getting to Moore again? What chance do I have of completing my mission?

I search my mind for alternatives, but I don't find any. The probability of success declines to nearly zero the moment I walk away from Lee.

I can't lose this mission, not when I've been sent to complete it.

If I go in now, Father and Mother might be angry with me. But if I finish the job quickly, how can they be anything but impressed?

The stronger soldier succeeds where the weaker soldier failed.

I will show The Program that I am the stronger soldier.

I look at Lee standing with one hand on the open truck door.

"Are you coming?" he asks.

"I'm coming," I say, and I climb into the truck.

"WHAT THE HELL IS HE DOING HERE?" A GIRL SAYS.

She's in the backseat of the truck, her face obscured in shadow.

"He's coming with," Lee says. "Dad invited him."

"And the night just gets weirder," she says, and looks out the window.

I slide in next to her, Lee following behind.

"Have you met my sister, Miranda?" he says.

"I haven't had the pleasure," I say.

Miranda doesn't acknowledge me.

"And I guess I won't now," I say.

I expect that to earn me a reaction, but I get none. The atmosphere in the truck is tense.

"I kind of thought I saved the day," I say. "Why's everyone in a bad mood?"

"You may find an assassination attempt funny," Flannel says, "but it's not funny to us. Not by a long shot."

I let shame bleed into my voice.

"You're right. Sorry. That was a dumb thing to say."

Someone knocks on the front window, a signal to Flannel. He

grunts and puts the truck in gear. He pauses briefly at the exit from the driveway, then, with a squeal of tires, he pulls out behind another truck. I note a third truck behind us, filling out the motorcade that will take us to Camp Liberty.

"Everyone's a little tense," Lee says by way of explanation. "Don't take it personally."

"I don't know what I was thinking," I say.

"You weren't thinking," Miranda says under her breath.

"Not unusual for me," I say.

I note her energy soften after I take a dig at myself.

Flannel drives quickly on the winding road, and I keep bumping into Miranda, our bodies touching in the darkness.

"Sorry. It's a little tight back here," I say.

"So you're not trying to feel me up?" she says.

"I move fast, but not that fast," I say.

She doesn't respond, just shifts her torso and brings her hands into her lap.

I have to be careful about flirting with Miranda. I want to win her over, but not at the expense of my relationship with Lee.

This mission is shifting with each moment. What was a direct assassination attempt has become something more like a standard assignment, in that I need to consider Lee and Miranda as marks that I can use to bring me closer to Moore. I will have to study them, quickly assessing how they interact with each other and with their father so I can keep myself safe as I make inroads toward Moore.

"We're clear of the signal blocking now," Lee says. "You can call your dad."

"Good idea," I say.

I pull out my iPhone. Miranda glances at it.

"Is that the new one?" she says.

"Yeah. Are you into tech?"

"We all are," she says.

"We?"

"At Liberty. It's part of what we do."

"We're a tech-heavy organization," Lee says, explaining. "My father believes if you don't stay on the cutting edge, you fall behind."

"I saw that he was using an iPad onstage," I say.

"Right. He's in love with that thing."

"It's cool when old people try to use tech," I say.

Miranda laughs. Flannel clears his throat in the front of the truck. A warning?

"No offense to anyone," I add quickly.

"I'm not offended," Lee says. "But if you say something like that at camp, you won't be around for long."

"Your father doesn't have much of a sense of humor," I say.

"It comes and goes," Lee says. "But when it goes, it's really gone."

"I'll be careful," I say.

"The camp is organized on a military model," Lee says. "That means you respect your superiors or you're out."

"Lighten up," Miranda says. "He's just coming for a tour."

"It's better he know now," Lee says.

Flannel interrupts from the front seat: "Daniel was about to call his dad."

Strange that he wants me to make the call.

"I'll give him a try right now," I announce to the truck.

I look at my iPhone. I can't risk putting it in secure mode with them watching me, but Father and I have protocols for that. I have a public number I can call, one that will pass the signal through a relay and connect me live to Father on a phone used only for this purpose.

The truck is silent as the number dials through.

Three rings, that's all it takes. I've used a public number on two occasions before, once on assignment in Ann Arbor, another during a mission in Austin, both in public circumstances where I was being monitored. Three rings and Father picks up. That's how it works.

I wait three rings now, but there is no pickup.

Four rings with no response.

Strange.

Five rings. Then six.

I let it ring ten times, but Father doesn't answer.

"What's up?" Lee says.

"He's not answering."

"Maybe it's the mountains," Lee says. "Signals have a way of getting distorted up here."

"But it's ringing," I say.

"Maybe he's ignoring you," Miranda says, her voice teasing.

"Yeah, you might have been abandoned," Lee says, picking up on Miranda's energy. The image of hyenas comes to mind, the way they can be in competition with each other one minute, then working as a pack the next.

I'll need to be cautious about this.

"Whatever it is, it's fucking weird," I say, letting them hear anxiety in my voice.

I dial again, and again it rings without Father answering.

"Nothing?" Miranda says.

I put the phone away.

"I'll try him in a few minutes. I have to let him know where I am or he gets pissed. Then you don't want to live in my world, you know?"

Suddenly the truck shudders and there's a loud flapping noise beneath us.

"Shit," Flannel says, managing to keep the truck under control as he brings us to a stop along the side of the road.

"Sounds like we got a flat," Lee says.

"Damn back roads," Flannel says, but there's something in his tone that sets me on edge. I replay his sentence in my mind, listening for variations in the speech pattern. That's when I know what it is:

He's not surprised.

The motorcade comes to a halt around us.

"Time for triple A," I say.

"Time for triple *me*," Flannel says.

"You need a hand?" Lee asks him.

Flannel looks from Lee back to me.

"That's a good idea," he says.

Lee slips out of the car, then Flannel pauses.

"You okay in here?" he says to Miranda.

"I've got my pepper spray," she says.

"No doubt," he says.

He turns off the truck and takes the keys out of the ignition, slipping them into his pocket as he goes. It's a smart security measure. You don't leave a running car in the hands of a stranger, even a car with a flat tire.

The door closes, and I'm alone with Miranda. I hear muffled voices outside the truck as Flannel and Lee determine the safest way to change a tire on a back road with no breakdown lane. It takes less than a minute for the air in the truck to go from ice-cold to the inside of an oven.

"Hot as hell," I say.

Miranda doesn't say anything.

"Are you going to pepper spray me if I unbutton the top button on my shirt?"

"You seem like a nice enough guy...." she says.

"Crap, here comes the let's-be-friends speech. Let me just get my seat belt buckled before I crash and burn."

The side of the truck tilts up several degrees as Flannel jacks up the car.

"Listen to me," she says. "I don't know why you want to come to Camp Liberty, but now is not the time."

"Why not?" I say.

I hear the sound of metal on metal as Flannel starts to twist off the wheel lugs. Miranda glances toward the back of the truck.

"I can't explain it to you," she says. "But trust me when I tell you you're in over your head."

"Maybe I like being in over my head. It's a challenge."

"You don't need this kind of challenge."

She reaches toward me suddenly and grasps my arm. Her hand is warm where it makes contact with my bare skin.

"It's not safe right now," she says more urgently. "The camp isn't safe."

Suddenly her door opens. She lets go of me, quickly letting her hand fall out of sight.

Flannel stands there, sweat soaking through his heavy shirt.

"Miranda, the other truck is going to take you in," he says.

"Finally," Miranda says, like she's had enough. Of the truck or me, I can't be sure.

She gets out, and I start to slide out after her.

"Not you," Flannel says. "Just Miranda and Lee."

"What about me?"

"You're waiting," he says.

"I'm sweating," I say with a whine. An annoyed kid used to getting his way.

"I'm betting you'll survive," Flannel says, and he closes the door.

The truck in front of us backs up until it's parallel to our own. Miranda glances at me, her eyes drilling into me one last time before she climbs in and disappears behind blacked-out windows.

I see Lee get in the other side of the truck, and two-thirds of the motorcade pulls away.

That leaves me alone on the side of the road with Flannel.

I hear the lug nuts going on one at a time with an electric drill. It doesn't take more than ninety seconds before I hear Flannel toss the flat tire into the trunk bed.

My internal alarm goes off.

If it was only going to take ninety seconds, why transfer Lee and Miranda to a different vehicle?

I look around the truck, searching out things I might use to defend myself. Loose tools on the floor, maps, even a tightly rolled newspaper is a weapon in the right hands.

My hands.

Flannel opens the back door.

"What's up?" I say. "Do you need a hand?"

"All done," he says. "You ride in the front now."

"Why now?"

"So I can see you."

"Girls tell me I'm easy on the eyes," I say.

He looks at me, not amused. He holds the door, waiting for me to get out.

"So much for limo service," I say, keeping my tone light and arrogant, consistent with the Daniel Martin I'm building on the fly.

I had one afternoon to prepare this identity. It was only deep enough to get me through a two-hour event at the community center until I could complete my mission. I did not anticipate having to be Daniel Martin in multiple conversations with people of varying agendas, all probing to know more.

"Out," Flannel says.

He waits for me to get out of the truck and into the front passenger seat. Then he closes the door behind me.

It would be fastest for him to walk around the front, but instead he heads toward the back, walking extremely slowly and disappearing from my vision.

He's keeping me waiting, building suspense. It's a classic interrogation move, designed to invoke fear.

He doesn't know that I don't feel fear.

His tactic buys me extra planning time, and I use it to recalibrate myself to the front seat, its angles and eccentricities, its dangers and possibilities.

When Flannel finally climbs into the driver's seat, he sits there for a moment, but he never starts the truck. He rolls down his window halfway and lights a cigarette.

I roll down my own window.

"My name is Francisco," he says, finally breaking the silence.

"I was calling you Flannel in my head."

He looks down at his shirt and nods. "Makes sense," he says. No smile.

"I'm Daniel," I say. "Nice to meet you."

"I know who you are. Who you say you are."

"What does that mean?"

"It means you're a liar."

"What the hell? Now you're calling me a liar," I say, letting Daniel get offended by this challenge.

I glance at the visor. Yanked from the roof at the correct angle, it would twist off a piece of metal piping that I could use to strike.

The throat. That's where I would aim first.

Francisco doesn't react to my mini-outburst. He simply says, "Everyone's a liar when they fill out an application."

"Not me."

"Everyone," he repeats. "People want to get into Camp Liberty. They don't tell the truth, because they don't think the truth will be good enough. And the funny thing, Daniel? The truth is the only way to get in. You have to tell the truth."

"Then I'm practically in already."

"I'll be the one to determine that."

"I thought it was already determined."

By Moore. In the parking lot a few minutes ago.

"You thought wrong," Francisco says, pinching the cigarette between two fingers and inhaling slowly.

It occurs to me that our truck didn't actually have a flat tire. I'm wondering if the whole thing was staged. To bring this journey to a standstill. To bring me face-to-face with Francisco.

"The question is not whether you lied," Francisco says, "because I already know you did. It's *why* you lied that I'm interested in."

"You already told me why. I wanted to get into camp."

"You haven't admitted that you lied yet. I want to hear it from you."

I could play dumb, but I don't think that's what he's looking for. Better to agree with him but add a twist.

"I didn't lie," I say.

I see his shoulders tighten, ready to attack again.

"I *embellished*," I say, giving the word the hint of an accent.

His shoulders relax a bit.

"About what?" he asks.

"I don't have a four-point-oh grade point average. I did last semester, but not anymore."

"What happened?"

I sigh like I've been caught.

"I fucked up in AP Physics and ended up with a B-minus for the semester. There was this girl in class, and maybe I got a little distracted. Whatever. No excuses. I went down in flames. It won't show on my GPA until next fall. I haven't even told my father yet."

Francisco nods, considering this. I've made it up on the spot, but I can always call it in to Father and ask him to doctor my school records. It's standard procedure for the hackers at The Program to get into the high school mainframe and insert a false student record there to support my cover story. I make a mental note to remind Father when I speak to him.

"You really want to get into Camp Liberty," Francisco says.

"Totally," I say.

"So much so that you're willing to lie."

"Embellish."

He nods.

"So be it," he says. "Now tell me something: Why Camp Liberty?"

"Because Weight Watchers camp rejected me."

"Humor works on Moore. Not on me."

"What works on you?"

He considers the question for a moment. He takes a drag of his cigarette and blows the smoke out the window. I can see him contemplating something, then he makes a decision.

"I'll tell you what," he says. "No more questions right now."

"Good, because I was starting to sweat through my shirt."

"I want you to call your father instead," he says.

It's the second time he's asked me to call. Why does he care about that?

I angle my body slightly, improving my defensive position if things get physical.

"You want me to call my dad?" I say casually.

"You said you needed to call. So call now."

"I tried him a few minutes ago."

"Try again."

"Good idea," I say.

He waits as I take out my phone. He holds the cigarette in his lips, his hands free somewhere in the darkness below the wheel.

I turn on my iPhone. He watches me as I access the home screen and dial Father's public number again.

"Put it on speaker," Francisco says.

"Why?"

"I want to know who you're calling."

"You ever hear of the Fourth Amendment right to privacy?"

"I know all about it," he says. "We don't have that at Camp Liberty."

"What do you have?"

"Transparency. That's how we know we can trust one another. If you want to be one of us, that's how you roll."

"Fine," I say. "Maybe you can talk to my father. Save me the trouble."

I put the phone on speaker.

It rings three times, the rings loud in the silence of the truck cabin. I wait for the pickup, knowing Father will stay in character on a public line, and hoping that will be enough to convince Francisco.

The phone continues to ring, but the familiar sound of Father's voice never comes.

There's no answer.

"Where is your father?" Francisco says, menace in his voice.

"I don't know," I say. And I mean it.

"No voice mail?"

We don't leave voice mail messages. Calls are securely logged and always picked up. There's no need for messages. But I don't tell Francisco that.

"There's no voice mail on his personal line," I say. "He doesn't believe in it. He's old school. You either get him or you don't."

"Unusual."

"He's an unusual man, no doubt about it," I say. "But he does read his texts. I'll send him one so he doesn't worry. He dropped me off tonight, so he knows I'm here. It shouldn't be an issue if I stay over at camp."

"You sure?" Francisco says. "I can still take you home."

"I'm sure," I say.

I type out a text to the public number, something that Daniel Martin might say to his father. Then I send it.

"All set," I say. "Are we going now?"

"Maybe yes, maybe no."

I've been playing chess with this guy, trying to satisfy his curiosity. But I'm tired of being on the defense. I decide to switch to offense and let Daniel Martin get pissed off.

"Hey, it's been a while since the others left," I say. "You needed a smoke, you had some questions. I get it."

"Do you?" he says, amused.

"But it's Moore who invited me to camp. So why don't you give him a call. You can tell him I answered all your questions, but now you're overruling his decision."

I watch his face closely to gauge the reaction. Does Francisco have the power to keep me out of camp? I note tension at the corner of his lip—just the tiniest amount—and I have my answer. This guy is reaching.

"Oh, and when you call Moore," I say, "how about you put it on speaker. You know, transparency."

Francisco chews the inside of his lip. I notice he doesn't take his phone out, doesn't even make a move to do so.

"I never overrule Moore. I share my opinion with him," he says.

"So you're just an adviser," I say, pushing him a little further.

"A *security* adviser," he says. "My job is to protect him. I'll do whatever it takes to keep him safe."

"I'm no threat to him," I say. "In fact, after what I did tonight, you might consider me the opposite."

Francisco drags deep on his cigarette. I see him studying my face in the soft glow of the cabin.

Finally he exhales and flicks his cigarette butt out the window.

"Point taken," he says.

He starts the truck.

"Finally," I say.

WE MAKE OUR WAY UP A TWISTING MOUNTAIN PASS.

Francisco navigates by memory, faster than anyone should be able to safely manage on this route. Eventually he slows to make a hairpin turn, and suddenly the road descends steeply for nearly a mile into a deep valley. At the bottom the forest falls away, leaving an open area of a hundred yards in all directions.

This doesn't look like the boundary of a normal kids' camp. It looks like the perimeter of a military facility. Cover keeps an encampment safe; lack of cover exposes the enemy. Together they make up the yin and yang of a good defensive perimeter.

We descend into the valley and drive through the clearing, and the wooden sign for Camp Liberty briefly lights up in our truck's headlights.

"Home, sweet home," Francisco says.

It's so dark in front of us I can barely make out a scattering of buildings spread across several acres, their profiles appearing and disappearing in the gray-blue moonlight peeking through the clouds.

I wasn't given a map of Camp Liberty in my briefing, because I'm not supposed to be here, so I'm going to have to find out everything I need to know on the ground.

Francisco seems to know where he's going. He pulls forward and brings us to a stop, a building rising out of the darkness.

"Ride ends here," Francisco says.

"Sorry if I was a little bit of an asshole earlier," I say, offering him an olive branch.

"A little bit?" he says, obviously not interested in taking it.

"Okay, then. See you around," I say.

"Guaranteed."

I open my door. A flashlight beam comes toward me out of the darkness. It shines in my eyes, briefly blinding me.

"You made it," Lee says.

The truck pulls away behind us.

"It wasn't the most enjoyable ride I've ever had," I say.

"Sorry we left you like that. It wasn't our call."

"I figured," I say.

"And Franky's not exactly the life of the party."

"Franky? That's what you call Francisco?"

"He's an okay guy once he warms up to you."

"How long does that take?"

"I'm still waiting," Lee says, and I laugh. "Anyway, he's head of my father's security detail now, so I'd rather he do his job than be a friend."

I note his use of the word *now*. Maybe Francisco got promoted recently?

"Follow me," Lee says. He starts walking through the darkness, turning his flashlight beam back toward the ground so I can see where to step. "It's easy to lose your bearings out here."

He's right. Without the flashlight, I wouldn't even see my feet hit the ground.

"By the way, I'm kind of worried that I didn't get through to my dad yet."

"Your phone won't work up here."

"Because of the mountains?"

"We have a central jamming unit. It makes the one at the community center look like a toy."

In my briefing Mother told me the compound was cut off from all communication.

"Why do you have to jam if you're way up here?" I say.

"Nothing in or out," Lee says, suddenly serious. "It's for our own protection."

"Protection from who?"

"Enemies," he says, pointing the flashlight in a sweeping gesture toward the mountains. The way he says the word, it sounds ominous.

"So there's no way I can call my dad?"

"We can get a message through to him if that would help."

I shake my head.

"I guess it can wait until tomorrow," I say. "I sent him a text earlier, and it's not like I'm going to be here forever."

"Who knows?" Lee says. "You may want to stay after you see what we're up to."

"It must be awesome," I say.

"You'll have to decide that for yourself," he says. "Follow me."

Lee guides me forward with the flashlight. He knows the place by heart, his footing sure despite the lack of illumination in the camp.

"So here's the plan," he says. "I'm going to show you where you'll bunk for the night, and we'll give you the tour in the morning."

I hear something in the distance, a rhythmic pounding like a hammer hitting metal accompanied by the faint echo of industrial sounds. Clanging steel, machinery, engine noise.

"That's a lot of noise for a deserted mountain," I say.

"That's the workshop," Lee says. "It operates twenty-four-seven."

"What do you make there?"

"It's one of the ways we earn money. Outsourcing electrical components."

"But I thought you only had kids here, right?"

"Mostly."

"What about child labor laws?"

"Ask my father that question," Lee says. "He'd love to discuss the subject with you."

"Is that a sore point between you two?"

"Don't get me started."

We walk deeper into the camp. There's no sign of any people, only the strange metallic pounding that continues to echo through the valley.

"How many kids are here at a time?" I ask.

"We generally take no more than two dozen for each camp session. But there are no session kids right now. Only permanents."

"Permanents?"

"Kids who live here full time."

I think about the English teacher with wild hair shouting about Moore taking her daughter. Is this what she meant?

"Kids can live here without their parents?" I say.

"Don't be so surprised. It's like military school. Or any other kind of boarding school. You know what that's like from Exeter, Daniel."

He says my name and for a second, it doesn't register that he's talking to me. I'm trained to take on identities one after the other, but adjusting to a new name still has a lag time associated with it.

Changing names is not as easy as people might believe. Your name is your identity, and you've heard it since birth. You associate everything about yourself with your name on a very deep and unconscious level.

I am Daniel, I remind myself. That is my identity now. Daniel Martin.

My own name, my real name, is buried in my consciousness. I neither use it nor access it.

"You okay?" Lee says.

"Thinking about something," I say. "It's not important."

As we walk through the dark, I can just make out the shapes of vehicles parked away from the buildings and facing toward the road. Another security precaution. Keep vehicles and their gasoline tanks away from wooden structures, turned outward, keys in the ignitions, ready to start at a moment's notice. There is no time for U-turns in a battle.

Is it possible this camp is being prepared for attack? The idea seems ridiculous, but the evidence is mounting. I'll know a lot more tomorrow when I examine it in the light.

Lee says, "My dad wanted to welcome you himself, but he's in meetings now."

"It's late for meetings, no?"

His tone turns serious.

"We have to discuss what happened earlier. And other things…" he says, his voice trailing off.

He looks like he wants to say more, but he stops himself.

He turns right at a small building and continues on a path that takes us farther away from what seems to be the central area.

"Just so you know, this kind of thing—the attempt tonight—doesn't happen to us on a regular basis."

"But it's happened before?"

"There have been threats," he says. "Nobody has gotten that close. Especially not someone—"

"Someone what?"

"Someone we know."

I imagine the scenario tonight. The English teacher has a daughter at camp, so they pass her through security without a thorough search, not expecting she has a gun in her purse.

"I can't stop thinking about that moment," Lee says. "How did you know she had the gun? You were on her practically before she got it out of her bag."

"Like you said before, I've got a real talent for this security stuff. Maybe I should join the Secret Service."

"Seriously."

"Okay, truthfully? My dad has a carry permit, so I've seen him take a pistol in and out of his work bag, like, a thousand times. It's hard to miss the gesture when you're used to it. My eye caught it."

He nods, processing the information.

"As for jumping her," I say, "that was pretty stupid. And pretty lucky."

"It should have been me," he says.

He pauses, staring into the dark.

"I saw the gun, too," he says, his voice dropping to a whisper. "But I couldn't move. I didn't know what to do."

"Most people wouldn't know what to do."

"I'm not most people. I'm Eugene Moore's son. He expects better from me."

The statement tells me everything I need to know about Lee. A powerful father, and a son who's not living up to his potential, at least in his father's eyes.

I was reading Lee wrong. The questions he was asking had nothing to do with me. They were about him and his guilt.

"I was just acting on instinct," I say, trying to make him feel better. "Who knows what I would do if it happened again?"

"Maybe you'd do the same thing."

"Yeah. Or maybe I'd poop my pants."

He laughs. "That would clear the room, huh?"

"Whatever gets the job done," I say.

"All kidding aside, maybe my father could use you on his security brigade. He needs another body up there."

"For real?"

"He's short a guy," he says, his voice low.

"How did that happen?" I say.

Lee does a quick circle with the flashlight, making sure nobody is close enough to overhear us.

"One of his bodyguards had to leave."

I think about the soldier from The Program. He was in this same camp four months ago, and now he's dead. Could this have anything to do with what Lee is talking about?

"This bodyguard," I say. "He wasn't doing a good job?"

"He wasn't loyal," Lee says, his voice turning cold. "So he was dealt with."

I don't say anything.

"Didn't mean to scare you," Lee says. "I'm just letting you know there's an opening."

Lee turns his flashlight toward a medium-sized square building set apart from the other structures. "We're here," he says.

The front door is locked, and Lee flips open a metal plate next to the door to reveal a digital keypad.

He moves to block my sight line with his body. I back up like I'm giving him his privacy, but I shift subtly so I can see over his shoulder. He holds the flashlight under his arm and types in a four-digit code.

9 6 6 4

He turns the handle, and the door opens.

"This is where you'll sleep," he says.

"I get my own place?"

"Pretty cool, huh? I'll get you settled, then I have to go over to the meeting."

"I hope you guys have cable," I say.

"We've got better than cable," he says.

"ARE YOU A GAMER?" LEE SAYS.

We're standing in what looks like a hotel room at a three-star property. A stripped-down space, but clean and obviously designed for guests. There's a large bookshelf filled with titles, but that's not what Lee is referring to. He's pointing to a sixty-inch LCD screen that fills the wall in front of us. It looks enormous in such a small room.

Even better is what's on the shelf underneath it. A state-of-the art gaming system, its wires running back through the wall and up out of sight into the television screen.

"'Gamer' is a little bit of a stretch," I say. "But I play once in a while."

I'm thinking of *Zombie Crushed Dead!*—the MMORPG world where I meet Mother for emergency conferences, the anonymity of thousands of players serving to obfuscate our operational communications. In fact, if I can get online here—

"I've got a game going right now," I say. "Can I log in and play it?"

"You mean out in the real world?" he says, pointing up and out. "No can do. It's an intranet setup. We only play each other."

"That's how you guys spend your time? I'm surprised your dad lets you play games. Mine hates when I do that."

"It's not just a game. It's training," he says. "I helped to design the whole thing."

"You programmed it?"

"Not myself. But I supervised the programmers. And I'm the one who came up with the idea behind the scenarios."

"So it's like a flight simulator?"

"That's a good comparison. It develops hand-eye coordination, strategic thinking, and familiarity with military maneuvers. 'Serious play,' my father calls it."

"So you go back to your rooms and play each other?"

"Only some of us have them in our rooms. But we have a couple game centers in common rooms around the property."

"Not a bad deal."

"Actually, it's a trade-off. We don't have computers, iPhones, or tablets of any kind."

"But you've got this."

"We do. Everyone in the encampment has a profile programmed in. Our characters have physical attributes and skills based on our real-world talents. As we train in real life and get stronger, our characters get stronger."

"Sounds amazing," I say.

"You have a profile, too."

"I do?"

"Preprogrammed, based on your application. And a few other things we know about you."

What do they know about me?

Lee says, "The game tracks your score and compares it to everyone else's in the encampment. Ranking is everything here. You'll see."

"I can understand why you guys want to live here," I say, smiling.

"Not yet, you can't," he says, suddenly serious. "But I'm going to show you. If you're interested."

"I'm here, aren't I?"

"You're here," he says. "In fact you're guaranteed to be here at least until morning."

"What does that mean?"

"I have to lock you in tonight. Standard operating procedure. Sorry."

"No problem," I say. "I can't see shit out there anyway. Where am I going to go?"

He laughs.

"See you in the a.m.," he says, and goes out.

I hear him walk down the hall. The exterior door opens and closes, accompanied by the sound of a lock clicking shut.

As soon as I'm sure he's gone, I take out my iPhone.

I move around the room looking for any indication of a signal, trying different angles and heights, testing the limits of the jamming system. The phone stays in search mode, unable to connect to a cell tower, to Wi-Fi, to anything.

No signal of any kind.

I look at the sixty-inch screen mounted on the wall. If I can't explore Liberty tonight, I can explore the game they play, acclimate myself to the culture. Maybe kick some online ass in the meantime.

I power on the system in my room. An avatar appears on-screen—a generic boy, roughly my height and size, rotating in space.

On the back of his shirt is written DANIEL X, as if he's wearing a sports uniform with his name stitched there.

I click the character, and I'm presented with a series of game scenarios:

Laying Plans

Waging War

Tactical Disposition

The Use of Spies

The Attack by Fire

I think about where I've seen phrases like this before, and it only takes a second for me to remember. *The Art of War*, Sun Tzu's classic text of military doctrine written in the second century BC. I studied it as part of my training.

I'm guessing this game is based on the military principles in the text.

I click to open LAYING PLANS, and I'm presented with a colorized map. I study it for a few moments, and I realize I'm looking at the planning schematic for the encampment. I see the main road coming in through the mountain where I drove with Francisco. Camp Liberty is designed as a large oval shape surrounded by mountains. One main road coming in, and a smaller service road exiting from the side. There are two larger buildings: a long rectangular house dead in the center of the configuration and another building that I haven't seen yet, set far back from the other structures, neatly tucked into the side of the mountain. The main building is surrounded by several smaller structures set at random intervals around it. I try to determine which structure I'm in, but it could be one of several.

I study the map more closely, and I see notations for defensive positions set up around the encampment.

Laying Plans

This scenario represents the positioning of forces to maximize the defense of the encampment. But why would they need to defend a camp for kids? Defend it from whom?

Maybe I can find out.

A dialogue prompts me:

Are you ready? Y/N

I press Y, and the map races toward me in 3-D, like I'm being beamed down from space. The world of the encampment comes alive around me on-screen. My avatar stands in the area near the main road. I hear him breathing in a way I never breathe. He is winded, his breath ragged.

There's a scream next to me. I turn and see a man on the ground at my feet writhing from a gunshot wound to the stomach. He turns over and I see a name on the back of his shirt: P. MERCURIO.

The earth jumps a foot from my feet. It's a gunshot impact. I see flashes coming from the main road.

I run.

I note a statistics box on the lower right, and I see there are fourteen active players currently in this scenario. Suddenly P. Mercurio's name pops up in red before the box fades out. Now there are thirteen active players.

I'm starting to get the hang of this.

I move through the digitized world of Camp Liberty. There are a lot more than thirteen players on the board. When these avatars turn their backs, they're identified numerically, for example as COMPUTER 1249, which means the computer is generating additional characters to populate the world. These characters stream out of the buildings, confused and upset. Some of them are caught in the open and mowed down; others carry weapons and run in a zigzag pattern like they know what they're doing. Almost everyone is moving toward the main building in the center.

The earth rumbles beneath me, and I hear large armored vehicles moving down the main road toward the encampment.

"Daniel, this way!" a character shouts.

He runs in front of me, motioning for me to follow him. The back of his shirt says L. MOORE.

It's Lee.

I follow him toward the main house. If the game world is as realistic as I suspect, I can use it to learn the layout inside the house.

I lose Lee in the throng of running people. Some of them are panicked and screaming, others calm. There are different entry points to the main house, and they seem to know which to head for. The ones who make it are let into the safety of the house.

I watch a character run through the front door. I make for the same door and turn the knob—

It's locked.

"Access denied," the game says, and sends a painful warning vibration through my controller.

Gunshots pepper the wood around my head. I duck low and run for a side door.

"Access denied," the game intones again.

I turn and see a figure watching me from across the way. There's something different about him, something unlike the other characters on the map. At first it seems like he might be dead because he's not moving while people pass by him.

But I note a subtle swivel of his head. He's standing still, but he appears to be monitoring me.

Who inside the game might be watching me? It's not Lee. I saw him disappear into the main house.

I move toward the unknown figure, trying to angle around to see the name on the back of his shirt. I slide along a wall, edging ever closer to him.

Suddenly a bullet impact throws wood splinters past my character's eyes.

I'm temporarily blinded. When my vision returns, the unknown figure is gone.

I hear shouts behind me. Men in blue jackets are racing into the encampment, the letters ATF emblazoned in gold across their front. They carry assault weapons.

ATF. The Bureau of Alcohol, Tobacco, Firearms and Explosives.

I'm beginning to understand why the camp is set up like it is. They think they're going to be raided by the government. Not just raided but attacked. And they're preparing to defend themselves against it.

I watch the ATF agents streaming into camp inside the game. My first feeling is that I should trust them. They work for the government, and though they'd never know it in real life, so do I.

In the game, I step out where the ATF agents can see me, and I raise my hands in surrender.

They lift their assault rifles and commence firing on my position.

This should never happen in real life, law enforcement firing on unarmed civilians. But in the ethos of the Camp Liberty game, it's us versus them. This ATF has shoot-to-kill orders.

I turn and run.

I make for a small house set apart from the main structure. I fling my avatar's body against the door.

"Access denied," it says.

I feel my pulse quicken as the ATF agents advance on the encampment.

This is just a game, I remind myself.

But it's amazingly realistic in its depiction. The screaming voices, the rumble of trucks, the hiss of tear gas cartridges falling and releasing their contents around me.

I even hear my character coughing. His movement slows. I press harder on my controller, but I cannot make him run faster.

I cannot get away from these agents with guns.

One last chance, a glass window in a small building off to the side. I run toward it and throw my character into the air, hoping to hear the window shatter.

Instead there is a loud buzzer.

"Access denied," the game says again.

That's when the bullets hit me.

A vibration passes through the controller along with a mild shock that causes the muscles in my hand to contract.

I look down at my character's stomach, blood seeping through his shirt.

I press the controller, but it's like trying to move through wet concrete.

I glance up to see an unknown figure standing passively to the side, watching me. It's the one from before, the one who was monitoring me.

My screen begins to dim.

The character turns and begins to walk away. I look at the back of his shirt through the encroaching haze. Every character has a name or a computer code imprinted on the back of their shirt.

Every character except his.

There is no name. His shirt is blank.

My screen goes black. There is the sound of wind, a low howl like a storm blowing through an empty field. A single word appears on the screen:

Terminated

A data block floats in and centers itself on the screen. These are the stats for my character, Daniel X.

Active player ranking: 14 out of 14

Chance of survival in an equivalent real-world scenario: 0%

Chance of survival in all scenarios: 32%

Universal ranking: 128 out of 128 statistical players

I'm not only dead, I'm dead last.

No matter.

Because in playing the game, I've seen a map of Liberty for the first time. Now I can find my way around.

Enough play. It's time to get my mission on track.

I have to call Father and let him know where I am.

I take my iPhone from the desk. I glance at it and see there's no service.

I think about how a group could accomplish electronic blocking in an environment like this. I imagine a primary device radiating from the center of the encampment, with additional devices, electronic repeaters, up in the mountains.

Up high. That's where I'll have to go to defeat the jamming and acquire a signal.

It's late now, well past midnight. It's time to use what I have learned from the game.

CALCULATED RISK.

That is what I am trained to assess. All actions carry risk. Stepping out of the house in the morning, walking on the street, getting into a car, flying. All of them are risky, but a normal person doesn't see it that way. Because once the level of risk falls below a certain threshold, a normal person no longer sees the activity as inherently dangerous.

Not me. I know the truth.

All actions carry risk, but the risk must be assessed.

Leaving my room in the dark and walking through an armed encampment? Attempting to escape into the mountain, high enough that I can get a signal and call The Program?

Extreme risk.

Staying in my room without contacting The Program, knowing that I am undertaking a mission that was not planned and for which I can receive no support?

Greater risk.

My decision, then, is simple. I have to talk to Father or Mother.

So I choose the lesser of the two risks and prepare to go outside.

I explore the room, looking for anything that might be helpful to me. When I open the closet, I find a row of forest-themed camouflage pants and brown T-shirts. I select something in my size and slip it on. I put my iPhone into a buttoned pocket on the camo pants. I make sure to wear my special glasses.

I walk down the hall to the door. I turn the handle. It's locked, just as Lee said it would be. But I know the code. I type it into the digital pad.

A moment later the door lock clicks open, and I step outside.

I walk out into a dark so profound that my eyes are useless.

No matter. I will use my other senses. I listen for the distant metallic pounding coming from the workshop. I track the way it bounces off the mountainside and triangulate that back to where I am standing. In this way, I can echo-locate the mountain and move toward it, making my way to the edge of the encampment.

I have one primary objective.

Ascend.

Ascend until I can get a signal on my iPhone, until I can inform The Program of my location, and together we can develop a contingency plan for this mission.

Ascend.

But I must remain undetectable as I do it, or my mission will end tonight.

IN THE DARKNESS, I USE WHAT I HAVE LEARNED FROM THE GAME.

I head behind my building, walking silently across dirt and grass, my arms in front of me feeling for obstacles. Several times I note sentries moving in the darkness, but I drop into a crouch and wait for them to pass, moving on their assigned rounds.

The moon moves out from behind the clouds, and I can make out the great mass of the mountain in front of me. I see that I am near the perimeter, the open zone between the edge of the encampment and the forest on the other side. It looks like a clear shot into the forest, but I doubt it's that easy.

I pause at the edge of the perimeter and study the scene before me.

The wind blows, picking up leaves from the forest and scattering them down into the open zone. I catch a glint of red light off one of the leaves.

I pick up a handful of dirt from the ground and rub my hands until it breaks up into fine particles. I move forward slowly, blowing dust in front of me as I go.

That's when I see them, quadruple red lines marking an invisible laser perimeter. The lowest line is maybe seven inches off the ground, the rest spaced at eighteen-inch intervals above it. Too low to crawl under, too high to jump over. A system like this will link to a monitored computer somewhere inside a building. In a forest setting, a regular laser perimeter would be riddled by false alarms—falling branches, animals, any number of things could break the beam and cause an alert. This system must be sophisticated enough to screen out false positives, so if a raccoon runs across the line, it won't trigger an alert that will call out the sentries.

I could take my chances and move through the beams low and fast, replicating the characteristics of an animal, but instead I blow another shower of dust, scope out the distance between the lowest two beams. If I do this right—

I back up several steps and I leap between the beams, flattening my body so I pass through without triggering the perimeter alarms. I roll up from my leap, then dart into the forest without hesitating.

I stop inside the tree line and listen. There are no guards, no shouts, no sound of a chase.

I am clear.

I move out now, zigzagging from tree to tree, not stopping until I know I am fully hidden by foliage. Then I pause to examine my surroundings, looking for the most viable path up the mountainside.

As I climb, I think about the idea of a central jamming unit radiating outward with repeaters placed in the forest around and above the camp. How high would those repeaters have to be in order to cap off all communication? At least as high as the tallest building, plus additional distance to overcome line of sight interference.

I estimate the height of the repeaters in the mountainside, and I move forward and up, working to ascend above them.

I've made it no more than ten meters when I hear a crunch in the woods below me.

I wait, listening.

A twig snaps, the sound coming from behind and below me. It's not an animal. The pattern of movement is human.

Someone has followed me from the encampment. I don't know who or how they've accomplished it, but I know.

I am being tracked.

I set off deeper into the woods, moving in a herky-jerky upward spiral, backing down and around my own tracks and making it as tough as possible on the person who is following me. An amateur will show himself quickly in a situation like this, either losing the track entirely or revealing himself without knowing it.

But whoever this is, he is not fooled by the spiral maneuver. He moves when I move, and stops when I stop with only the barest overlap.

I'm impressed. He's good.

But I'm better.

When I start out again, I feign movement without going anywhere. I stay behind a tree, stepping in place, allowing my footsteps to get louder and softer, using different angles on the tree to bend the sound, drawing the person closer to me. A genius tracker might be able to discern what I'm doing, but anyone at a level below that will fall for it, eventually flushing himself out.

Half a minute later I hear footsteps approaching, and I see the outline of a figure with a hoodie pulled tight around his head.

He stops when he comes close, sensing something is amiss. This may not be the highest level of tracker, but he is close. He waits and he listens.

I allow the tiniest sound to escape, no more than the whisper of fabric against bark like a pant leg brushing against the base of a tree. I want to draw him toward me, let him think that he has located me.

I note caution in his steps as he changes position, circling back around and moving toward the source of the sound from a different angle, perhaps thinking he's going to surprise me.

It's a good move. Just not good enough.

I dart noiselessly to a nearby tree and I wait.

I count down the steps until he's on top of me. Three, two—

The figure passes by, and I step out from behind and grab him, one hand around his chest, another at head level. I don't mean to harm him, only take him down, neutralize any threat until I know who I'm dealing with. Then I will decide what comes next.

As I clamp down, he tries to spin away, and I feel something soft across his chest. Surprisingly soft.

A woman's breasts.

I release my grip too quickly, and the figure spins back toward me.

"Let go of me!" Miranda says.

I see her face now, an angry scowl outlined by the hoodie, red hair tucked out of sight.

"You snuck up on me," I say.

"You broke curfew and got out of camp," she says. "You're lucky it's only me who snuck up on you."

"What are you doing out here?"

"Following you," she says.

We stand facing each other in the middle of the woods. She's right that she could have called the guards, raised an alarm, prevented me from getting this far.

But she didn't.

I remember her warning to me in the back of the truck when we had a flat tire. Why did she help me then, and why now?

She adjusts her jacket around her breasts.

"Did I hurt you?" I say.

She puckers her lips. "It's a sensitive area," she says, "but I'll live."

Her eyes track me in the darkness.

"I heard you pass by me in the woods outside of camp," she says. "How'd you get out?"

"I walked."

"That's impossible. You would have triggered an alarm."

I shrug. "You got out without a problem, didn't you?"

"I know how."

"Then I guess I got lucky,"

"Twice in one night, huh?" she says.

"What do you mean?"

"First you grab a gun, then you get through a laser perimeter. You must be the luckiest guy in the world."

If she wanted to turn me in, she would have done it already. So I play it brazenly, showing her the arrogant side of Daniel Martin.

I say, "Actually, I got lucky three times in one night."

"What's the third?"

"I'm in the woods with a cute girl."

That stops her short. But only for a second.

She says, "You didn't come out here for the hot singles scene. So why are you here?"

Just then my iPhone chimes. She glances toward my pocket.

"You're trying to make a call!" she says, thinking she's figured something out.

Most operatives would be tempted to lie and cover their tracks in a situation like this, but I've learned that the truth is the most power-ful tool I have.

I take out the phone and hold it up. "You got me," I say.

I glance at the screen, hoping it's a return text from Father, but it's a simple reminder about a school assignment that's due Monday. The iPhone has been preprogrammed with the data of the fictional student named Daniel Martin.

"You know there's no reception in camp," she says, "so you snuck up here hoping to find a signal."

I see her putting it together. They're used to playing strategy games in this camp, solving riddles. Maybe I can use that to my advantage.

"You're right. That's why I'm here," I say. "But who am I calling?"

"Let's see," she says, intrigued by the question. "You're trying to make a call in the middle of the night, which is stupid. You sneak out of the compound to do it, risking getting thrown out. Also stu-pid. And you get caught, which is—"

"Stupid," I say.

"Right. So I have to ask myself: What makes a guy do stupid things?"

"What's the answer?"

"A girl."

I laugh.

"You have a girlfriend, don't you?" she says.

My laugh stops.

A memory of my last mission pops into my head, Samara and me running through the rain in Central Park.

I push it back down, burying it deep in my unconscious, where I will not have to deal with it.

"I don't have a girlfriend," I say.

The phone screen glows brightly in the dark of the forest.

"You want to call someone pretty badly," she says.

There's an edge to her voice now, anger creeping in where before there was only curiosity. I have to defuse it.

"It's not my girlfriend," I say. "It's my mother."

I see her body relax.

"You're a momma's boy!" she says, finding her answer at last.

Now I show the sensitive side of Daniel, allowing myself to appear vulnerable in front of her.

"My parents don't know where I am," I say. "I mean, I sent my dad a text earlier, but he's notoriously unreliable when it comes to passing on info to my mom. That's if he's talking to her at all right now."

"But why call her in the middle of the night?"

"She'll be up. She's a worrier."

"I wish *my* mom were a worrier," she says.

It's a curious response.

"She's not?" I say.

Her body posture deflates, her voice dropping to a whisper.

"No. She's more like a traitor."

"What do you mean?" I say, shocked at her use of the word.

"She left last year," Miranda says.

"Your parents got divorced?"

She shakes her head.

"She just fucking left," she says. "Him. Us. This place. Our way of life. All of it. She packed her bags in the middle of the night and left without telling anyone."

I try to imagine a woman who would leave her husband and children without telling them. It could be a woman who is mentally unstable. It might be a woman who fell for another man and got lost in love and obsession. Or it could be something else, a woman so afraid for her life that she thought she had no choice but to run.

It would be helpful to know which it was.

"Why did she leave?" I say.

"I don't really know. We haven't spoken since that night."

"Never?"

"A postcard. That's what I got. One postcard, no return address."

"That's messed up."

"Completely."

"So you never found out why?"

She shakes her head. Perhaps she knows more, but she seems unwilling to go there.

Miranda is tough, a survivor. I appreciate that about her. And I sense that now is not the time to press her for more information.

The screen on my phone goes to sleep, casting us back into darkness.

"If you want to call your mom, you should," Miranda says. "But don't call from here."

"Why not?"

"We're too close to the encampment. They monitor everything and they can triangulate the signal."

"Where should I call from?"

"Follow me," she says, and she starts up the mountain.

SHE WALKS AHEAD OF ME, HER MOVEMENTS NEARLY SILENT.

To walk through a forest quietly is extremely difficult. To move through a forest quietly while hiking up a mountain in the dark is nearly impossible. But she achieves it almost effortlessly, her body moving in patterns both trained and reflexive. It tells me a lot about who she is and the life she has led up until now.

It also tells me that she doesn't know how to hide her skill set from me. This is the difference between a soldier and an operative. A soldier is a soldier all the time, but an operative is myriad things, each of them adjusted to time, place, and situation.

This girl is a natural, but naturals need to be developed to become operatives. This camp has taken her only so far. I wonder what she could become with the proper guidance.

A troubling memory comes to me. It's a memory of Mike and me in gym class years ago. It was before he killed my parents, before I knew about The Program.

We were doing a basketball rotation, and the coach had us running wind sprints on the court—free throw line and back, midcourt line and back, full court and back, each with a 180-degree turn to develop our flexibility and speed. Mike ran next to me, matching me move for move.

When we were walking back to the locker room after, he turned to me.

"I saw you out there," he said. "You've got natural skills."

"Nah, I'm too short for basketball," I said. I was only twelve, and I hadn't hit my growth spurt yet.

"Not just for basketball. In general," Mike said.

The comment passed without my thinking much about it.

That was almost five years ago, but I think about it now as I walk behind Miranda.

I am assessing skills, just like Mike did. In his case, he was secretly recruiting a new operative.

But what am I doing?

I am keeping myself safe. No more than that.

I push the memory away.

As I move behind Miranda, I make sure I do not give away my own skills. I step on fallen branches from time to time, brush against dry leaves, take two steps when only one is needed. I may have made it out of the encampment and snared Miranda during a tracking maneuver, but I can muddy her impressions of me now, lead her to think that luck played a greater role in my success than it did.

We walk without speaking for several minutes until we crest the top of the ridge. She comes to a stop. I hear the sounds of a river flowing nearby.

"This is the place. It's safe here," she says.

"How do you know?"

"Because they've never caught me."

She reaches into her pocket and comes out with something small and black. I can't see what it is until she turns it on and her face is lit by the glow of her own iPhone.

"You're allowed to have a phone?"

She shakes her head.

"No one knows," she says. "And it has to stay that way."

"Who would I tell?"

"Wrong question."

"What's the right question?"

"Who would believe you?" she says.

A warning. For a moment, her face looks ghostly in the screen's light.

"Who do you call from up here?" I say.

"There's nobody to call. I read the news, look at YouTube. I want to see what's going on in the real world."

"I'm surprised."

"Why? You thought I was a good girl?"

"Something like that."

"Well, I'm not."

"Then what are you?"

She looks away from me, stares into the woods.

"Complicated."

It's quiet now, the evening punctuated only by the call of night birds and the distant sound of running water.

"Is that a river I hear?" I ask.

She nods. "Liberty survives because of that river. It leads down into camp. We use it as our water supply."

"What about in the other direction? Where does it go?"

"I've never followed it there."

She presses something on her phone.

"I'm going to read the paper," she says. "Why don't you make your call? We don't want your mommy to worry about you."

"Hey, I said I was a momma's boy. I've got no shame about it."

"Eventually you have to leave the nest."

I gesture toward her phone. "Is that what you're doing? Breaking your father's rules?"

"We're not talking about me right now. I notice you have a brilliant way of turning conversations around."

"Maybe I'm uncomfortable talking about myself," I say.

"So it's a defense mechanism?"

"One of many."

"What do you have to defend yourself against?"

I point to the world around us, mirroring Lee's line from earlier:

"Enemies," I say.

She stares at me.

"You're an interesting person, Daniel."

"I'm interesting now, and you hardly know me. Imagine what I'm going to be like in a few days."

"I hope you make it a few days," she says with a devious smile.

I wink and turn my back to her. I'm planning to be here only as long as it takes to finish the job. That's why it's critical that I talk to Father.

I use the unique finger gesture to open the alternative operating system on my iPhone.

The phone instantly goes into secure mode, giving me access to a suite of security apps unimaginable to the average user. I open the Poker app, arrange a hand of cards that represents Mother's phone number.

If Father isn't answering the temporary public number, I'll dial into the permanent secure number that guarantees a nearly instantaneous connection with Mother.

I glance over my shoulder at Miranda. She's turned her back to me, giving me privacy.

I listen in the digital silence, waiting for the inevitable click of a line opening and Mother's voice answering. Any time of day or night, anywhere I call from, she is there. This has been true over two years and across multiple missions.

It's not true tonight.

There is only silence.

First I check the cellular signal. Four bars. Full reception.

Then I backtrack, closing the app and reopening it. I rearrange the poker hand, checking to make sure the cards are in the proper order by number and suit.

Again, I wait for the connection, and again nothing happens.

I turn off my phone.

"Did you speak to her?" Miranda asks.

"You were right," I say. "She must be sleeping."

"So much for being a worrier."

"She's also an Ambien user. The two kind of go together."

I walk toward Miranda, slipping my phone into my pocket.

"I want to ask you something serious," I say. "Earlier tonight in the truck, you told me to stay away."

She lowers her voice to a whisper. "Things are changing here, Daniel."

"How are they changing?"

"It's not just a camp anymore. My father. He's different since my mother left. I think she kept him calm in some ways. No more. Now he's got plans."

"What kinds of plans?"

She comes even closer, our faces nearly touching.

"Frightening plans," she says, her breath soft on my cheek.

"I don't understand what you mean."

"I can't say more," she says.

I lean toward her, our faces inches away from each other.

"But you didn't even know me when we were in the truck. Why bother to tell me anything?"

She looks at the ground, suddenly shy.

"I liked you right away," she says.

"You've got a funny way of showing it."

"I'm used to being around military-type guys," she says. "I guess it's made me kind of tough."

"But the warning?" I say, getting her back on track.

"I didn't think it was fair to bring you here without you knowing what you were getting into."

"I'm trying to register for the next camp session. That's a good thing, right?"

"My father canceled the next camp session. That event was just for show."

"There's no camp this summer? Then what am I doing here?"

"He wanted you here. From the very beginning, the moment you walked into the community center. They were talking about you before the event. I overheard them."

"Them?"

"Francisco and my dad."

"That's strange."

Moore rejected me after his speech and refused to meet me. He was trying to keep me out, not bring me in.

So why would she say the opposite?

"Nothing happens without my father wanting it to," she says.

"Nothing?" I glance at her phone.

"Almost nothing," she says.

Maybe it's the night, or the girl, or the sense of danger all around us. I just know I want to step forward and kiss Miranda.

It could help my mission or harm it. I can't be sure.

So I step back.

"It's getting late," Miranda says, obviously uncomfortable. "We should probably go back before they notice we're not in camp."

"It was fun while it lasted," I say, and she laughs, a sweet laugh that makes me wish I had kissed her.

But I am a soldier. I am here to accomplish a mission. Nothing else.

Miranda moves away from me through the forest.

"Hey, what's the best way down?" I call to her.

She keeps moving.

"You were talented enough to make it up here," she says, her tone suddenly teasing. "Can't you find your way back?"

"I can if I follow you."

"I'm going down alone," she says. "I don't want to risk us being seen together outside of camp."

Her outline is faint now.

"Either I'll see you at breakfast," she says, "or I'll see you after the search party finds your body."

"Wait a second...." I say.

But she doesn't. She disappears into the night.

I'm alone in the dark now, thinking about what just happened.

It's not getting down the mountain that's the problem. I'm on a ridge peak next to a river that flows south and feeds the encampment. So direction is not the issue.

Nor is getting back through the laser perimeter.

It's what it will say about me if I do. Miranda took me off the path, led me higher into the mountain, and left me here. If I get back down, that says a lot about my skill set. Too much.

And if I don't make it down, they'll search for me and the entire camp will know I breached security. There will be questions, doubts, maybe even censure.

So I have to make a choice.

Before I decide, I take out my phone again, open a secure connection, and try Mother.

It is the same as before. Silence.

I try Father, both public and private lines.

Nothing.

It's possible the mountains are causing interference with the signal. It's possible blocking tech from Liberty is affecting the ability of the phone to uplink to the satellite.

Possible but unlikely.

What exactly is going on?

I don't know.

I only know I have to stay in the moment, and the moment requires me to make a choice.

Follow the river back to camp or play lost? Either could work, either could fail.

Life is about risk. Mission dynamics are no different. It's just that the stakes are higher on a mission.

Much higher.

I make my choice.

I head south, moving silently through the darkness, walking back down toward Camp Liberty.

IT'S A COUPLE OF HOURS BEFORE DAWN WHEN I GET BACK.

It's my experience that a security detail loses focus closest to dawn when it nears the end of its shift. The end of a shift is like the last minutes of a job, of school, of nearly everything. By that time you're just waiting for it to end so you can get home and do what you want to do.

That makes it a perfect time for me to explore.

I watch from the cover of the woods. I listen for the clang and whir of metal fabrication, and then I follow it toward the workshop building, moving along the tree line outside of camp, my body turned inward so I can watch for trouble.

When I get closer to the source of the sound, I move into the encampment, slip through the laser perimeter, and instantly make my gait casual, like a guy who is taking an early walk because he can't sleep. I turn a corner, and I see it, a factory building with double doors wide enough to drive a truck through. I recognize the building from the game, the second of the two largest structures in camp. Even in the dark I can see the doors are sealed tight with huge padlocks.

The windows of the workshop are blacked out, but I can make

out flashes of light coming between cracks in the paint. The flashes stop, then start again in a staccato rhythm. At first I'm not sure what I'm looking at, but after a moment the pattern becomes familiar.

Arcs from a welding torch. Something is being assembled in the workshop in the middle of the night.

I look down the road at the white vans parked there. They look like utility trucks, but there's no branding on their sides.

Lee said they outsourced components to earn extra income. That might explain the vans, but it doesn't explain the all-night fabrication processes.

I move toward the workshop, heading for a bank of high windows on the side. If I can find something to stand on, I might be able to get a sight line—

"You can't be back here," a voice says.

A flashlight beam snaps on in my face.

I recognize the voice. It's Moore's bodyguard, Swivel Neck.

How did he find me back here? And how did he get close without my registering it?

I haven't slept in nearly twenty-four hours, and I'm starting to make mistakes. Miranda tracked me into the forest, and Swivel Neck snuck up on me. These are bad signs.

But I can't do anything about them now. I have to react.

I hold my hand up to my eyes and feign surprise.

"Hey, what's up?" I say, and then I pretend to suddenly recognize him. "You work the night shift, too?"

"I work all the time," he says. "And you're not allowed to be out here now."

"I couldn't sleep. I was taking a walk and I heard some noise."

"Curfew lifts at dawn. The camp is off-limits until then," Swivel Neck says.

"There's a curfew? Nobody told me."

He plays the beam across my face.

"*I'm* telling you," he says.

"Off-limits. It's all good," I say with a shrug. "By the way, what time is breakfast served? Unless waffles are off-limits, too."

"Funny man," he says. "Follow me."

He turns, and his flashlight beam catches a small flash of red on the ground.

I follow him, stopping briefly to tie my shoe. I scoop the little piece of red into my hand and close my fist around it.

"You coming?" he says.

"Right behind you. What's your name, by the way?"

"Why do you need to know what my name is?"

"Relax, guy, I'm trying to fit in here."

He points the flashlight in my face again.

"My name is Aaron," he says.

Then he swings the flashlight back around and beckons me to follow him to the building with my sleeping quarters.

"Breakfast is in the main house at oh seven hundred," he says, using the military designation for seven AM.

He blocks the keypad with his body while he dials the code. The lock clicks, and he opens the door and waits for me to go inside.

"Thanks, Aaron."

"How'd you get out in the first place?"

"It was unlocked."

"Lee," he says, shaking his head. "Sloppy."

He closes the door, and I hear the lock click.

I go back to my room and flip on the light.

I open my fist to examine what I found on the ground outside.

It's a thin red curlicue of rubberized plastic insulation. The shape tells me it's been stripped from some type of wire. It could be from a car or some other machine, an engine that was being repaired. It could be from electrical wiring in a building.

It could be anything at all.

I button it into the side pocket of my camo pants, then strip down and go to bed.

I DON'T SLEEP.

For the rest of the night I lie awake, thinking about The Program and why I am unable to communicate with them. I come up with three major hypotheses:

1. Technical interference, either man-made or spontaneously occurring.
2. They've cut me off on purpose, either because it's not safe for me to communicate with them or for other reasons I cannot fathom.
3. They are themselves cut off, in trouble, or otherwise compromised.

Of the choices, I deem number two to be the most likely. If our communications system has been breached by Moore's people, the only choice would be to stop communicating with me until a message can be passed safely.

But if that's true, what does it mean for my assignment? Do I continue forward until I get to Moore, carrying out the last directive

I was given? Or do I default to primary objectives, protecting The Program first and myself second?

I run through the options again, but I don't come to any conclusions.

After a while I get up and sit in a chair. Sleep research has found that after lying in bed for thirty minutes without falling asleep, it is better not to fight sleeplessness. It's more effective to get up and do something else for a while, change location and tasks, thereby allowing your body to find its own sleep rhythm. You will get tired later and go back to bed without having to force it.

So I sit in a chair and think about everything I've learned about Liberty up until now. I think about Moore, where he might be sleeping, what it would be like to sneak up on him unprotected and complete my assignment.

And maybe for a second I think about Miranda, the softness of her chest against my arm when I grabbed her in the forest.

I stay in the chair for the rest of the night.

I don't sleep.

The next thing I know light is creeping between the window blinds, and I hear distant bangs, a sound both distinctive and chilling.

It is the sound of gunfire.

IT BEGINS WITH A SINGLE SHOT.

One becomes two, two becomes cascades of rifle fire, the echoes bouncing around the valley.

I drop from the chair and crawl away from the window, expecting shattering glass and the sound of rounds hitting the wall above my head. None come.

The shooting stops. For the briefest of moments I think I dreamt it, and then it begins again, another volley of gunfire.

This is not an attack. It's training.

I walk down the hall and hit the head quickly, pause to look at myself in the mirror.

I see a boy with bags under his eyes, his face puffy from lack of sleep. I see that my tight haircut is in need of a trim. I note that I lost some weight in the sports camp and on the journey to New Hampshire. This causes my muscles to appear too pronounced. Normally I like to hide my physical abilities behind a couple of extra pounds, just enough to lower expectations.

I see this too-thin, too-tired boy who has been up most of the night, first on a mission and then on postmission planning, and I transform his energy into that of a boy who had trouble sleeping because he is nervous about the day to come. A sixteen-year-old desperate to impress, yet confused about who he is and what he is here to achieve.

In short, I make myself into Daniel Martin, the new recruit at camp.

Finally I stretch out my T-shirt, loosening it up to make myself appear smaller and less athletic.

When I'm done, I look away from the mirror, draw my attention back to the morning and the moment.

The sound of shooting continues in the distance.

I walk to the exit door down the end of the hall.

Last night it was locked from the outside. Today it is open, an invitation to the game.

I take the invitation.

LEE IS WAITING FOR ME.

He is lost in thought, leaning against the wall of my building, his hands jammed deep in his camouflage pants pockets.

"You're awake," he says when he sees me.

"How long have you been standing there?"

"Not long. Dad asked me to let you sleep. He said trauma can exhaust a person emotionally and physically."

Trauma. Tackling a crazed woman with a gun and narrowly escaping being shot. Just seeing that would be too much for most people, triggering days of anxiety and post-traumatic stress. And being in the middle of it? That would indeed be traumatic.

But I am not traumatized. Not by a long shot.

Another volley of gunfire echoes across the camp. I note a brief lag between the shot and my reaction to it, which doesn't please me. My response time is dulled from lack of sleep.

"Is someone being executed?" I say.

"We only do that on Wednesday," he says. "Today is Saturday."

"It's nice to have something to look forward to."

He smiles and motions for me to follow him.

"We train every day," he says as we walk. "You're going to get a taste of life here."

"How about a taste of breakfast first?"

"Plenty of time to eat afterward," he says.

He takes me around the back of the structure and we walk toward the camp perimeter. I'm memorizing details as we go, matching the small, dark wood cabins and larger white buildings to the images from the game last night, creating a mental map of the compound so I can navigate by day or night.

We walk through what was an active laser fence last night, out past the perimeter, and around to a gun range. It's set several hundred yards away from the camp facing out toward the mountain. Any stray rounds will continue on for a time until they impact in the forest, where they can do no harm.

There are about two dozen teens out here, half in shooting positions, half watching from behind, awaiting their chance on the firing line.

Shooting practice.

It's one thing to receive weapons training for self-protection or so one can be a safe and knowledgeable hunter. But that's not what I see here.

These teens are on their bellies firing assault rifles from combat positions.

I recognize the range master from the community center last night. He's the man in his early forties with a shaved head, the one Moore trusted to talk with the parents.

The range master calls for a cease-fire on the shooting line, and the teens fire off their remaining rounds, pop the magazines, and check their chambers. These kids know what they're doing, and they exhibit proper range etiquette. The range master walks the line like a pro, inspecting weapons and correcting where he finds error.

Then he crosses to us, giving me the once-over.

"This is the guy I've heard so much about?" he says.

Lee nods. "Daniel, this is Burch," he says.

"*Sergeant* Burch," the range master says, correcting him.

"You were at the community center last night," I say.

"So were you. And you did a hell of a job, son. Pleased to meet you."

"Thank you, sir."

He extends a callused hand to shake. I let him crush me a little with his grip, allowing him to assert dominance right off the bat.

A true military man.

"I'd like to give Daniel a chance to fire off a few," Lee says.

Sergeant Burch's face grows troubled.

"That's not a good idea," he says.

"I think it's a great idea," Lee says. "What do you think, Daniel?"

I've been trained to shoot, but I don't like guns.

The nature of my work doesn't call for them. There's no such thing as anonymity with propulsive weapons, no way to use them quietly, to fully control the damage inflicted, or to obliterate the forensic evidence that remains after the fact.

For all their power, guns are inefficient for someone like me.

"It's not up to me whether I shoot," I say, deferring to Sergeant Burch.

"That's right," Burch says with an appreciative nod. "Nothing personal, young man, but we don't allow the new people—"

"He's going to shoot," Lee says, interrupting. "We all shoot here." Something angry passes across Lee's face, a dark energy that surfaces seemingly from nowhere and disappears just as quickly. "Besides," he says, "it's important to shoot because it improves your player stats in the game. And let's be honest, you could use some improvement."

"How do you know my stats?" I say.

"Everyone knows," he says. "The scores are public."

Light laughter around me. The group of teens have been listening in, their attention focused on us.

I say, "Funny for you guys, maybe, but I was locked out of all the buildings. How is that fair?"

"It's a realistic simulation," Lee says. "That's what would happen if our perimeter were breached now. You'd be out in the open with nobody to protect you."

"You wouldn't let me in the building?"

"It's not up to me," Lee says. "You don't have security clearance. You know what that makes you?"

"What?"

"SOL," he says. "Shit out of luck."

He snaps his fingers rapidly, the edginess returning.

"Let's get back to business," Sergeant Burch says to the group. "B-Group to the shooting line. Load your weapons and await my command."

He turns to Lee.

"Why don't you take your friend for a walk while we finish training."

"Don't tell me what to do. You're not my father," Lee says.

A look passes between them.

"Burch gets confused sometimes," Lee says, directing his comments toward me. "He thinks that because he and my father served together, he can give me orders."

Sergeant Burch's face stays passive, but he cranes his neck sideways until it cracks.

"I want Daniel to shoot," Lee says.

"You said yourself that he doesn't have security clearance."

"I'm giving it to him now."

"I'm not going to put a weapon in a stranger's hands," Sergeant Burch says. "It's a breach of protocol."

"Who says he's a stranger? He was invited by my father, and he's my personal responsibility."

"You vouch for him?" Burch says.

"I do," Lee says.

"Then by all means, let's give him a rifle," Burch says, then shouts, "Clear the line!"

The teens in firing positions lay their weapons on the ground and retreat to the safety of the observation bench.

Sergeant Burch selects a rifle from a table and walks it toward me. I recognize the profile of the M4 carbine, a military-issue weapon that has become the successor to the M16 for U.S. combat troops. A true M4 is illegal for private sale or ownership. It's possible that I'm looking at a legal variant, a civilian knock-off without a fully automatic mode. But I can't be sure without firing it.

"Do you know your way around a combat rifle?" Sergeant Burch asks.

"I learned a few tricks during my three tours in Afghanistan," I say.

Sergeant Burch stares at me without so much as cracking a smile.

"So you've never fired a weapon like this," he says.

"Nope. I'm only sixteen."

"I've got thirteen-year-olds who can handle this weapon."

"Well, then it sounds like I've got some catching up to do."

"Fair enough," Burch says with the calm demeanor of a good instructor. "If we're going to do it, we're going to do it properly."

With Lee looking on, Burch gives me a one-minute tutorial on loading and firing the weapon and the safety procedures associated with it.

When he's done, he passes me the weapon.

"This is not a toy," Sergeant Burch says. "I need your entire focus and concentration."

"You have it," I say.

I take the weapon from him. I press the telescoping stock into my shoulder, aim downrange, and sight down the barrel.

That's when Moore comes striding onto the range with Aaron and Francisco following close behind.

I shift toward Moore, and his eyes widen as he sees the rifle in my hands. Francisco and Aaron react quickly, moving in front of him as Aaron quick-draws a pistol from under his arm.

Moore puts a hand out to stop Aaron. Then he steps between Aaron and Francisco, exposing his chest as he moves slowly toward me.

"What's going on here?" he says quietly.

"They asked me if I wanted to shoot," I say.

"*Who* asked you?" Moore says.

I glance at the crowd of teens watching us, moving my eyes but not my body.

"Lee asked," I say.

Moore walks toward me. Francisco and Aaron tense behind him but hold their positions.

Twenty degrees of rotation. That's what it would take to bring the shortened barrel of the M4 in line with Moore's chest. At this distance, the round would impact with devastating effect. A double tap, two bullets to the chest, and it would be over.

Moore must know this, but it doesn't deter him. He stays in the open, exposed to danger.

"The rifle," Moore says, spreading his arms wide. "Do you know how to use it?"

"Sergeant Burch showed me," I say.

"Lee vouched for him," Sergeant Burch says.

"Very well," Moore says. "Daniel, I want you to aim the rifle at my son."

Lee's eyes widen.

"I can't do that," I say.

"Why not?"

"You don't aim a weapon at anyone you're not willing to kill," I say.

"I told you to aim, not fire."

"They're the same thing," I say. "I've had shooting lessons. I know to consider them the same."

I sense movement behind me. It's Sergeant Burch. He's picked up a rifle and trained it on my back. He's not shy about aiming.

"What if I command you to aim at my son?" Moore says.

"I don't take orders from you," I say.

Tension ripples across the faces of the kids watching us.

Moore nods, considering what I've said.

"Do you take requests?" he says.

"If they're reasonable."

"Put the weapon down."

I make sure the rifle is on safe, and I pull the magazine. I place them both on the ground at my feet.

I feel Sergeant Burch relax behind me. Aaron and Francisco move back into position next to Moore.

Suddenly Moore whirls and charges toward his son.

"You gave a weapon to a newcomer?" he shouts at Lee.

He glances at the assembled teens, then at Sergeant Burch. Nobody dares speak.

"I did," Lee says, putting on a brave face in front of his father.

"Why?" Moore says.

"The game," Lee says. "I wanted to establish a skill level for him—"

Moore reaches out and puts his hand on the boy's shoulder. At first it seems like a benign gesture, but his fingers turn white as he grips, pressing into Lee's flesh the same way he pressed into mine in the parking lot of the community center last night. I see Lee working hard not to react while Moore bears down, putting intense pressure on his nerve plexus. Sweat breaks out on Lee's forehead and his face goes pale, but he doesn't make a sound.

Moore lowers his voice, leaning in toward Lee.

"I love you," he says, "and I wouldn't do anything to hurt you. But you have to learn that decisions have consequences. You put yourself in danger with your actions here. Do you see that?"

"Yes, sir," Lee says, his voice faint.

"You put all of us in danger."

"I understand."

"I'm not always going to be here to protect you," Moore says.

He looks at Lee's face with great concern, then he releases his grip from Lee's shoulder.

Lee inhales sharply. I can see him holding back tears.

"Very well, then," Moore says, brushing himself off. "Sergeant Burch, we'll talk about this later."

"Yes, sir."

Moore slowly looks across the line of teens, a silent challenge.

Nobody says a word.

"Daniel, why don't we take a walk together," Moore says. "If you don't mind."

I adjust the glasses on the bridge of my nose.

"I don't mind," I say.

I need to find a way to get Moore alone for a few minutes. This could be my opportunity.

BUT MOORE IS NEVER ALONE.

Flannel and Aaron tail us as we walk, never straying more than a few feet from Moore.

"I'm sorry to use you like that," Moore says.

"Use me?"

"To teach my son a lesson."

"What would you have done if I'd followed your order and aimed at him?"

"I would have given you a second order," Moore says.

"To drop my weapon?"

"To shoot."

I look to Moore for some sign that he's joking. I don't see any.

"And if I had followed the second order?" I say.

"So be it. A lesson is learned either way."

I think about what kind of man would be willing to sacrifice his son to teach him a lesson.

Then I think of Father, his hand over mine on the cyclic in the helicopter yesterday. Was he really willing to crash our helicopter to make his point?

"We have rules about newcomers," Moore says. "They're not to get live ammo until they've been fully vetted."

"I can understand that. But if you were truly concerned about me being new, why did you walk in front of me when I had a loaded rifle?"

"Not in front."

"Nearly."

"If you had turned even an inch toward me, you would have died."

I glance back at Francisco, find him watching me, his eyes scanning regularly from Moore to me.

"Okay, but if I were a bad guy. I might have gotten off a shot."

"Doubtful," Moore says. "But whatever happened, I would have had my answer."

"Your answer to what?"

"To the question of whether or not you're dangerous."

"That's what you want to know?"

He nods.

"I didn't shoot you, so I'm in the clear, huh?"

I react like Daniel Martin would, wiping fake sweat from my brow.

"Not exactly in the clear," Moore says. "There's a difference between a zealot and a professional. A zealot acts without regard to personal safety. A professional is doing a job and wants to go home at the end of the day. You didn't shoot, so I know you're not a zealot. But that's all I know."

I watch Moore closely, trying to understand his intent. Is it possible he knows who I am?

I want to defuse the situation, so I say, "To be honest, I haven't had breakfast yet, and this conversation is making my head hurt."

"We're not done talking yet," Moore says, danger radiating from him.

"What do you want to talk about?"

"I want you to tell me the truth about who you are."

Truth. It's the same thing Francisco talked about last night.

"The truth? I'm a guy who wants to get into Camp Liberty," I say.

"Why?" Moore says, his focus intensifying.

I think about my mission briefing with Mother and Father yesterday, the doubt they wanted me to show Moore. Normally I would have time to develop this persona earlier in a mission, before I even got close to my target, but now I have to do it in real time, in front of Moore.

I take the arrogant Daniel Martin and I go deeper, probing beneath his surface attitude to the boy who might be suffering quietly.

"Maybe I want to get away from my parents," I say.

The sentence surprises me a bit.

"What's so bad about your parents?" Moore says.

"They're liars."

Moore nods, waiting.

"They expect me to play by the rules, but the rules keep changing. How the hell am I supposed to deal with that?"

"That's not fair to you," Moore says.

"No kidding. I get blamed for shit that's not my fault because they changed it up on me, and then they want my respect. But you have to *earn* respect, don't you? It's not something you get automatically because you call yourselves parents."

I sense something personal inside me threatening to surface, so I think instead about Daniel's story, redirecting the focus of my rant.

"My parents say they don't believe in the system and then do everything in their power to stay a part of it, even to excel within it. My father is willing to give money to organizations like yours that want to change things, but what does he really want? I mean, he's giving money to change a system he benefits from, and the organizations themselves only exist because people make money off the system so they have something to donate. To me it looks like one big feedback loop of bullshit."

I'm expecting Moore to be offended, but he smiles at me.

"I understand how you might feel that way," he says. "It's a system, that's true, but everyone has a role to play."

"What do you mean?"

"An army, for example, has different elements. There are the soldiers on the ground who do the actual fighting, there are commanders whose job is to see the big picture and guide the fighting, and then there are the money men, who pay for it all. Without everyone playing their role, there is no army."

"I never thought of it like that before."

"So you may not like the role your father plays in this ecosystem, but he plays a role nonetheless. An important one. Not everyone can do the fighting."

I nod, signaling my understanding. "The ecosystem you're talking about—I know which role I want to play."

"Which role is that?"

"Soldier."

Moore smiles. "I thought so," he says.

He signals for Francisco to come forward.

"He's ready," Moore says to Francisco.

"Ready for what?" I say.

WHITE VANS LINE THE ROAD LEADING OUT OF CAMP.

Unlike the other day, they are pointed out toward the mountain pass, their engines running. I see teens in the driver's seats, waiting impatiently.

Francisco walks me toward the back of the line, where a number of kids are gathered in a group. I slow down as I pass, noting that most of them are dressed in black from head to toe. I see Lee talking with people in the center of the group, his arms gesticulating wildly. He notices me and signals for me to join him.

"Go ahead," Francisco says. "I'll catch up with you in a minute."

I walk over to Lee.

"Hey," Lee says. "My dad called to say you were coming with us. I'm glad."

"I'd be glad, too, if I knew where we were going."

"The Hunt."

"What's The Hunt?"

Lee smiles. "A scavenger hunt. We go out and look for things. Are you interested?"

"Sure. Maybe I can call my parents from the road?"

He nods. "Come on, then. You're riding with us."

He walks me toward a van near the rear of the pack. He opens the side door and waits for me to climb in. Then he slides in behind me.

Francisco nods a greeting from the driver's seat.

"Everybody locked in?" he says.

"Safety first," Miranda says, buckling her seat belt in the front passenger seat.

Lee pats me on the back. "We're good to go," he says to Francisco. Then he leans forward to his sister. "Daniel is one of us now, Miranda. Can you believe it?"

"Did you clear it with Dad?" she asks Lee.

"It was Dad's idea. Isn't that right, Francisco?"

"That's right," he says.

"It's official. I'm coming with," I say.

"The more, the merrier," she says, unimpressed. Then she turns around and slumps in her seat.

"Let's roll out," Francisco says, and he starts the van.

"You're going to love this," Lee says quietly. "It's a total blast."

THE VANS SPLIT UP OUTSIDE OF CAMP, MOVING OFF IN DIFFERENT DIRECTIONS.

I sit in the back with Lee, trying to monitor our direction in case I have to report on it later. There are no windows on the side of the van, so I look through the front windshield, memorizing details as we go.

I recognize Manchester as we cross into the city limits.

My phone chimes.

"What is that?" Francisco says quickly from the driver's seat.

I pull out my phone. It's another fictional reminder for Daniel Martin, this time for a school book fair that's happening next weekend.

"It's just my phone," I say.

"Off," Francisco says.

I look to Lee. "But you said I could call my dad."

"Later," Lee says. "If your phone is on, you can be tracked. *We* can be tracked."

He motions to all of us in the van.

"So what?" I say.

"You don't want to be tracked right now. Believe me," he says.

He watches as I turn the phone off. I glance up to see Francisco also looking at me in the rearview.

"It's off," I announce to the van.

Francisco nods and steers the van down a busy stretch of road. We pass store parking lots filled with cars.

"What would they think if they knew we were out here now, driving among them?" Lee says.

"Who?" I say.

"The people. The nice, law-abiding people."

"If *they're* law-abiding, then what are we?"

"Save it," Francisco says from the front seat.

Lee grits his teeth. I'm noticing he doesn't have much of a poker face.

He leans toward me and whispers: "You'll see what I mean."

Miranda flips down the mirror in the front seat. Ostensibly she's fixing her hair, but when I glance at her, she's looking at me from the corner of the mirror, her eyes large.

She doesn't say anything, so I don't, either.

I try to piece it together. What are they planning?

We make one stop at a gas station, and I notice Francisco pulls a baseball cap low over his forehead before he gets out to pump gas. When he gets back in the car, he has a bag full of energy bars, beef jerky, and trail mix. He tosses it back to me.

"What's this?"

"Lunch for everyone," he says. "It's the best we can do."

"Anything is better than nothing," I say.

I haven't eaten all day, and I missed breakfast because I was talking to Moore, so I dig into some trail mix, eating slowly to replenish my energy without shocking my system.

"Okay, time to do some reconnaissance," Francisco says.

We head out of Manchester, driving east for several miles until we pass signs for Lake Massabesic, just east of Manchester.

"It's up ahead," Lee says.

"I can read the signs," Francisco says.

"You're not from around here, so I'm just making sure."

"Thanks for your concern," Francisco says.

"Enough," Miranda says. "All this dick swinging is boring the crap out of me."

The road is mostly empty, but Francisco drives cautiously, obviously unfamiliar with the territory.

"Where are you from, Francisco?" I say.

"Lots of places," he says.

"He was a stray," Lee says, "until my father took him in."

"That's not nice," Miranda says, putting her hair into a bun and tucking it under a nondescript baseball cap. "We're all in this together."

She passes a similar cap back to me, motioning for me to put it on.

"It's not nice, but it's true," Lee says.

Francisco keeps his cool in the front seat. Instead of responding to Lee, he says simply, "It's time to focus on the task at hand."

Lee slips on a baseball cap as Francisco takes the turnoff for Lake Shore Road. We drive for a few miles, hints of the lake popping up through brief clearings in the forest.

"We're going to drive around twice, nice and easy," Francisco says. "Keep your eyes open."

We do two laps around the lake, and then Francisco slows, searching for something on a nearby road. A moment later he finds it, a wooded cul-de-sac hidden from the main road. He pulls in and turns off the engine.

Miranda reclines her seat back. Lee rests his head on the side of the van and pulls his cap over his eyes like he's going to sleep.

"What's happening now?" I say.

"Now we wait," Francisco says.

"For what?" I say.

"For nightfall."

THEY NAP THROUGH THE AFTERNOON, BUT I DO NOT.

I use the time to sort through my mission timeline, attempting to look at it both from The Program's perspective and my own.

Twenty-four hours since I began the mission at the community center, and Moore is still alive. From my perspective, the mission has been delayed, but not abandoned. If anything, I'm getting closer to the inner circle, more comfortable there, integrated and accepted.

But what is The Program's perspective?

I haven't talked with The Program or received any communication since I stepped out of Father's car.

It seems like they have disappeared, but if something has gone wrong with my iPhone or the comms link, perhaps I'm the one who seems to have disappeared. The thought is troubling to me, but there's nothing I can do about it now.

I hear a crinkle of paper, something being unwrapped. I look over at Lee. He's awake, surreptitiously peeling and eating a chocolate bar, gobbling it down a square at a time.

He notices me watching him.

"What?" he says, his mouth full. "It's an energy boost."

"Where did you get it?" There were no chocolate bars in the bag Francisco brought us.

"I smuggled it from camp," he says.

He reaches into his pocket and pulls out another one.

"You want?" he says. "Our secret."

"I'll pass," I say.

An alarm goes off from some kind of timer in the front seat. Miranda reaches for it and turns it off. Then she stretches and yawns loudly.

"Who would have thought that changing the world would be so boring?" she says.

"Did you guys get some rest?" Francisco says.

Lee and Miranda answer in the affirmative. I join them, even though it's not true for me.

"Let's get started," Francisco says. "Everybody ready?"

Lee finishes off the chocolate bar in one big bite, then wipes his mouth with the back of his hand.

"I'm ready," he says.

"What about you?" Francisco says as he turns toward Miranda. She nods.

"I need a verbal confirmation," he says. "You know the protocol."

"Ready and willing," she says unenthusiastically.

"And you, Daniel? Are you ready?"

"Don't I have to know what we're doing before I know if I'm ready?"

"Are you ready to trust us?" Francisco says. "That's all we need for now."

"Sure," I say.

"Then let's go," Francisco says.

He hops out and opens up the back of the van. He pulls out a single duffel bag, which he slings over his shoulder.

"Do you have your comms?" he asks Lee.

"I've got them, and I've checked them," Lee says.

"Check again," Francisco says.

"I checked already."

"We can't afford any errors," Francisco says.

"There won't be any errors," Lee says, and I see his hand balling into a fist. He grudgingly pulls a cell phone from his pocket, checks for a signal, then types a text into the phone.

A second later, a text comes back with a faint ping.

"You see? It's working," he says, and stuffs the phone back into his pocket. "The only time we get cell phones, and I can't even download any apps."

Francisco sighs. He turns to Miranda. "What's our timeline?"

Miranda presses a button on her digital timer.

"Thirty minutes," she says.

"What's the timeline about?" I say.

"That's how long we have to get in place and accomplish the mission," she says.

"Mission?"

"The Hunt," she says.

"T-minus thirty," Francisco says. "That means we have to hustle."

With a hiss of air through his teeth, he starts up the side of the road, motioning us to follow him.

THE ROAD IS DESERTED.

I sense the lake to our right, a low-slung stone wall defining the boundary of the property around it. We pass the occasional cabin to our left, and Francisco diverts us into the woods, out of sight, switching back to the road only after we're a good distance away. Only once do we spot headlights coming toward us down the lake road, and Francisco quickly moves the group behind the foliage until the car passes.

As we get closer to whatever our destination is, Francisco staggers us so we're not as obvious a group, or as large a target. I use the opportunity to drop back a little ways to where Miranda is.

"You guys have done this before," I say.

"A few times a year," she says. "For two years now."

"Same group?"

"Different groups. But they usually keep Lee and me together."

"It's like a camping trip of some kind?"

"It's no camping trip," she says. "It's a hunting trip."

"No talking, please," Francisco says.

He's fallen back within earshot.

He stops the group by putting up a fist, then he points from his eyes to a spot in the distance.

A utility road opens out of nowhere, marked only by a single rustic wooden sign:

MANCHESTER WATER WORKS
WATER TREATMENT PLANT

"What is this place?" I whisper.

"It's the water processing plant for the city of Manchester," Lee says. "The lake provides drinking water for one hundred and sixty thousand people. All of it passes through here to get purified before it winds up in their homes."

"What are we doing here?" I say.

"We're just taking a tour," Lee says. "An unauthorized, nighttime tour."

"Don't look so serious," Miranda says. "This is the fun part."

Without another word, she hops over the stone wall and disappears into the darkness. Lee does the same, then whistles for Francisco and me to follow.

ONE SENTRY DRIVES THE ROAD AT NIGHT.

One sentry, every two hours or so, unless something draws his attention before that time. It's our job to make sure nothing draws his attention. That's what they tell me.

We come to the locked side door of the treatment plant.

Miranda pulls a small kit out of her pocket and leans down in front of the lock.

"We're going to break in?" I ask Lee.

"Not exactly. We sneak in, find what we're looking for, and leave undetected. That's how The Hunt works. They can never know we were here. Or else our team loses points," Lee says. "We're scored on our performance, then the scores are tabulated and added to our game profiles back in camp."

"The game I played last night."

"The one you tanked on," he says with a smile.

"Keep it down," Francisco says.

"Yeah, I'm trying to concentrate," Miranda says.

She holds a miniature flashlight in her teeth while she expertly works the lock.

A minute later, the door opens.

"We're in," she says. "Sixteen minutes."

"Let's do this," Lee says.

We slip inside and close the door behind us. I'm surprised that I feel the same rush I do when I embark on a Program assignment. The danger, the excitement of possible discovery, the need for a focus so intense that it shuts out every other thing in your life to the point where all your problems seem far away.

I look at Lee and Miranda, and I recognize the expression on their faces: the excited buzz of doing something forbidden.

Then I look at Francisco, and I see something else.

He is calm.

He glances over to find me watching him, and his entire physicality changes in an instant. His shoulders rise and his jaw tightens, his body taking on tension.

It happens so quickly it's easy to think I misread him in the first place.

Francisco hisses under his breath, drawing our attention, and then he guides us to a wall, pointing down a hall and up to the ceiling, where a camera is mounted in the corner.

"No motion detector," he says. "Just a digital recording system, but an older one that rotates and records with a slow frame rate."

The frame rate is not unusual for a security camera. Regular video records at thirty frames per second or greater. But most surveillance video runs at six to ten FPS to save energy and storage space. Although playback will have a herky-jerky quality, it's still easy to make out the motion of the figures on the video, the way they're dressed—

And their faces.

The good news is that Francisco knows about the system and where it's located. It's not only old, it's badly placed, midway down the hallway and against the wall, sweeping left and right. That makes it easy to wait until it's aimed away and move below it.

We pass down the hallway until we're clear of the camera. Then we move into the main chamber of the water treatment plant, a massive room filled with complex machinery and the computers that monitor it. Francisco pulls out an iPad mini, bringing up a schematic of the building before focusing in on the room and the machinery all around us.

"We're looking for this," he says, pointing to a piece of machinery on the screen.

"What is it?" I say.

"It's the chemical feed system. That's where they add the chloramine," Lee says.

Chloramine. I've heard that term before. It's a compound of chlorine and ammonia that some municipalities use in their drinking water as a disinfectant in place of pure chlorine.

Lee says, "They feed the chloramine into the water in late-stage treatment to kill all the nasties."

"Why do we need to find that?"

"Maybe we want the nasties left in there," Lee says.

And he smiles.

Francisco interrupts him. "We find it because that's the game," he says. "We don't ask questions."

I don't like what I'm seeing here.

Nobody would imagine a terrorist threat in the middle of rural New Hampshire, in a place where the greatest threats are weather and wildlife. But a hundred and sixty thousand people is a tempting target. And how many targets like this exist throughout the United States?

The scope of it is staggering. If you were to disturb the water supply for a city like Manchester, then every water supply of this size and greater would suddenly need to be protected. The cost in security, man hours, and structural upgrades would be prohibitive. How can you protect every municipal water plant, every Department of Public Works, nuclear facility, university laboratory, electrical facility? Trying to do so would bankrupt the U.S. economy.

"Six minutes, guys," Miranda says.

"What happens if we're late?" I say.

"We lose points if we're late, and we can't let that happen," Miranda says.

"Over here," Lee says.

He's tracing a piece of machinery along the wall, following a large pipe across the room, where it disappears into the floor.

"Damn, it's in a separate room," he says. "Let's go."

He starts down a metal ladder.

THE ROOM BELOW.

That's where we find the chemical feed system, the last stop before the water is distributed into the community.

Miranda uses Lee's phone to take a picture of the machinery. "We got it," she says.

I see her check the photo and close her camera app.

"We can go now?" I ask.

Miranda shoots a nervous glance toward Lee. "Not exactly," she says.

Francisco puts the duffel bag down at his feet.

"What's going on?" I say.

I get no response.

"A minute forty-five seconds," Miranda says, studying the timer on her watch.

I look at the duffel bag.

"What's in the bag, Lee?"

"Something we add to the system," he says.

I look at the feed pipe in front of me, the top of it with a latch and round handle that turns like a metal steering wheel. Pop the latch, and you have an opening directly into the system.

"What are we adding?" I say.

Lee and Francisco look at each other. They don't answer me.

"A minute fifteen," Miranda says.

Lee pulls thick gloves from out of a side pocket of the duffel bag. He holds the gloves out to me.

"For you," he says. "You're the guest of honor."

"What do I do with those?"

"Put them on. You're going to be handling a hazardous substance."

"I thought this was a game," I say.

Lee shrugs, noncommittal.

"Leave him alone," Miranda says. "He doesn't know what's going on."

"He'll find out soon enough," Lee says to her, then turns back to me. "If you're with us, you'll put them on."

"I can't be with you unless I know what we're doing."

I look at Miranda, but she won't meet my eye.

"We're poisoning the water supply," Lee says.

I glance at Francisco. He's watching me carefully.

"Why?" I say.

"Because those are my father's orders," Lee says.

"And you're okay with that?"

"I don't question orders. I carry them out."

The words are so familiar it's like they're coming out of my own mouth.

I look at the gloves being dangled in front of me.

Is this real, or is it a game?

Judging by the serious expressions on the faces around me, it's no game.

My mission is to take out Moore. Anything I do is in service of that goal alone.

If helping them commit an act of terrorism would bring me closer to Moore, then in theory I should do it.

But why was Moore targeted in the first place, if not to prevent something like this from happening?

Is my loyalty to the mission or to the purpose behind the mission, or at least what I perceive that purpose to be?

Without being able to talk to The Program about this, I'm going to have to make a judgment on my own.

As I look at Lee holding out the gloves, I realize I already have.

I can't stand by and watch these people poison the water supply, even if acting against them will destroy any chance I have of completing my mission.

Miranda is peering at the timer on her watch. "One minute to go."

"Well?" Lee says.

I look at the gloves, but I don't reach for them.

Lee grunts and snatches them away.

"Never send a boy to do a man's job," he says, putting them on.

"Slow down," Francisco says calmly. "We don't do anything until we get the signal."

Lee glares at him. "Unzip the duffel bag, Franky."

"Not until we have confirmation," Francisco says.

Lee is sweating, the veins in his neck popping out. Francisco, on the other hand, is relaxed, his gaze steady and unblinking.

"Goddamn it," Lee says. "Open the bag."

"Wait," Francisco says calmly.

"Fifteen seconds," Miranda says, her voice tight with tension.

"I hate you," Lee says to Francisco. "You're not even one of us."

"I *am* one of you," Francisco says. "Your father trusts me with his life."

"I don't trust you. Not at all."

"Whatever your feelings about me," Francisco says, "we follow procedure."

"Fine," Lee says. He makes a huge gesture of taking the phone out of his pocket and holding it in front of him.

"Countdown starting," Miranda says.

I watch Lee, judging the distance between us, planning how I will take him out if he reaches into the duffel bag. My only question is order of attack—can I move fast enough to neutralize him before Francisco and Miranda realize what's happening and respond? Based on what I've seen up until now from Francisco, I decide it would be prudent to disable him first before going after Lee.

Miranda says, "We go hot in three, two, one . . ."

There's a ping from Lee's phone.

He looks at it, and his shoulders slump.

"Goddamn it," he says. "It's just the game."

Miranda exhales loudly.

"What did I tell you?" Francisco says. "No need to even open the bag." He betrays no emotion as he says it.

"Sending the picture," Miranda says, and I see her using her phone to text the photo of the feed pipe.

"Wonderful," Lee says with a sneer.

"You'll keep first place in the rankings," Miranda says, trying to make him feel better.

"That's kids' stuff," he says. "I'm talking about the real thing."

"You shouldn't be in such a rush to get to the real thing," Francisco says.

"Whatever," Lee says, pulling off the gloves and throwing them into the bag.

"All right, let's focus," Francisco says. "We still have to get out of here undetected and get back to camp."

"Maybe we should make Daniel walk back," Lee says.

"Stop it," Miranda says.

"I don't know whose side this guy is on," Lee says.

"I'm here, aren't I?" I say.

"But are you loyal?"

Francisco and Miranda pause, waiting for me to answer.

"I don't give my loyalty away," I say. "It has to be earned."

"That's a good answer," Miranda says softly.

"We haven't earned it?" Lee says, challenging me.

"Not yet," I say.

Francisco nods. "Fair enough," he says. "Now let's get out of here before we have a bigger problem on our hands."

WE MAKE IT BACK TO THE VAN.

Francisco drives us to camp with Lee sitting in the front seat this time, slumped down, a cap pulled over his face as he naps.

When we're clear of Lake Shore Road, Francisco turns on the radio, finding a jazz station he likes and keeping it low.

I lean over to Miranda in the backseat.

"I don't understand what happened tonight," I say quietly.

"The teams are sent to scout different places and bring back a picture of what they find as proof. We get points for every successful mission."

She lowers her voice, and I move a little closer to her in the van.

"If it's just a game, why is Lee so upset?"

"We have to treat it like an actual op until the text comes in."

She glances toward the front seat.

"He wants it to be real," she whispers, "but it never is. It's my dad's version of a mind fuck."

"That's a relief," I say.

"You wouldn't have gone through with it?"

I detect the change in her tone as she asks it, her voice serious.

"Killing innocent people?" I say. "It sounds a little crazy to me."

"It's not about killing people. It's about shaking up the system in a profound way."

She looks at me, her face hidden in the dark of the backseat.

"I'm all for shaking things up," I say.

"I thought so," she says.

She reaches over and runs her fingers down the length of my arm. The sensation makes me shiver.

"My father wants us to confront questions like these. It's a part of the game."

I think about a camp full of kids being trained for military operations on American soil. That doesn't sound like a game to me.

A large component of soldier training is desensitizing recruits to the stimuli they will receive in an actual battle situation, so when the soldier finally gets into battle and the explosions start around him, he doesn't freak out. He's already experienced it, albeit in the relatively safe environment of the training facility.

Moore is doing the same thing with these kids, bringing them to the brink time and again, without them knowing what is real and what isn't.

I think about the operation tonight, imagining a dozen white vans, some heading down to Boston and into western Massachusetts, others staying in the immediate area. I think like Moore, considering targets he could hit if that was his intent: Natick Labs, the main research and development center for the U.S. Army; Raytheon; Boston Scientific; various tech labs at MIT; the campuses at Harvard, BU, or any of the other sixty or so colleges and universities there. The possibilities are endless, and from Boston, it's a short hop to New York and Washington. Suddenly Camp Liberty's location in the mountains of New Hampshire doesn't seem so remote.

"You have to admit it was a rush, wasn't it?" Miranda says.

"It was," I say, placating her.

She slips her hand in mine.

"What are you two whispering about?" Lee says, waking from his nap.

"Daniel is telling me how much fun he had tonight," Miranda says, pinching my palm at the same time.

"Yeah, right," Lee says. "Lots of fun."

THERE IS A FIRE AT LIBERTY.

I can see it as we pull in: the glow of flames against houses, the trail of smoke rising from the center square of the valley.

"Is something burning?" I say.

"It's a bonfire," Lee says.

"We have a party after The Hunt," Miranda says.

Francisco parks the van, and Miranda hops out fast.

"Let's go," she says, pulling me along beside her.

"I want to talk with Lee. I'll catch up with you in a couple minutes," I say.

"Fine," she says, obviously disappointed.

I don't like being caught in the middle of this competition between Lee and his sister, but I need to talk to Lee about what happened tonight.

Lee gets out of the van, walks around, and opens the back door.

"How are you doing?" I say.

"How am I doing?" he says angrily.

He reaches in and pulls the duffel bag toward him. He unzips it and holds it open to me.

I look inside. There, in the bottom of the duffel, are two sacks of unbleached flour, double sealed inside plastic bags.

"I'm fantastic as long as we're going to a cake-baking contest," he says.

He rezips the bag and pushes it violently into the truck.

"You wanted to poison those people?" I say.

He kicks the bumper, and suddenly all the anger drains from him.

"No," he says, his head hanging down. "That's not what I wanted. I wanted—"

Francisco comes around the van, and Lee stops in midsentence.

"Lee, let's go talk to your father," Francisco says, his voice gentle.

"Not now, Franky. I'm not in the mood."

"I think you should," Francisco says. "You'll feel better."

"I don't care what you think," Lee says. "*Especially* not you."

Francisco looks back and forth from Lee to me, then he throws up his hands and moves on.

Lee slumps down on the back bumper.

"I didn't want to poison those people, but I want to do something. Somewhere. Sometime. We talk and talk and never do anything. It makes me so angry, I can't even speak to my father anymore. He's just like the government he pretends to criticize. All talk, no action."

He looks up at me, angry.

"You're the same way," he says. "I offered you the gloves and you wouldn't take them."

"That's not fair."

"Either you're one of us or you're not."

"I came to learn about your father's ideas. You can't throw me into something like this and expect me to be okay with it."

"Maybe you're scared," he says. "Maybe you don't have what it takes to sacrifice yourself for a cause."

"We'll see."

"We will. I agree." He slams the van doors. "If you stick around. And if my father ever decides to do something for real."

"This camp is for real," I say, trying to get back on his good side. "What he's teaching everyone here, the training he's giving them that they'll take out into the world."

"Sometimes I think it's all a scare tactic," Lee says. "He builds this big weapon and never uses it, just waves it in people's faces."

I hear Lee's frustration, but I disagree. You don't send kids out on mission ops unless you intend to use them someday. Why risk getting caught? Why risk dealing with the authorities at all?

So I think Lee has it wrong, but I understand his frustration with his father. Maybe I can use his frustration to get closer to Moore.

"Have you talked to your father about it?" I say.

"Ad infinitum," he says. "But it doesn't matter. You see how he treats me, how he dismisses me."

I glance down and see Lee's fists clenched by his sides.

"One day I'll be in charge," he says, "and it will all be different. Believe me when I tell you."

"I believe you," I say.

"You do?" he says, looking up.

"Really."

"You think I have what it takes?"

"I do. I saw it tonight."

He smiles.

"Sorry about earlier," Lee says. "Maybe I was wrong about you."

"Maybe I should have taken the gloves. I don't know."

"We'll have another chance."

"I hope so."

He starts walking toward the main square, and I follow.

"Do you think your father will let me stay?" I say.

"We'll see," he says.

"Where is your father now?"

"I don't know. He usually lies low during parties. He's not much of a celebration guy."

"What about you?"

"Not in the mood. But you should go."

"Maybe I'll hang out with you instead," I say.

He smiles.

"I'd rather be alone," he says. "Besides, my sister will have a hemorrhage if you don't show up at the party. I think she likes you. Did you see how she stuck up for you tonight?"

"I think she was doing that just to piss you off."

He laughs.

"Seriously, are you okay if I hang out with her? If not, I'll—"

"It's fine with me," he says. "But be careful. She only *seems* nice. She's tough under the surface."

"She's tough *on* the surface, too."

He laughs.

I think of Mother, the woman who runs The Program.

"Anyway, you don't have to worry about me. I can handle a woman with a temper," I say.

"You think you can," he says. "But she might surprise you."

I HEAR THE SOUNDS OF MUSIC AND KIDS LAUGHING IN THE DISTANCE.

I follow them into the main square, where a large bonfire is lit. Nearly the entire camp is here, girls and guys celebrating together, singing songs and talking about their various exploits from the evening.

A couple of girls invite me to join them, but I politely shrug them off, looking instead for Miranda.

I don't find her.

And I don't find Moore.

Instead of staying at the bonfire, I head back through the darkness toward the building where I bunked last night.

The door is unlocked. I flip on the lights in the bedroom and find everything as I left it last night. Only the bed has been made.

Suddenly a toilet flushes down the hall. I leap up and turn out the light. Then I hear footsteps coming toward the room.

I press myself behind the door, waiting to see who is coming and whether they are a threat to me.

A figure comes into the room and pauses, sensing something is wrong.

I can't see her in the dark, but I don't have to. I smell her.

Miranda.

"What are you doing here?" I say.

"You don't sound happy to see me," she says.

"You said you'd meet me at the bonfire."

"I changed my mind. Too many people out there."

"So you came to my room?"

"It's not like I could call you and let you know I was stopping by," she says. "Actually, I could have called you because you have a phone."

I hear the teasing tone in her voice as she reminds me of what happened last night in the forest.

"What if someone saw you come in?" I say. "I'm not sure your father would be happy."

"You shouldn't be thinking about him right now."

"He's all I'm thinking about."

"All?" she says, and she flips on the light.

She's wearing a bath towel cinched tight above her breasts, her hair wet against her shoulders. I look down and see her legs, long and bare beneath the towel.

"Maybe not all," I say.

She walks toward me, her face coming close to mine, her voice dropping to a whisper.

"Do you know what would happen if my father found out I was here?" she says.

"I'm guessing it would involve Sergeant Burch and a shotgun escort out of camp."

She nods. "Something like that. And you'd be lucky compared to me."

"That sounds like a good reason for you to leave."

"To me it sounds like a good reason to stay."

"How do you figure?"

"There's nothing more exciting than breaking the rules," she says. "Didn't you feel it at the water treatment plant tonight?"

She puts a hand on my chest, one finger lightly moving against my T-shirt. Her breathing is heavy. I feel my body stir, the heat building in my groin.

"Besides," she says, "we have nothing to hide from each other. We already know each other's secrets."

My body tenses beneath her touch, and I step back.

"What secrets?" I say, preparing to take action against her if need be.

"I know about your phone, and you know about mine. So we're evenly matched. Did you ever learn about the Cold War doctrine called MAD? Mutually assured destruction. As long as we both have the same weapon, we're safe."

She drops the towel and faces me. Her breasts are large, nipples hard in the cool air of the room.

"I see you've got different weapons than me," I say with a grin.

"You never got the birds-and-bees speech?"

"It's been a while. I might need a refresher course."

"I can help you with that," she says. "You just need to put your arms around me."

I step in and we kiss, a long kiss, our tongues playing against each other.

"I asked if you had a girlfriend before," she says when we come up for air.

"Are you asking again?"

"I've been thinking about it," she says.

"My answer hasn't changed," I say. "No girlfriend."

"You hesitated when you answered. Which means there was someone, wasn't there?"

Miranda is very perceptive. I like that about her, but it reminds me that I need to be cautious.

"There was someone."

"Someone special?"

"Very special. And very over," I say, wanting to change the subject. "How about you? What's your status?"

"Single and available," she says. "And missing my shirt."

"I noticed that."

I glance down and see she's wearing tiny black lace panties.

I say, "I think your jeans might be missing, too."

"Is that a problem?"

"Not for me. But I'm surprised you don't have a boyfriend here."

"It's not like I have a lot of choices."

"The camp is full of guys your age."

"Guys so beholden to my dad that they wouldn't dare do anything to upset him."

"Why do you think I'm different?"

"I know you're different," she says. "You're not afraid of anything. Including my dad."

She pulls my T-shirt over my head.

"Now we both have our shirts off," I say.

"Isn't that a coincidence," she says.

She runs her hand across my chest, tracing the muscles there. She stops when she comes to the knife scar on my pec, probing the hard flesh.

"What is this?" she says.

"I got burned when I was a kid," I say. "I barely remember it."

"No more talking," she says, and steps in to kiss me.

"Wait," I say, gently pushing her back.

It's possible that sleeping with Miranda would bring us closer, thereby giving me access to Moore. It's possible, too, that it would complicate things, creating emotion and attachment where it is unnecessary, maybe even alienating Moore.

I can't tell Miranda any of that. But I step away from her.

"Why are you stopping?" she says.

"I don't even know if I'll be here tomorrow. Your father could change his mind and ask me to leave, my parents could call and—"

"We don't know if any of us will be here," she says, interrupting me. "Sometimes you have to take a chance."

"Carpe diem," I say.

"*Verum est*," she says. She runs her hand softly down my cheek. "But if you did stay—"

She pauses.

"What?"

"It could be like this every night. Wouldn't that be nice?"

"You, naked every night? It would be a change of pace, I'll say that much."

"You're such a guy," she says.

I grin.

"I didn't mean just sex," she says. She takes my face in her hands and brings it close to hers. "I meant us every night."

Us.

There's something powerful about the word. I let it wash over me, then feel some relief when it passes.

The mission is everything. And I have work to do.

"What are you thinking about, Daniel?"

"I'm thinking we'd better send you back to your room before something happens."

"Maybe I want it to happen."

"There's no rush," I say.

She opens her mouth like she's going to contradict me, then she stops herself.

"You're right," she says. "There's no rush."

She dresses quickly. I want to stop her half a dozen times, but I don't.

When she's done, she pecks me on the cheek and slips out the door.

It hurts to watch her go. Not in my head. Someplace else, someplace deeper.

Closer to my heart.

I CLOSE MY EYES FOR A WHILE AFTER THAT, BUT I DON'T SLEEP.

I lie in bed thinking about Miranda, the things she's shared with me since I've come to the camp, her dreams of the future, the way she's torn between duty to her father and the life she wants to live.

I think about it for a while, and then I let it go.

It's hard to focus now. It's been almost forty-eight hours since I've slept. My body is trained to function with little sleep, but at a certain point I begin to lose operational awareness. I've learned how to take micronaps, small bursts of REM sleep that allow me to stretch the time between periods of full sleep. But even those seem out of reach now.

The disappearance of Father, the operation at the water treatment plant, my interactions with Lee and Miranda, all of these conspire to keep me awake.

Eventually I give up and sit in a chair, attempting to slow my thoughts and move my focus back to where it belongs, not on Miranda or Lee, or even on The Program.

I focus on the mission.

On Moore.

I think about Moore sending teams of young kids through the countryside at night, searching out targets.

They call it a game. I call it something else.

Domestic terrorism.

During my missions I am never given the reasons why a target has been assigned by The Program. I am trained not to ask questions, to focus only on target acquisition and removal, leaving the why of it to others.

But living among Moore and his people, I can't help but see the danger they represent.

This, more than anything, helps to steady my intentions. Whatever the purpose of this mission from The Program's perspective, I have my own purpose now.

I have to stop Moore.

I sit in the chair thinking of ways to do it. By the time I glance at the clock, it's seven AM.

I ate some trail mix last night, but that's not enough to fuel multiple days of mission operations. I need real food.

I dress quickly and head for the main house, following the smell of bacon in the air. In the central square, I see the ashes of last night's bonfire being raked up by two young kids, one of whom collects trash in a large plastic bag.

I walk past them unchallenged and head toward the main house.

I press the handle on the front door, but unlike in the video game, it is unlocked.

I ready myself, and then I open the door and step inside for the first time.

IT'S MOORE.

He's standing in the hallway inside the door as if he's been waiting for me. Francisco and Aaron are by his side.

"Good morning," I say, like I'm happy to see him.

"You're in a good mood," he says.

"Absolutely," I say, but not for the reasons he might think.

"How was last night?" he says.

For a moment I think he's talking about Miranda being in my room, but I doubt he'd be smiling if he knew.

"You mean the treatment plant?" I say. "That was interesting."

"Not the word I was expecting."

I shrug. "It's a lot to process all at once."

Teens pass by us heading to breakfast. When they see Moore and me talking, they hug the wall, giving us plenty of space.

"Lee told me what happened," Moore says. "It sounds like you had some doubts about the mission."

I want to be real with Moore, letting him hear my concerns, at least up to a point.

"That's a fair way of characterizing it," I say.

"I thought you wanted to be a soldier," Moore says.

"I do."

"Last night was preparation for the battle."

"The battle against the dangerous people of Manchester, New Hampshire?"

Moore's face reddens. I see the tension ripple through Aaron's shoulders as he prepares for trouble.

"Explain it to me," I say quickly. "Help me understand."

Moore nods, his face returning to normal.

"Are you familiar with the shot heard round the world?" he says.

"The first shot of the American Revolution."

"That's right. It was the Battle of Lexington and Concord, where the patriots fired against their colonial oppressors for the first time. It was in that moment that the world changed."

"What does that have to do with last night?"

"We are modern-day patriots," Moore says. "We who choose to live at this camp. We are practicing for that first shot. We don't know when or how it will need to be fired, but we know we must be ready. You said you wanted to be a soldier—"

"More than anything."

"That's what a soldier does. He trains for the day when he will be needed by his commander."

I pause, thinking about what Moore has said. He has a masterful way of using truisms to support his ideas. One can easily agree with the truth of the surface statements without questioning the ideas themselves.

It makes it easy for me to agree with Moore, at least for the time being.

"I understand what you're saying."

Moore smiles. "I know you do, Daniel. I have confidence in you. So does Lee. He told me so last night."

"Is that right?" I say, wondering what Lee said to his father.

Moore signals for Francisco to come forward.

"Francisco's going to take you home now," Moore says.

"Home?" I say, my voice rising.

I feel myself getting upset, lost in the character of Daniel. He's opened his heart and now he's being rejected by Moore.

"Please. I don't want to go," I say.

I play it up, letting myself get desperate in front of Moore. If he throws me out, my mission is over.

Moore holds up his hands, trying to calm me.

"I'm sending you home because I want you to make arrangements with your parents," he says.

"Arrangements for what?"

"To come back and stay with us for a while."

"For a camp session?"

"There is no camp session, Daniel. Not anymore."

This is what Miranda was trying to tell me in the forest the first night.

"What about the recruiting event?" I say.

He waves his hand as if it was insignificant.

"That was for appearances. We've moved beyond camps and temporary fixes and on to the next phase of our growth."

"What phase?"

I want to ask another question, but Moore steps closer and looks me in the eye.

"Do you trust me, Daniel? Even if you don't fully understand my methods?"

"I do."

Moore reaches out and puts a hand on my shoulder. It would not be out of character to flinch, especially after getting squeezed in the parking lot the other night and seeing Moore put the pincer movement on his son the first night.

But I don't flinch. I let him touch me.

His hand is firm and steady on my shoulder.

"Do what you have to do to convince your parents," he says. "Then come back to us."

"I will," I say. "As soon as I can."

"YOU GOT THE BIG INVITE," FRANCISCO SAYS.

"It's not like I'm the first," I say.

We're walking away from the main house together, heading toward an area where vehicles are parked.

"No," he says, "but Moore sealed the compound last month. The fact that he let you in is a miracle."

"Why did he close it down?"

"Safety precaution," Francisco says simply.

I think about the dead soldier. Father said he got into the compound. Assuming he was discovered, could that have been the trigger for Moore sealing the compound from the real world? If so, why would he open it now to let me in?

We turn the corner, and I glance back toward the main house.

"You know, I've never been inside the main house. Not past the front hallway at least."

"You'll get there eventually," he says. "It took me a while. Now I live there."

"Is it nice?"

"Not nice," he says. "But I'm close to Moore. That's what's important."

At that moment I see Lee walking around the corner, heading for the main house.

"Lee!" I shout.

"I'll grab the truck and meet you over there," Francisco says, pointing to a paved area to the side of the building.

I nod, and he hurries away.

I look back at Lee. It's obvious he's seen me, but he keeps walking.

"Hold up a second," I shout, jogging over to him.

He hesitates, then stops to wait for me.

"How are you doing?" I say.

He shrugs.

"Your dad asked me to stay for a while. I'm going home to get my stuff."

"That's great news."

"He said he talked to you about me last night. Whatever you said, it worked."

"I told him the truth. That's all."

"There are a lot of ways to tell the truth."

"Not with my father. There's only one."

He looks at me, his face serious.

"Always tell him the truth, Daniel. He's going to find out anyway. If you lie, it's just going to be worse for you later."

A horn beeps. A truck pulls up to the side of the building, Francisco in the driver's seat.

"That's my ride," I say. "Maybe we'll get to spend some time together when I get back."

He nods, noncommittal. I want to leave him with a positive impression of me.

"Thanks for helping me get in here," I say. "It means a lot to me. Really. I couldn't have done it without you."

He smiles.

"Okay, okay," he says. "I can't take any more ass kissing."

"Just one more thing," I say. "Will you take me to the shooting range when I get back? That combat rifle scared the shit out of me."

He laughs.

"See you when you get back," he says.

TWO BOYS WITH RIFLES STAND GUARD AT THE ROADBLOCK.

It has been fortified since we drove past it yesterday, a thick wooden barrier placed across the road with a spike strip below it that would puncture the tires on any vehicle smaller than a half-track.

When the armed boys see Francisco, they nod. One of them pulls back the spike strip while the other opens the gate.

"That's a pretty serious roadblock," I say after we pass through.

"These are serious times," Francisco says, but he doesn't elaborate.

I inventory the security measures I've seen: one road in and out of the valley, a military-style roadblock at its base; a laser perimeter around the camp with sentries at night; high-tech digital signal blocking around and above. And these are just the defenses I've identified. There are likely more hidden out of sight.

What exactly is Moore protecting inside Camp Liberty?

We drive the steep mile-long incline that leads out of the valley.

"Look over your shoulder," Francisco says.

I look back. In the daylight, Liberty looks almost quaint, a scattering of buildings nestled in the green embrace of a mountain pass.

"What do you think?"

"It's small," I say.

"From up here, you see that it's lucky to exist at all."

"That's why you work so hard to protect it?" I say.

"I work hard because it's my home now."

"Are you a permanent?"

"Where did you hear that term?"

"Lee told me."

"Yeah, I'm a permanent," he says. "Something like that."

"How did you persuade your parents to let you stay?"

"They didn't have a choice."

"What do you mean?"

"I'm nineteen now," he says. "My parents don't get a vote anymore."

Usually I can tell someone's age, but it's been hard to determine with Francisco. The long hair and beard make him appear older, but when I look at his eyes now, I can see that he's just a few years older than me.

"Must be nice," I say. "To be independent, I mean."

"It's got pluses and minuses," he says.

Three white panel vans approach us heading toward the camp. It's a narrow road, and Francisco has to slow and move to the very edge to allow them to pass. As they go by, he toots his horn once and waves. The lead driver waves back.

I glance through the window of the second van, and in the moment it takes to pass, I see her.

The English teacher with wild hair. The one who tried to kill Moore.

At least I think it's her. She's in the passenger seat, looking away from me, a wool cap pulled low over her hair. I'm rarely wrong about things like this. My memory works like a photographic database, logging facial structures, eye shapes, hairstyles, and postural quirks.

If it's the English teacher, why would she be invited back to camp after what happened at the center?

I consider asking Francisco about it, but I decide against it.

A few seconds later the vans are gone, and Francisco pulls back out onto the road. We start around the long curve that leads to the other side of the mountain and civilization.

"Why do you think Moore invited me to stay?" I say.

"I know why."

"I'm all ears," I say.

"Moore will have to tell you that himself when and if he decides. But I can guarantee you it wasn't a spontaneous decision. We were up half the night talking about you, and then we took a vote."

"We?"

"He and I."

"Not Aaron?"

"I'm head of security, not Aaron."

He sits a little straighter in his seat. It's obviously a point of pride for him.

"Not much of a vote with just the two of you," I say. "Tough to settle deadlocks, too."

"Not really. His vote counts twice."

We come down the other side of the mountain, Francisco's speed increasing as the road widens.

"Which way did you vote?" I ask.

"I voted for you to stay. Does that surprise you?"

"A little. Yeah. Especially after you were such a dick that first night."

"It's not my job to be nice. Not to strangers."

"What *is* your job?"

"Assess. And defend if necessary."

"Have you assessed?"

"I have. I watched you very closely last night."

I look at Francisco. He's a lot more astute than he appears at first. It's easy to be thrown off by his wild-man appearance.

"And what did you decide?"

"I voted to keep you here."

"I haven't done anything to prove myself."

"It doesn't matter. I voted for potential."

"You think I have potential?" I say.

"More than you know."

"But I didn't even take the gloves last night," I say.

"You think taking the gloves was the right thing to do?"

"We have to follow orders. That's what everyone keeps telling me."

"We follow," Francisco says, "but not blindly. It's a choice."

"What the difference?"

"Everyone in the world is a follower. They follow an agenda, whether it's set by school, parents, a job, society. The only question is who or what they choose to follow. Most people don't even realize there's a choice to make, so they end up stumbling blindly through their lives, wondering why they're so unhappy when they're doing everything right."

"You've made a choice. That's what you're telling me."

"Yes."

"Are you happy with it?"

"Most days. Yes."

He pops down the sun visor, squinting as we take a ramp that briefly turns us east.

"Liberty is much better than where I was before," Francisco says.

"Where were you before?"

"In hell."

Francisco turns the corner, and I recognize the neighborhood near the house where I prepped with Father two days ago.

"You said you lived near here, right?" Francisco says.

"You can let me off at Cumberland Farms up here. I'm going to grab something to eat before I go home. You guys had me so busy I didn't get any food. Except for that stale trail mix you gave me yesterday."

Francisco grins.

"We'll feed you plenty when you come back," he says. "*If* you come back."

"I'm coming back," I say. "Believe it."

He pulls into the parking lot and stops the car.

"Door-to-door service," he says.

I sit there for a moment without saying anything. I hated Francisco at first, but I'm beginning to feel different about him now.

He says, "Can you find your way back to camp, or do you need a pickup?"

"I'll probably drive myself back."

"Stop at the roadblock when you get there. I'll tell them to look out for you."

"Thanks, Francisco."

I get out of the truck and head into Cumberland Farms.

From inside the store, I watch him pull out of the parking lot and head down the road.

I look at the neighborhood outside. I spent the afternoon in this neighborhood—was it really only two days ago?

Thursday night the soldiers came for me. Friday night I was at the recruiting event with Moore. Saturday night was The Hunt. Now it's midday Sunday.

It seems like more time has passed, but that's one of the effects of sleep deprivation. Fatigue degrades cognition, dulls the sense, slows decision-making processes, and distorts perception. A minute can seem to stand still, yet things that occur slowly can pass you by.

I buy several carbohydrate drinks and a handful of protein bars. When I get out of the store, I stand under a tree out of the line of sight from the road. What I really need is a good meal and a full night's sleep, but this will have to do.

I slowly chew a bar, interspersing it with swallows of carb drink. In this way I refuel, allowing my strength to return along with some of my focus.

I take out my iPhone and put it in secure mode. Here, away from the camp, the digital blocking, the obstruction of the mountains, away from all possible means of interference, I can truly test it.

I dial the prearranged number, Father's secure number for this assignment.

I will inform Father that I am bound for the safe house. He may be there waiting for me already. If not, he will be there soon to meet me.

I'll have to explain the reasons why I went into Liberty. Father may be unhappy at first, but once I tell him what I've learned there, I'm sure he will reward my initiative. Besides, the mission is even more critical now that I have a sense of Moore's plans.

I hear three rings through my phone followed by a click. The line goes dead.

I start again, this time trying Father's public number.

There's no answer.

I don't know what's happened to Father's communication ability, but I know our fallback procedure.

I finish off the last of the protein bars, and I head down the street to the protection of the safe house.

The neighborhood is quiet. A normal Sunday afternoon, nothing that flags my suspicions.

I proceed down the street until I come to the familiar white-and-yellow house.

Number 578. Same silver Escape in the driveway.

I move with the relaxed energy of a kid coming home after a morning hanging out with friends. I walk up the stone path to the front door and turn the knob.

It's locked.

I try it again in a different direction. Still locked.

Strange.

I walk around the side, look in a window. I'm expecting the electromagnetic film to prevent my seeing in, but that's not the case. I'm staring at a set of vases over the mantel place.

Suddenly the front door opens.

"Excuse me," a woman's voice says.

I whirl around, preparing to meet the challenge.

I find myself looking at an attractive thirty-five-year-old woman in jeans and an oversize sweater. No threat to me. Just a little agitated to find a boy standing in her flower bed.

I collapse my posture into the slouch of a low-key teen boy.

"Who are you?" she says.

"Who are *you*?" I say with a shrug.

We look at each other.

"I'm the woman who owns this house. You're a kid sneaking around my yard."

"I'm not sneaking," I say. "I'm looking for my dad."

"Your dad?"

"He lives here."

"I'm sorry. You're mistaken."

A man I've never seen comes to the door. He puts a protective arm around her.

"What's going on, honey?"

"This boy seems to think he lives here."

"This is *our* house," the husband says, his voice cautious but friendly, still wanting to clear up the misunderstanding. "I should know. I pay the mortgage every month."

"It wasn't your house two days ago," I say.

"It's been our house for six years," the husband says.

I look at the number again. 578.

Correct street, correct number.

"Are you sure it's your house?" I say.

I watch carefully, waiting for them to break character, show themselves to be operatives for The Program, maybe a recovery crew of some kind. I wait for the nod inviting me in to safety.

But there is no nod. These people seem like the real thing.

I feel the confusion growing inside me.

That's when I see their skin appears darker than it should be for this part of the country, even in the summer.

"Why do you have tans?" I say.

The husband looks at me strangely. It was a stupid thing for me to say, but I'm not thinking clearly.

"We won a trip to the Caribbean," the husband says. "We were on vacation, and we just got back. Not that it's any business of yours."

"I'm confused," I say.

My mind is racing, trying to put together the lack of communication from The Program, the strange circumstances at the safe house, any of it, all of it.

They must see that something's wrong, because the woman says, "Are you feeling all right?"

I don't like how she's looking at me. Like I'm a lost kid of some kind.

"Do you want to come in for a minute?" the wife says.

"Hang on," the husband says. "We don't know who this is."

"He needs some help."

"Then we should call the police."

"We don't need the police," the wife says, like her husband is being ridiculous.

"Maybe he's on drugs," the husband says.

I can't allow the police to become involved. I have to pull myself together.

"I'm sorry," I say. "I guess I made a mistake. We just moved to Manchester. All the streets look alike."

"Come in for a minute," the wife says. "I'll get you a glass of water."

"No," I say.

"Please."

Something about her draws me in. The warmth of her voice or the way she smiles at me like she's concerned.

"Maybe I'll come inside," I say.

Not only do I need a drink of water, it would be a good idea for me to go inside and look around the house, make sure I'm not mistaken about the location. I can buy myself some time to analyze the situation and figure out my next move.

I look toward the husband. He shakes his head as if he's been through this before—having to live with decisions his wife makes that he disagrees with. He sighs and steps aside, gestures for me to come in.

"For a minute only," he says.

"Just a minute," I say.

I step into the house. I recognize it instantly. Same fireplace, same green blanket thrown over the sofa.

I was here two days ago. I'm sure of it.

So what happened to the safe house?

I sit on the sofa, and the husband sits across from me in an armchair. We look at each other uncomfortably while the sound of clinking glasses comes from the kitchen.

A minute later the wife comes out with two glasses of lemonade, one for me and one for her husband.

"I hope you don't mind lemonade," she says to me.

"It's great," I say.

The sugar is a good supplemental energy source. It will help right now.

The man drinks. I drink. The woman looks on.

"How long have you lived in Manchester?" the husband says.

The glass is cool in my fingers. I drink the lemonade in measured sips, trying to make it last.

I think back to the briefing I received two days ago, the story of the boy whose life I'm supposed to be living now.

"We've been here a few months," I say.

"A minute ago you said you just moved," the husband says.

"This year, I meant. My parents came here for work."

"Would you like us to call your parents for you?" the wife says, trying to be helpful.

I laugh then. It's inappropriate, and it instantly sets them on edge. I note the woman's eyes dart to the corner of the living room.

That's when I see it. A pink kid's scooter propped up against the wall near the front door. The woman notices me looking at it.

"That belongs to our daughter," she says, like she's warning me against doing anything dangerous, some action that might disturb the peace of this family.

Family.

These are not Program operatives. I see that now. They are a real family, back in their home after a vacation, completely unaware of what has gone on here while they've been gone.

I think of my father sitting in the living room of our home in Rochester. We didn't have a TV when I was a kid. My father spent his time at home listening to classical music and reading books. He'd sit propped on the corner of the sofa, his nose deep in a new novel. Sometimes my mother would lay a blanket across his lap and lie down next to him to read.

My real parents, together and reading. Back when everything seemed normal.

A feeling wells up in my chest, so powerful that it causes me to moan.

The wife unconsciously places a hand on her husband's shoulder.

A united front. That's what they're showing me. A partnership that will expel the intruder if need be.

The intruder. That's me.

I do not belong in this house.

"I appreciate the drink," I say.

I stand up.

The wife looks relieved. Her husband maintains his caution.

I smile, attempting to set them at ease.

"You know what I just realized? I think I'm one street over from where I'm supposed to be."

"Oh, *that's* what happened," the husband says, as if it's an honest mistake on my part.

"I feel silly," I say.

"It's no problem," the husband says.

"I'm sorry to cause you any trouble."

"No trouble at all," the wife says.

She turns toward the front door. She makes it two steps before the living room window shatters behind us, exploding inward and sending deadly, razor-edged shards of glass raining down on the wood floor.

IT HAPPENS QUICKLY AFTER THAT.

The glass shatters, bullets thudding into the wall across from us, each one raising a plume of plaster dust like a tiny volcano.

The husband screams. The wife leaps away from the source of the noise but toward her husband, her body covering his.

Even as I drop to safety, I am processing this: It's not a normal reaction for a civilian. An overprotective mother or wife might cover a loved one with her body, but this woman moved like she has been trained, tackling her husband at knee level and pulling him down, perhaps sensing that the high muzzle velocity of a weapon like the one that sent these bullets is likely to pass through her body and into his if she remains standing.

She may not be from The Program, but she is some sort of pro, perhaps a former police officer who left the force to have a family. I can't be sure.

I am only sure that we are under fire and that suburban houses do not come under automatic weapon fire in the middle of a Sunday afternoon in a small city in New Hampshire.

Selective fire, I should say, because six bullets hit the wall. A double burst from a semiautomatic rifle.

I spin and roll from the couch to the floor, staying beneath the sight lines of the window, and I belly-crawl to the couple, now cowering on the floor.

"How many entrances in the house?" I say.

"Two," the husband says, at the same time that his wife says, "Four."

They look at each other.

She says, "Front, back, side, garage."

"That's right," he says.

I like this woman. She has operational intelligence even under fire.

More glass shatters behind us as a second burst comes through the front door, three pings in rapid succession.

That means at least two men, advancing and anticipating our reaction inside the house.

"Grab the back of my waistband," I tell the wife as I crawl in front of her. And then I tell the husband, "You grab the back of *her* waistband. We'll move together in a line. Stay low, follow me, and I'll get you out of here."

The man starts to ask a question when a line of bullets slams into the wall high above us. That ends the conversation for the time being.

I duckwalk them toward the side door. That's where we are most likely to get out safely.

I select the side because of the way the attack is unfolding. If you want to take a house quietly, you surround it on all sides and send in an insertion team. If you want to take out a guy and not get your hands dirty, you shoot him through the front window. It's crude but effective, barely a couple steps above a drive-by. But since that's the way this attack is happening, the men are likely to be massed in the front yard.

I glance out the side door. It's clear. I begin to open the door, but the wife stops me, grabbing my arm.

"Our daughter will be home from her friend's house soon," she says, fear in her voice.

"How soon is soon?" I say.

"Ten or fifteen minutes."

"It will be over by then," I say. "She'll be okay. I promise you."

She looks at me, judging whether she can trust me.

A look passes between us. I let her see I am a professional.

"Who the hell are you?" she says.

I hear wood shattering at the front door.

"They're here," I say. "You have to get out now or you're going to die."

The man's eyes are wide and unfocused. He's going into shock. The woman starts to hyperventilate.

"Your family needs you," I tell her. "Pull it together."

I see her accessing a deeper part of herself, and her breathing slows.

I fling open the door and go out before them, eyeing both directions.

"Get at least four houses away," I say. "Is there someone you trust in the neighborhood?"

The husband is uncertain, but the wife points to a green house several backyards away.

Behind us I hear men breaking through the front door and moving roughly through the living room.

"I don't understand what's happening," the husband says.

"Go and call the police," I say to the woman, and she pushes her husband out the door, squeezing next to him as they pass through the bushes into the next-door neighbor's yard.

I could follow them and get out to the street, but where would I go?

I need the black comms rectangle in the toolshed so I can contact The Program, and I need to find out who these men are.

So while the couple makes their way to safety, I slip into the backyard.

There is one man there watching the back door. Heavyset with wide shoulders.

He stands at a slight angle, his rifle cocked but trained on the ground at his feet, ready to rise at a moment's notice. It's a decent operational posture, but only if he has another man backing him up, watching his six.

He does not.

I slip up behind him and I choke him out with a pincer motion, catching his throat in the crook of one elbow, then closing the vise by grasping my wrist with the opposing arm. It's not the pressure that does it so much as the placement. The neck is the nexus of the nervous and arterial systems, both located close to the surface. It does not take much to gravely injure a person at throat level.

I don't have time to find out who this man is or why he is doing what he's doing.

I only have time to neutralize him.

I do it quickly, ignoring the hiss and gurgle as his body fights for breath beneath my grip. Rather than think of these noises as a man trying to live, I've been taught to think of them as the sounds of danger.

When the sounds stop, the danger stops with them.

In this way, it becomes easy to protect myself, overriding the natural human instinct for compassion.

The big man goes slack in my arms. I let him fall to the ground, and I race away from the house, toward the toolshed.

I'm halfway across the lawn when I see something is wrong.

The padlock on the toolshed, the one designed to open with my digital thumbprint.

It's missing.

I race over to the shed and throw open the doors.

There is no black rectangle, no weapon mounted on the wall.

It's a normal toolshed packed with gardening equipment.

It doesn't much matter now, not with danger rushing at me from the house. One man is dead, but at least two men are still here, coming for me.

The back door slaps open, and a tall man steps out in a hurry. If he were smarter, he might slip out the door carefully, but not this guy. He throws open the door and it crashes against the wood frame of the house.

Which means I have to move quickly.

I scan the shed. A bag of mulch at my feet. Small garden tools scattered about, any of which could be deadly but none of which will work effectively in this situation.

I swing around to meet the man coming out of the house, and I see it: a garden spade propped up against the door.

I grab it in both hands, and I turn.

The tall man has been distracted by his partner's body on the ground. He's kneeling down to check for a pulse.

That is a mistake.

I rush him, covering the distance across the lawn in less than two seconds. By the time he looks up, the spade is already in motion. The back of the blade whacks him across the bridge of his nose. I hear a sickening crunch and blood spurts.

As he falls back, he brings up his gun to fire, but I step on the barrel with a free foot and the bullet goes wide. He is fast, his other arm reaching for a knife in his belt. I hear a noise inside the house then, a third man reacting to the rifle shot.

There can be no hesitation. Before the tall man can get to his knife, I swing the spade into the side of his skull, hitting him hard enough to take him out for the duration.

I fling myself against the house, waiting for the next man.

He is smarter, which is to say more cautious. He pokes the barrel of his rifle through the door first—slowly. A gunshot and two bodies on the ground are enough to give him pause, and the rifle barrel starts to recede back through the door.

I do not let it happen.

I grab the barrel, yanking hard enough that the man holding it comes flying out the door, trapped by the rifle strap around his shoulder.

I think I have him, when he reaches up and hits a quick release on the strap, falling back into the house and tripping me at the same time, taking me down with him. The spade catches in the door frame and slips through my hands.

Now the fight is up close and personal, the two of us wrestling for dominance on the floor of the house. He is brutal, his muscles thick, his ability to use elbow and knee superb.

I take some punishment. But I do not flinch. Not until a young girl's scream freezes both of us in place.

It is no more than a split second of distraction, but it is enough for me to get the upper hand, using a knee at his throat and a twisting motion to snap his neck.

I leap up, grabbing the spade as I go, and I throw myself inside the door.

There is a fourth man.

He has found the side door of the house and slipped out without my hearing him.

He's found more than just a door.

He's found the couple's daughter.

She is about nine years old, in jeans and a yellow tank. The collar of the tank has little white flowers on it. Above the collar is a man's hand.

Around her throat.

In the other hand, he holds a semiautomatic pistol.

This is the girl the wife mentioned to me. She is an innocent civilian, caught in the wrong place at the wrong time, an unlucky witness to events that have nothing to do with her.

I should not care about this girl, but I make the mistake of looking in her eyes.

They are wide and dark brown, fear dilating the pupils. I don't see a stranger, a witness, or a civilian.

I see someone's daughter.

The man watches my face as I look at the girl. He is a professional. He knows I am weak now.

He glances around, noting his partners splayed on the ground around the yard and in the rear doorway.

He nods to me, almost like he's congratulating me for doing a good job, for making it this far.

This far but no farther. Because it's payback time.

He clamps his hand harder on the girl's throat, and she starts to cough, an involuntary reaction to strangulation.

I put down the spade.

I put my hands up in a nonthreatening manner, and I walk forward. He smiles. His grip lessens but does not release.

He takes the gun from her head and aims it at mine.

It's a bit of a cowboy move, this aiming at someone's head. It's designed to create fear, and at that much it is effective. But it's not a great shooting strategy.

Heads are small. Heads move in space. Heads can distract from the things bodies are doing.

My head does not move. I keep it still as I walk toward him, allowing him to think he has me. In a sense he does. He holds a girl by the throat, he holds a gun in his hand, and I am unarmed.

But there is an expectation here, an unspoken one that not even a trained soldier like him is aware of. I'm about to risk my life on it.

The expectation is that I'm going to stop walking.

It's hard enough to walk toward a loaded gun, but if you do it, if you're ordered to do it, it's a foregone conclusion that you will get close to the gun and stop.

Nobody walks into a gun.

Nobody who is not fearless.

Nobody but me.

When I hit the point where a normal person would stop, I speed up. Three quick steps that take him entirely by surprise.

I use the heels of both hands as weapons, a lightning strike to the sides of his temples like I'm crashing a cymbal. The skull is designed to protect the brain from injury, but a forceful impact will cause the brain to collide with solid bone. If I'm able to create sufficient impact, I will temporarily short out the brain's electrical system.

I strike hard and fast, and I see his eyes roll up into his head as his grip releases on the girl's neck.

But not before the gun fires.

Into the air and over my shoulder.

In the extra second I've earned, I grab the girl away from him.

"Run and hide behind the toolshed," I tell her, and I turn and attack, not allowing the man's brain time to come back online.

I flip him over on his back, and I grab the rifle from around his shoulder.

He winces like I'm going to shoot him, but I don't shoot him. I turn the gun upside down and hold the barrel so the blunt stock is pressing into his throat.

I push down, slowly crushing his windpipe.

"Why are you here?" I say.

He eyes dart from side to side, hoping one of his partners has revived. He doesn't know I've removed that possibility.

"It's just you," I say. "There's no help coming."

He refuses to speak. I press the gun stock harder into the soft structures beneath his neck. He starts to choke, and I back off the pressure the tiniest bit.

"Who sent you?" I say.

"I don't know," he says.

I press harder, feel the beginning of tissues giving way in his throat.

"Who?"

"Freelance," he says. "We're just a freelance team."

"For who?"

"Different employers, different assignments."

"Are you military?"

"Ex."

"You're not affiliated?"

"We're affiliated with whoever pays us."

I imagine the life he must lead. A former soldier, once loyal to a cause, who now sells his services to whoever pays the rent.

For a moment, I pity this man. Even though he came to kill me and he would have willingly allowed a girl to become collateral damage.

I pity him. Maybe that's why I decide to let him live.

But the moment I lift the gun stock from his throat, he is in motion, elbows dug into the ground to propel him up toward me, legs moving into striking position.

I swing the rifle in a pendulum motion, hitting him in the head hard enough to rattle him.

But he is resilient. It does not stop him.

He was a good soldier. I can see that now.

He must have been very good in his day. Before he turned, before he became this other thing.

Not now.

Now he reaches for his pistol on the ground, the one that has fallen but remains within arm's length.

I wanted to save this man's life, but he's given me no choice.

I bring the stock down onto his head.

Once. Again. A third time.

His hand was reaching for the gun. Now it twitches and stops moving.

Police sirens in the distance. That means the parents made it to safety. From the sound of the sirens, I've got four to six minutes to finish here.

I step away from the dead man, glance across the backyard at the bodies scattered there. I don't have to take a breath. I've been breathing all along, evenly and calmly, even as I've defeated these four men.

I lean over the body of the man I've just killed, checking his pockets. I find something at chest level.

An iPhone.

I swipe the phone. For just a moment, I expect The Program's secure apps suite to pop up, but that's ridiculous.

Why would The Program send a team to kill me? Especially a team like this, unaffiliated and crude in its tactics.

The Program is smarter than that.

But I can't dwell on this now. I check the iPhone log for recent calls. It's amazing how many operatives will not pause to wipe their phone clean before embarking on a mission. It's arrogant and foolish at the same time, but on some level it's understandable. Almost nobody heads into a mission thinking they're going to fail, and remembering that even in failure, they must protect their organization.

But this man was good. He cleared his phone's memory before he arrived. There's no information for me to find.

I reach to put the phone back in his pocket, and I feel something hard against my knuckle. I probe the pocket. It's empty.

I tap the outside of the pocket, and I feel it, a small hard object.

I reach in and tear the pocket lining. I find a tiny black micro SDHC card. A secure digital high-capacity memory device.

I slip it into my own pocket.

I hear soft footsteps in the grass behind me.

I spin around, ready to strike.

It's the daughter. She's looking at me, her eyes wide.

Moving slowly, I place the rifle on the ground. I step in front of the ex-soldier's body, blocking her sight line because I don't want her to get scared and scream.

She doesn't scream.

"You're just a boy," she says. "How did you do those things?"

She watched me kill a man. She should be terrified, not asking questions.

I forget how resilient kids are. This girl in particular. She's her mother's daughter.

I move closer to her, my voice gentle.

"You have to go to the neighbor's house. Your parents are there," I say.

"Where?"

"Four doors down. A green house. Do you know it?"

"Ms. Weiss."

"Go there now and wait for the police."

"What about you?"

"I can take care of myself."

I lead her through the bodies, blocking her view as best I can. I open the gate and when I'm sure it's clear, I let her out, watching as she runs down the street to safety.

The police sirens are close now. I hear the screech of tires as they turn the corner onto the block.

Neighbors are grouping on the street, emboldened by the sound of the police on their way.

I move in the opposite direction, passing quickly through several backyards until I come out a distance from the house.

I walk slowly so as not to attract attention. I'm thinking like the freelance team might have thought, where they would stage for this assault, how they would move toward the house, how close they would have to be to get away after they were done. I'm looking for a particular kind of vehicle, something generic enough to go unnoticed yet parked in a way that shows me it's not from the neighborhood. I pass a few likely suspects, check them briefly, but all the vehicles look well-used. While it's possible these guys stole a car, it's doubtful. Not for an operation like this, where they needed to get loud and then get away unseen.

I find it a quarter mile away on the side of the road, a Chevy Silverado, parked at a slight angle as if it were stopped too quickly. I pass by and note the truck is completely empty inside, not even a coffee cup in the holder.

I kneel down as if to tie my shoe and reach into the front driver's-side wheel well. My hands close around a key fob.

I was right. It's the truck they came in.

It's standard operating procedure to leave the keys with the vehicle. You don't let someone carry the keys if you're not sure all of you will make it back. You leave the keys with the vehicle, thereby allowing an escape under any circumstances.

Before I get in, I put my hand on the hood.

The metal is cool to the touch, about the same temperature as the outside air.

Depending on climate and usage, it can take an engine two hours or more to cool down after being driven. If these men followed me from the camp, they would have parked here less than half an hour ago. The engine block would still be warm.

But a cool engine means they were already here, waiting for me.

Which means they knew where I would be.

I open the truck door and get in. At first examination, the truck is empty, the seats clean, the change tray empty.

Inside the glove compartment I find a legal registration and insurance in the name of a generic fleet-leasing company.

I reach down into the space between the seats, and I find a black knife with a three-inch retractable blade.

I don't like knives, but I slide it into my pocket just the same. I may need it.

I fire up the engine. I drive out of the neighborhood at normal speed, avoiding the police cars rushing past me into the neighborhood.

I need to find someplace where I can think for a while, sort through the things that have happened to me in the last twenty-four hours without worrying about my safety.

I need someplace large and public. Someplace busy on a Sunday afternoon.

THE MALL OF NEW HAMPSHIRE.

I drive into a three-quarters-full parking lot, find a corner space with a view of both the mall and the parking lot entrances, and back the truck into it. I keep the engine running for a full ten minutes as I wait, scanning the parking lot and monitoring all traffic coming into and out of the mall. There are no tails, no suspicious vehicles or foot traffic, only a mall security patrol in a small electric cart moving in a lazy circle at five miles per hour around the perimeter of the mall.

I turn the engine off and lean back into the seat, the tension bleeding from my body for the first time in hours.

I pull out my iPhone. There's no use trying to call Mother or Father again, but maybe there's another way to get a message through.

I put the phone in secure mode and open the Instagram app. I lean out the window and take a photo of a trash can. In the description I write, "What a mess!" Then I geotag the photo, not to the mall but to the neighborhood where the safe house was located. Under normal circumstances, I could upload this to a monitored Tumblr blog, and it would trigger an investigation by The Program as well as an immediate call to my phone to check up on me.

But now the photo will not upload, a progress wheel perpetually spinning on the screen. I check the phone and see that I have reception, but no access to the special server.

Every means of contacting The Program has been blocked.

Why?

I run through the facts.

First I lost communication with Father and Mother, now with The Program as a whole.

The safe house was gone and sanitized.

Finally I was attacked by a freelance team, waiting for me at the location of the safe house. The team may or may not have known who I was, but they knew enough to be there.

None of it makes sense.

I back up and go through the list again, this time starting with the disappearance of the dead Program soldier.

There's something I'm not understanding, some critical fact that's missing.

I need more data if I'm going to make an informed deduction.

But how can I get it?

I am trained as a solo agent, a soldier alone in the world, my only links to Father, Mother, and The Program.

With those links severed, there is no help for me.

Not Program help, at least.

There was only one time during a mission when I breached protocol and sought help outside The Program.

It was from a boy a few years younger than me.

His name was Howard.

I STOP AT A BEST BUY INSIDE THE MALL.

I buy a new iPhone with cash, set up an account under an assumed name and e-mail address. I have credit cards under a dozen names, the numbers memorized in a sequence algorithm that exists only in my memory. These numbers are anonymized, even within The Program, a firewall to protect against the one-in-a-million-chance scenario where The Program's data is breached.

I type in the memorized credit card number and security code, and I wait as the wheel spins in the prompt box.

A moment later, the card is accepted.

I take the phone to an isolated section of the mall. I find a bench and I sit down.

I send a text to a special number, a throwaway phone I purchased for Howard from an electronics shop in New York City.

My text is a simple, prearranged message: CAN'T SEE YOU NOW. CALL YOU LATER.

If Howard remembers the protocol, he will write down the number from this text message, destroy the first throwaway phone, then call me from a second phone that has never been used before. It should take no more than two minutes.

That's if he remembers, if he hasn't lost courage in the weeks since I left New York, and if nothing bad has happened to him because of the secrets he learned after meeting me.

It takes ninety seconds for my new iPhone to vibrate.

"Howard?" I say.

"Holy shit," Howard says. "It's really you."

"It's me."

"Holy shit holy shit holy shit," he says.

"Nice to talk to you, too," I say.

"Are you kidding? It's great to talk to you. It's *incredible*. I thought you would forget about me."

I remember the first time I saw Howard in the cluster group at an Upper West Side private school in Manhattan. He was pale, curly-haired, and excessively sweaty, never participating in the social life of the school but watching everything from the sidelines.

The memory makes me smile.

"How could I forget?" I say.

It was during my last mission that Howard used his hacking skills to help me research my target, the mayor of New York, and sort truth from fiction. In the process we became friends. I told him things about who I am and what I do. Things that put his life in danger.

When I left the city, I told Howard that I might call on him some-day. I didn't know that day would be so soon. Or how much trouble I would be in.

"What's going on, Ben?" he says.

Benjamin. That's the name he knows me by from my last mission.

I have to be very careful what I say to him on an open line. Even with our call bouncing through the crowded digital traffic of the Northeast.

"It's good to hear your voice," I say.

"Where are you?" he says, then interrupts before I can dismiss the question. "Wait, that's a stupid thing to say. I can't ask a question like that, can I? Let me think of a better question."

"Howard—"

"I'm going to think of one. Just give me a second. This is much harder than I thought it would be."

"Please, Howard…"

There's silence on the line.

"You sound strange," he says.

"I'm going through some things."

"What kinds of things?"

I think about what it might mean if I tell Howard what's happening. The risks he'll take without fully understanding them, the risks I'll take by opening myself up to him again.

It's one thing for me to take risks. I'm trained for it, but Howard's innocent, a high school hacker with a Japanese girlfriend he's only met in avatar form online.

"Ben?" he says.

"What?"

"Whatever it is, you can tell me."

The lessons of The Program ring in my head. I am a solo act. I can handle things on my own, without assistance from anyone or anything. When in doubt, I am to trust my instincts and intuition.

But what if The Program has been breached? What if Mother or Father need my help?

The freelance team revealed that I am in danger. My mission may even be compromised.

I am trained to work alone, but I can't figure out this situation on my own. With Howard's skills, I might be able to determine what's happened to The Program, the reason for the communication blackout and disappearance of the safe house. I can't tell him the story on an open line, but in person—

"I need your help, Howard," I say.

"What can I do?"

"Come to New Hampshire."

I TELL HIM TO TAKE THE TRAIN TO EXETER.

A fourteen-year-old boy traveling by train to Exeter on a Sunday afternoon won't attract any notice whatsoever. I make arrangements to pick him up there in several hours. Then I hang up the phone.

It's done.

I've broken from Program doctrine for the second time in my life.

I have hours to kill before Howard arrives, and I need to stay in public. Luckily, I have the perfect cover. I am a boy at the mall on a Sunday.

I start by walking the mall, doubling back on myself, watching for reflections in storefront glass, popping into several stores then out again, scanning all the time for unusual movement around me.

There is none.

Instead I see something else.

A couple holding hands on a date. A family arguing about which store they will go into first. A group of teenagers laughing at some inside joke.

I see normal life, a life that I do not live.

When in doubt, emulate.

I've been trained to fit in anywhere, matching the patterns and the energy of the people around me. That's what I do now. I move through the mall like the teens I see around me. Unlike them, I use the time to recuperate from killing four men.

I get a haircut. I order a small pizza in the food court. I sit in a massage chair at an electronics store. Then I go to Barnes & Noble, and I find a corner of the magazine section and comb through the news and culture magazines.

Because I do not live in one place, I have to work hard to stay up on current events. Without the daily pattern of attending school, talking with friends, and watching television, it's easy to fall out of sync with the world. I have to feed myself a stream of information so I can understand and stay connected to current events and be able to converse with those around me without seeming like a visitor from a foreign country.

I pick up a *New York Times* and read a follow-up article about the death of Mayor Goldberg's daughter in New York City, a death I know more than a little about. The article reflects on the incidence of rare and unexplained mortality in young people due to natural causes.

Natural causes. My specialty.

According to the article, Mayor Goldberg has gone into a media blackout while he grieves for his daughter. Something about the image of this lonely billionaire losing both his wife and daughter has caught the imagination of the world, raising his profile and bringing him attention on an international level. There is talk of him running for president in the next election.

I think back to my time in New York. The memory is painful, like pressing a bruise that has not fully healed.

I questioned The Program, and a girl is dead because of me. She was not innocent, but she was special to me, even if only for a brief time.

But that was before. And I've been taught how to handle *before*.

You put it away and replace it with *now*.

I toss the *Times* back onto the rack.

I check my watch. The entire afternoon has passed, and the mall is beginning to close.

It's time to get Howard.

I make one last stop at Gap to buy some new clothes and a duffel bag to carry them in.

I pull the tags from the clothes, crumple them into a ball, and stuff them into the duffel so they'll wrinkle and look more worn. I change into a fresh T-shirt and pants in the bathroom, slipping my old clothes into the Gap bag and dropping it in the large covered trash bin as I leave the mall.

HOWARD IS STANDING ON THE SIDE OF THE ROAD BY THE EXETER TRAIN STATION.

I pull up in the Chevy Silverado and beep the horn to draw his attention. He sees me and his face lights up. He grabs a small duffel from the ground, swings a large computer bag over his shoulder, and hops into the truck.

"Hey," I say, and he quickly puts a finger up to his lips to silence me.

He reaches into his duffel and pulls out a square electronic device with three mini antennas jutting from one side. He flips a switch and the device lights up and emits a single chirp.

Howard's face scrunches in concentration. He moves the device around, trying to pick up the source that is causing the beep. He crawls over the seat, nearly kicking me in the head in the process. He scans the backseat but finds nothing. Then he comes into the front and the device chirps again.

It's me. I am the source.

Howard looks concerned. He starts at my feet and moves up my body, the chirps increasing until he arrives at chest level, when the device emits a steady tone.

He points to my right pec, one finger up at his mouth to warn me not to speak.

I reach into my right pocket and take out my phone and hand it to him.

He scans the phone, but the device does not register anything.

If it's not the phone, what is it?

He holds the device to my chest again, and again the chirping becomes a steady tone.

He points toward my chest, indicating that the signal is emanating from there. We look at each other.

He reaches slowly toward my chest, touching the pocket there. He reaches into the pocket and comes out with the micro SDHC card I took off the leader of the freelance team at the safe house. I forgot I'd transferred it to the pocket of my new shirt.

He examines the micro SDHC card, then exhales. He turns off the device with the antennas.

"It's safe to talk?"

"Nothing is transmitting," he says.

"What's that device you have?"

"A little something I brought along. I knew you were in trouble, so I came prepared."

He holds up the micro SDHC card, flipping it between his fingers like it's a poker chip.

"Do you know what this is?" he says.

"I know it's some sort of data card. I took it off a bad guy."

"It looks like a normal data card, but it's not. I can see that the contact points are different. You need some kind of a special reader, or the card is useless."

"I don't have the reader," I say.

"You don't need the reader," he says. "You have me." He smiles. "Now aren't you glad you called me? Because I am fucking awesome."

I laugh and slip the truck into gear. "It's good to see you, Howard."

"I missed you," he says.

"I missed you, too, buddy."

More than I realized. Having Howard around was the highlight of my last mission. It was my first experience having someone to rely on, someone I could trust who had no agenda but to help me.

"You don't look good," Howard says.

"I haven't slept for a while."

"Is it because of a mission? I know you couldn't talk about it on the phone."

"We'll get to that," I say, wanting to hear more about Howard first. "How have things been at school?"

His face darkens.

"You want a lie or the truth?"

"The truth is always better."

"It sucks," he says. "People were mellow for a while after—it—happened. Then I went back to being Hard-On Howard and they started beating the crap out of me again. And Sam isn't around to protect me."

Samara. The girl I loved. The girl I killed.

"She was my only friend," Howard says.

"Not your *only* one," I say. "Not anymore."

He smiles. "Thanks, Ben."

"My name is Daniel now," I say.

"You have a different name?"

"Different mission, different name. I'm trained to switch identities. I was only Benjamin for a short time."

"How do you keep the identities straight?"

"I don't attach."

"To the name?"

"The name, the place, the circumstances of the assignment. None of it."

"What about the people?" Howard says.

I shake my head. "Especially not the people," I say.

He bites at his lip, troubled by the idea.

"So what about me?" he says.

"You're special," I say.

"I knew it!" he says, beaming. "But wait, what should I call you?"

"Call me Daniel. It will help to keep us both on the same page."

"Will you tell me your real name sometime?"

There are only three living people who know my real name.

Father and Mother. And Mike.

"Sometime I will," I say. "I promise."

"Daniel," he says. "That works for now."

"For now."

"You sounded bad on the phone," Howard says. "So tell me what's going on."

I hesitate, wondering how much I should reveal to Howard. But he's already here, already exposed. He's risked everything to come here and help me.

"I'm in trouble, Howard."

"Does it have something to do with this card?"

"That's just a part of it."

"I'd like to hear all of it," he says.

I take a breath, hovering between talking and putting Howard back on the train and asking him to forget everything.

It takes me less than a second to make a decision.

I pull away from the station.

As I drive back to Manchester, I tell Howard about the camp, about Moore inviting me in, about Father and The Program disappearing, about my attack at what was supposed to be a safe house. He listens, his head bobbing, not freaking out even as I share details about The Program and some of what I do for them.

I don't tell him about previous missions or targets, but I give him enough information to endanger him forever, to threaten the lives of his family and anyone he's ever known or cared about in the world.

To his credit, he listens closely, occasionally asking questions or inquiring about details, but respecting when I set a boundary.

I finish as we pull into a Holiday Inn near the Manchester airport.

We sit in the parking lot while he considers all of it. He leans forward and rubs his fingers through his curly hair over and over again.

"I see why you called me," he says. "It's a confusing situation."

"I've been running scenarios, but I don't have the answers. Not yet."

He leans back in his seat, still pulling at his hair.

"I think we should start with the SDHC card and see what we find. If I can crack the card, you'll know a lot more about this— what did you call them?"

"A freelance team."

"Right. This freelance team and the people who hired them. That will tell us some of what we need to know."

"That sounds like a good starting point," I say. "What do you need from me?"

"Power," he says. "And Cheetos. Lots of them."

"We can get those," I say.

I RENT A SUITE AT THE HOLIDAY INN.

I politely ask the desk clerk for a suite in a quiet part of the hotel with nobody next door. With vacancy rates high, they are more than happy to comply.

The minute we get into the room, I jimmy the lock to the adjoining suite and open the door. Now we have two connected suites, one under a false name in the hotel's computer system, the other not in the system at all.

I go back into the first suite and I see Howard emptying his duffel, removing power cords, multiplug outlets, surge protectors, coaxial cables. A miniature electronics store comes out of the bag.

"Did you bring any clothes?" I say.

"Why?" he says.

"To change. You might be here a few days."

"Hackers don't change," Howard says, like it's a crazy question. "We have priorities."

He runs extension cords from the outlets in both rooms, then he sets up double laptops, an iPad and iPhone, a power unit, Wi-Fi cards, and various other small machines that I haven't seen before.

"All right. Let's take a look at the card."

I pass him the micro SDHC card pinched between two fingers.

"This is an SD card reader right here," he says, showing me a small device attached to one of his laptops. "But I'm not going to put it in there."

He flips the card around in his hand, examining it from every angle. Then he places the card on a piece of white frosted glass, and a schematic registers on the laptop screen behind him. I see a printed circuit board and assorted electronics, all miniaturized inside the confines of the card casing.

"Just what I thought," he says. "It's not really an SDHC card at all, more like a secure communications device posing as an SDHC card."

"That's unusual, isn't it?"

"I've never seen anything like it. It's very sophisticated. What do you know about the guys you took it away from?"

"Not very sophisticated," I say.

"Which means they were given the card along with some kind of special reader at the same time. That would allow them to access the data, but if they lost the card or it got taken away from them, nobody else could read it. I'm guessing if you put this in a regular SD reader, it destroys itself."

"Can you get into the card, Howard?"

Howard examines the schematic, whistling softly under his breath.

"It's going to take a while," he says.

"Stay at it, as long as it takes."

He brings up some application on his laptop. I see numbers flying by as a cursor scans the schematic on the screen.

"Tell me about Moore's camp," Howard says. "What's it all about?"

"They think the government is weak, and they're trying to do something about it."

"They're right, don't you think?"

"What do you mean?"

"The government *is* weak. I mean, I could hack the banking system right now if I wanted to. I could probably even get inside the Homeland Security network if I had a few days, and there are only, like, a dozen guys who could even begin to try to stop me. A dozen guys protecting the entire government."

"There's got to be more than that."

"Okay, a hundred guys. Two hundred. I guarantee the IT department at Google is bigger than the cybersecurity core of the U.S. government right now, and Google pays a hell of a lot better, too."

"You could hack all that stuff, but you don't do it," I say. "Why not?"

"Because I'm not a dick."

"But other people do it."

"They are *Phalli giganticus*. I can't speak for them."

"But you understand them."

Howard groans, like he's having to explain something boring to a child.

"Why do people do it?" Howard says. "Because they can. Because it's fun. It makes them feel like hotshots to get behind the infrastructure and see what's in there. I understand the impulse. You know in those old movies where kids break into school on the weekend, get into the gym and play some hoops, or rifle through a teacher's desk to see if they can find the answer key for a quiz?"

"I've seen those movies. But there's a big difference between that and hacking the U.S. banking system."

"Sure. Hacking is easier. You do it from home in your underwear while you're eating trail mix. And then you announce it to the online community, so a few thousand friends are applauding you and watching your every move. Then they try to top you by going further, doing a little more. It's a big competition. You can see the attraction to that."

"I can see it, and I know it's fun to break the rules. But the U.S. is already under attack from foreign powers. You'd think kids would want to defend against that rather than contributing to it."

"I don't think they see it like that," he says. "Some people think of it more like a global government. Hackers versus the establishment, us versus them."

"Us versus them. That's how Moore thinks of it."

"That's why you've been sent after him?"

"I never know why I'm sent. I don't *need* to know. I'm a weapon."

I think about the things I've seen in Moore's camp over the last two days.

"But in this case," I say, "I think I figured out why. It's critical that I stop him."

I glance at my iPhone, checking the time. If I'm going to get back, I should try to get there before morning.

"So you're going back to the camp?" Howard says.

"I have a mission to complete."

Howard pulls an iPhone out of his bag. "I bought this before I left New York," he says. "We can stay in contact."

"I can't call you on a number that can be traced—"

"I know that," he says, interrupting me. "I used a credit card number I snagged from Verizon corporate. It gets billed back to them as an internal department expense. It will take them months to figure it out. By then I'll have wiped the data."

"I'll keep my phone on," I say. "The same number I called you from the first time. There's signal blocking throughout the camp, but if you need me, send a text and I'll check for it when I can."

"Can I have your special iPhone number, too?"

"My Program phone? Why do you need that?"

"If we lose contact. If it's an emergency."

I hesitate, wondering if I should trust Howard with my phone number.

Which, of course, is ridiculous, because I've already trusted him with my life.

I pass him the phone.

He handles it delicately, cradling it in two hands.

"It's an iPhone, Howard, not a baby."

"I've never held a baby," Howard says, "but I know how to respect other people's digital property."

He gently taps open the Settings folder and takes a snapshot of the information with his own phone. Then he hands my Program phone back to me.

"I'll let you know the second I've decoded the SDHC card."

"I don't know what I'd do without you, Howard."

"Your life would be considerably less awesome," he says.

"That's true."

"Really?" he says, delighted that I'm agreeing with him.

"You risked everything coming up here. "

"I know," he says softly.

"It means a lot to me."

Before I can stop him, Howard rushes forward, squashing me in a bear hug.

I say, "I've got to be honest. It makes me uncomfortable when you do that."

"Just once," he says. "Then you can go back to being a tough guy."

I LEAVE THE SILVERADO IN THE LONG-TERM PARKING LOT AT THE AIRPORT.

I don't want to bring it into Camp Liberty on the outside chance it might be recognized because the freelance team was hired and equipped by Moore. After considering what Howard told me about the SDHC card, I have to ask myself who has the sophistication to place their own electronics inside a storage card.

Moore's people might be able to do it, but why would they invite me to stay, then try to take me out the moment I left camp?

Still, it's a risk I cannot take.

So I leave the truck in the long-term parking lot, where it will not be scrutinized for days, and I look for a replacement vehicle, something with the engine still warm. If someone just dropped off their car in long-term parking, I can get at least forty-eight hours of use out of it before it's reported missing.

I walk the parking lot in the middle of the night, making myself appear like a weary traveler who just got off a plane and can't remember where he left his car. It's not much of a stretch. I actually stumble going up the ramp, a reminder of how tired I am and the fact that even trained muscles will start to misfire at some point.

I find a new-model Honda Accord, open the Travel Channel app on my iPhone. It's an app with a built-in database, and it should work without needing to connect to a Program server.

I click on SELECT A DESTINATION. I find JAPAN on the scroll wheel, then wait as the app searches its database for the master key code for the Accord. When it finds the right code, it transmits a remote signal.

I hear the familiar click of the locks being disengaged, followed by the engine starting up. I get in and drive out of the parking lot. I use the ticket I got a few minutes ago, explaining to the girl at the pay gate that I messed up and drove into long-term when I only needed short-term.

"You can charge me for five minutes if you need to," I say with a smile.

She winks at me and opens the gate.

THE SUN IS COMING UP BY THE TIME I GET BACK TO CAMP LIBERTY.

I pull up to the roadblock outside camp in the Accord.

Rifles come up. A girl with a gun walks to my window. She stares at me for a moment, and then her expression lightens.

"I know you," she says. "I saw you at the community center the other night. You're a legend."

"I don't feel like a legend. I feel like a guy who needs to go to the bathroom and get some breakfast. No offense."

"Girls go to the bathroom, too," she says.

"I don't have a sister," I say, "so I never learned these important details."

She laughs. "They told us we might see you today. I'm glad you're back."

"Me, too," I say.

"Always nice to have a new brother."

I allow myself to feel what Daniel Martin might feel: proud for persuading his parents to let him come back, nervous about returning here, excited about being a part of something new.

The girl signals to her partner at the roadblock to lower his weapon.

"By the way, you timed it perfectly," she says.

"For what?"

"Breakfast," she says.

She motions to the boy, and he opens the security gate and pulls the tire strip from the road, clearing a path for me.

I PARK THE ACCORD AND JOIN A GROUP OF KIDS HEADING INTO THE MAIN HOUSE FOR BREAKFAST.

There is a large dining area off the main hall where Moore stopped me yesterday.

I follow the group through the double doors and I'm met by loud conversation and laughter. Members of the community sit at long tables with large shared platters of food running down the center.

Family style.

I look around the room for a free place to sit.

On most missions where I sit, when I sit, how I enter a room like this is vitally important. If I were in a high school setting, I'd be concerned with status, social proof, defining myself through the hundreds of cues that create ranking. But a community like this has different standards of evaluation, and I have to recalibrate my thinking.

I am a guest here. A guest does not have to fit in or look comfortable. The opposite, in fact. I allow myself to appear uncertain, not knowing where I should go or what I should do. I let my body reflect

261

that, tensing my shoulders and breathing in a shallow way that is unnatural to me.

I use the opportunity to scan the room as if I'm looking for a place to sit.

But I don't care where I sit. I'm looking for Moore.

I need to know his patterns. Where he eats, where he takes meetings, when he goes to the bathroom, anything and everything.

Because I need this to be done.

"Daniel!" Lee shouts.

He's sitting at a table across the room with Miranda next to him. I raise my hand in greeting and move toward him.

"Good morning," I say.

"Look who's back!" Lee says.

Miranda nods to me briefly, then returns her attention to a half-eaten bowl of oatmeal.

"Join us," Lee says. "Grab some food. You know how it works here?"

"No. It's my first meal with the group," I say.

"It's every man for himself," he says. "Especially at breakfast."

"Sounds rough," I say.

"It's only rough if they run out of bacon," Lee says, and that earns him a laugh from the table.

I take an empty spot across from him at the table, look down the row of faces at kids who greet me.

"I'd introduce you to everyone," Lee says, "but you've met a hundred people in the last couple days. I'm sure you won't remember anyone's name."

"I barely remember my own name at this point," I say, and the group laughs.

"Anyway, you all know Daniel," he announces to the table. "Or if you don't, you're going to get to know him. Because he's staying with us for a while."

That earns me appreciative nods.

I grab a plate and dig into some eggs.

I say, "You're in a good mood this morning, Lee."

"Why not? My father invited you to stay, and it looks like you took him up on the invitation."

"Amazing that I got invited after The Hunt," I say.

"The Hunt went well," Lee says. I note heads perking up around the table. "He reviewed all the stats the day after, and he said we did a good job."

Some kids fist-bump each other around the table.

"*You* did great," I say. "No thanks to me."

"What do you mean?" a blond girl next to me asks.

I glance at Lee. He nods, like I can say whatever I want about it.

"I wasn't exactly a supersoldier," I tell the girl.

"It was your first Hunt," Lee says generously.

"I guess," I say. "I'm still playing catch-up with how you do things here. It's a lot of information all at once."

"We're not so different from other places where people live together. Universities, boarding schools—"

"Oh yeah," I say. "It's just like Exeter. With guns."

The kids at the table laugh.

"There's a long history of alternative communities in the United States," Lee says. "In a sense, even our forefathers were an alternative group. They weren't living in the way that British society dictated, and they were resisting the laws that their British masters attempted to enforce."

"Are you comparing our government to the colonial British?" I say.

"There are similarities," Lee says. "A large and powerful governmental body that becomes cut off from the source of its power. It grows distant and ineffectual over time, more concerned with servicing the needs of the rich and powerful than the common man."

"There are parallels, I agree. But there's one big difference. It's *our* government and *our* country. We can change it if we like. We're not a colony."

"You've heard of 'too big to fail'?" Lee says.

"Sure."

"We're too big to change."

"I thought change was inevitable," I say.

"You guys are boring me," Miranda says.

Lee's face tenses. "These are important issues, Miranda."

His voice is suddenly loud enough to be heard across the room.

Miranda meets his stare. "Vitally important," she says. "So much so that they shouldn't be discussed casually over pancakes."

Lee's shoulders relax. "Agreed," he says. "There's a time and a place for everything."

Suddenly a siren wails through the encampment.

The entire room stands in unison, people moving in a quick but orderly fashion to exits all around the room.

"What's going on?"

"It's a drill," Miranda says.

"You don't know if it's a drill," Lee says.

"It has to be a drill," she says.

They look at each other, concerned.

"What does the sound mean?" I say.

"It's a warning siren," Miranda says, quickly coming around the table.

"A warning of what?"

"That we're under attack," Lee says.

"We have to hurry," Miranda says, and she grabs me and pulls me out of the room as the siren blares again.

PEOPLE ARE RUNNING THROUGH THE BUILDING.

I am herded through a side door where an assigned monitor stands with a clicker, making a head count of everyone entering the hallway. There is controlled chaos through the house as the siren continues to wail. Guns start appearing, rifles and snub-nosed shot-guns. People are strapping on holsters, moving to assigned positions around the house. I glance into rooms as we move down the hall, and I see at least two armed people by each window taking up shooting positions around the perimeter.

Sergeant Burch comes running toward Lee, thrusting a walkie-talkie into his hands.

"My father?" Lee says.

"Secured upstairs," Sergeant Burch says.

"It's just a drill, right?" Lee says.

"No such thing," Sergeant Burch says. "It's real until we hear different."

"But my father would tell you if it was a drill."

"Not anymore, he wouldn't," Sergeant Burch says. "Not since—"

He glances at me. He chooses his next words very carefully.

"The troubles," Sergeant Burch says.

Lee's face goes dark.

"I have to take off," he says to me. "Miranda, would you take care of him?"

"What do you want me to do with him?" she says.

"Stash him someplace safe, then take your position."

His walkie crackles, and he moves off quickly.

"Why do I need to be stashed?" I say.

"Everyone has assigned positions," Miranda says. "It's not safe for you to be walking around on your own."

"Can I come with you?"

"Not a good idea," she says. "I'm going to put you in an interior room, and I'll let Lee know where you are. It's almost certainly a drill. But if anything happens, one of us will come get you."

She rushes me down the hall, knocks hard twice at a door, and when there's no response, she opens it.

It's a windowless utility closet. She motions me inside.

"I'm sorry it's not nice," she says. "It's the best place for you right now."

"I'll be okay," I say. "I can defend myself with a mop if I have to."

"About this morning at breakfast—I was ignoring you because I don't want people to know about us."

"I understand."

"Do you?"

She steps into the closet with me, closing the door behind her. She kisses me hard on the lips.

"I was thinking about you all night," she says.

"I was thinking about you, too," I say, which is mostly a lie. I was thinking about my mission.

The siren is still wailing, a cycle of ten-second blasts, followed by ten seconds of silence, then another set of blasts.

"I have to go," she says, and she turns and runs out of the room, closing the door behind her.

A moment later, I hear a key going into the door.

I give it a minute and I check the knob. It's locked.

I hear multiple sets of footsteps passing by in the hall outside, people hustling to get into position.

The community is on high alert, heavily armed, at the height of paranoia. But all their energy is facing outward, toward an unseen enemy.

I am inside. I am close.

Somewhere upstairs is Moore.

It's the perfect moment for me to act.

I reach into my pants pocket, find the knife I took out of the freelance team's truck last night. I press a button and watch as the three-inch blade slides out.

I wait for the siren to start up, then slide the knife blade into the doorjamb, twist it hard to create a space between the door and the frame, then jiggle the blade back and forth over the lock, applying pressure until it slips back into the door.

I twist to remove the knife and open the door, and I am free.

People are running through the hallway on the way to their ready stations.

It makes it easy for me to step into the hallway, close the door behind me, and join the flow of people moving through the hall.

People nod as they pass me in the hallway, assuming I know
where I'm going. I ignore them.

They have a job; I have a job. This is what I want to project.

I move toward the center of the building. It's a long, rectangular three-story structure with a basement. Moore is upstairs. That's
what Sergeant Burch said.

Moore is a commander. He will want to direct the action.

There is strategic advantage to the high ground. Line of sight,
an ability to understand the battlefield, to position troops and
ammunition.

So I follow the hallway on the main floor until I arrive at a
staircase.

There are guards here, two of them.

They raise their weapons as they see me coming.

"Lee needs me," I say.

"We're not supposed to let anybody up," a boy says, nervous.

The siren is still wailing through the building, bodies in motion around us.

"I'm in a rush," I say, pressuring him. "Why don't you call up there right now?"

"There's no way to call," he says, biting his bottom lip.

"They didn't give you a walkie?" I say, like I can't believe it.

He looks toward the ground, embarrassed. "I'm not C2," he says. "I don't get comms gear."

C2. Military slang for "command and control," the officer elite charged with directing battle plans and defining strategy. That means only the top guys have comms, and the rest of the kids stand at their stations until otherwise notified.

"What do you want to do?" I say impatiently.

If you put too much responsibility on a nervous guy who isn't used to it, he's likely to make a mistake.

"You say Lee needs you?" he says.

"That's what he told me."

He looks to his fellow guard, uncertain.

"You'd better hurry," he says, stepping aside.

"Will do," I say. "Thanks."

I take the stairs two at a time. Near the top I miss a step, my toe slipping down and almost causing me to lose my balance. I catch myself without going down and pull myself to the top of the stairs and around the corner.

I pause there for a moment. I don't make mistakes, not when I'm operating at full capacity.

I remind myself to slow down a bit, not let myself go faster than sleep deprivation allows.

I know this is a three-story building, but the stairs end here. There seems to be no way to get to the top floor.

I'm confused for a moment, and then I remember something from my studies.

There's an old, maze-like section of Tokyo called Edo that was the former seat of power for the shogun. It's said that it was intentionally laid out in a confusing manner, so if enemies ever penetrated the city, they would become lost and could be slaughtered before they caused harm.

I'm guessing this building has been designed with alternating stairwells to make it tougher to get up or down quickly. I turn down the second-floor hallway, trusting my instinct, looking for the hidden staircase that will lead me up to Moore.

I go only a few steps when I sense that someone is shadowing me.

I pause in the middle of the hall, trying to determine whether the shadow is behind or in front of me. But when I stop, I can't feel him.

No shadow. Nothing at all.

For some reason I think of the dead soldier and the things that might have happened to him inside the camp. Was he tracking Moore one morning, just like me? Did he get close? And if so, what went wrong?

I should not be thinking about this. Not now, when I am moving toward Moore, when I might have an opportunity to get him alone at last.

The shadow, or whatever I thought it was, is gone.

Now there is only me, moving toward my target.

I round a corner and note a staircase up ahead, tucked into the corner of the building. There are two guards, both of them armed, one of them shouting into a walkie-talkie. I can't risk having him call my information in to Lee or Sergeant Burch.

I quickly reverse direction, walking toward another hallway in a more deserted section of the house.

This stairway is unmanned.

I stop. My intuition is telling me something is wrong.

An unmanned staircase, all the way in the far corner of the house.

Part of me feels it is a lucky break. Part of me senses a trap.

The problem is I am too tired to know which part to listen to.

Move forward or abandon the mission and wait for another opportunity?

I quickly assess the risks, and I decide this is not the time to hesitate. So I take the stairs two at a time, accelerating as I ascend, not stopping until I arrive, undetected, on the third floor.

The command floor.

Moore.

I hear his voice coming from a room at the end of the hall. He is giving orders, adjusting the position of forces throughout the main house.

A moment later two men step out of the room carrying rifles. They rush away from me, not bothering to look back, where they would certainly see me.

A lucky break. I may not get another.

I take a long, centering breath, and I step into the room.

It's a war room, maps pinned to one wall, a schematic of the compound on the table with troop positions marked out with colored pins.

A man with long hair is studying the wall map, his back to me.

He turns. It's Francisco.

"What are you doing up here?" he says.

"I thought I heard Moore."

"You did hear him, but he's gone. Now answer my question."

"The alarm went off when I was at breakfast. Lee and Miranda told me to wait."

"Wait downstairs?"

"Yes."

"Then why are you upstairs?"

"I was curious," I say.

He doesn't seem surprised.

"You're a very talented guy," he says.

"I don't know what you mean."

"You made it past all the security checkpoints, and if I'm not mistaken, a locked door." He takes a step toward me. "I find that remarkable."

"I just wandered up here," I say. "Besides, everyone's running around like chickens with their heads cut off. I don't know how remarkable it was."

"Let's take a walk," Francisco says. "Just you and me."

"Where to?"

"I have to fix a relay station. You can help me."

"I was hoping to finish breakfast," I say.

He takes another step toward me. His voice is firm but steady.

"Grab a protein bar and eat it on the way," he says. "But now I'd like you to come with me."

"Do I have a choice?"

I measure the distance between us, use my peripheral vision to scan the room for weapons.

"There's always a choice," Francisco says.

He spreads his arms wide. I can't tell if it's a gesture of friendship or an invitation to fight.

I look at him, judging whether I should go with him or whether I should end this now.

One-on-one, I believe I could take Francisco. But that's not the issue.

The issue is Moore. If I take on Francisco, it's sure to attract attention, and I'll have a lot of explaining to do. My cover could be threatened, or even blown.

That's assuming it's not blown already.

I look at Francisco staring at me from across the room. His face betrays nothing.

Moore is gone, and Francisco is offering me a carrot.

"Let's take that walk," I say. "Where's the relay station?"

"It's in the mountains."

"I guess I'll need hiking boots, then, won't I?"

"We're about the same size," Francisco says. "You can borrow mine."

WE STOP BY FRANCISCO'S ROOM IN THE MAIN HOUSE.

I wait outside in the hall as he gathers some things for the journey. He leaves his door open, and I glance in to see a bare room without decorations on the walls. Either Francisco lives like a monk, or he moved in here not too long ago.

A minute later he comes out with rope, a tool kit, and an extra set of boots.

"These should fit you," he says.

"How do you know my size?"

"Your profile."

"What profile?"

"In the game. I looked at your stats. And we just happen to be the same size."

"Convenient," I say.

"Very," he says.

We walk together toward the edge of the encampment. The sirens stopped a while ago, signaling the end of the defense drill, but the grounds of Camp Liberty are still empty. We are alone with the exception of a single sentry in the distance.

Francisco pauses at what should be the edge of the laser perimeter. He removes a square gray device from his bag.

"What's that for?" I say.

"We have some security provisions. This turns them off for a few seconds."

He's talking about the lasers, but I don't want him to think I know about them.

He presses a button. "Are you ready for an adventure?" he says.

"Always."

He moves forward through the perimeter. I follow him up a path into the mountain. It's a different path from the one I used the other night, one that begins cloaked in trees at the base of the hill behind the encampment but quickly opens into a narrow and well-defined trail.

"How are you keeping up?" Francisco says after we've gone a few hundred meters.

"I'm fine."

"New boots can be tough."

"*I* can be tough," I say.

My foot hits the ground wrong, twisting my ankle as I stumble. Francisco stops.

"Are you sure you're okay?" he says. "The climb gets more difficult up ahead," he says.

I walked through these woods silently three nights ago, but now I am unsteady on my feet, lack of sleep breaking my concentration and affecting my stride.

"I can handle myself," I say to Francisco.

He glances at my feet and grunts, and then he starts out again.

He stays ahead of me on the trail, legs strong, sweat appearing around the neck of his flannel shirt, then under his arms, then across his entire back. He sips from a canteen as he hikes, but he never complains about the heat or effort, never even rolls up his sleeves.

I do my best to keep up with him, making sure I drink two sips for his every one, keeping myself hydrated as limited defense against my exhaustion.

We hike for another hour before he pauses at a place where the trail splits in two directions. He takes a moment to judge both ways, then confidently moves to the left.

I'm watching the whole time, doing my best to memorize terrain, not knowing whether I'll need to get back home alone.

Or get away from him.

We come out onto a clearing on the ridge, open to the sky.

It's midafternoon now, but the elevation has caused the temperature to drop several degrees.

Francisco stops by a large tree with a small satellite dish about halfway up hidden among the branches.

"That's the satellite uplink," he says. "You want to spot me?"

"I can do that," I say.

"I'm going to clip us together," he says.

He snaps a rope into a carabiner on his belt, knotting one end, then does the same on my belt. He hands me the section of rope.

"I can trust you, right?" he says.

"Trust me not to throw you off the mountain?"

"Trust you to hang on if I fall."

"You can trust me," I say.

I've got no reason to harm Francisco. Not unless he gives me one.

He climbs halfway up the tree, makes a few adjustments on the satellite uplink, then climbs down without incident.

"Look there," he says.

I turn, and I can see the entire basin beneath us, the encampment laid out like toy buildings, and the road beyond that winds up the mountain and disappears out of sight.

It's barely been three days since I came to this place. It feels like a lifetime.

"What do you think of our home?" Francisco asks.

"It looks small from up here."

"It's small, but it's ours. How many people can say they have something like that in their lives?"

He steps closer to the edge, inadvertently kicking a stone that rolls for half a meter, then falls off the edge.

"You can step out farther," he says, tugging lightly at the rope on his belt. "I've got you."

I check to be sure we're still clipped together.

I take him up on his offer, stepping forward. The ledge is narrower than it first appeared, dropping off suddenly into nothing.

I stand at the very edge. I think back to a time just a few days ago at the sports camp in Vermont. I stood at the edge of a cliff. With Peter watching, I took the plunge into the cool water below.

But there is no water here. Instead there are a thousand meters of rugged cliff face.

A single wrong step and I would plunge off the side. If Francisco is strong enough, he could stop my fall. If not, we'd both go down together.

"You could have taken anyone up here with you," I say.

"But I chose you," he says.

"Why is that?"

He looks out over the valley. "Perspective," he says. "Sometimes you need to see what you're up against to understand who you really are."

"What are you up against?"

"Not just me, Daniel. Us."

He points to the vista in front of us, a small valley surrounded by mountains on all sides.

"We're up against the world," he says.

"It looks like these mountains will keep out the world."

"For a time maybe. Not forever."

I track his position behind me, looking for any indication of a move toward me, an adjustment of his body that might portend danger to me.

"You haven't been at Liberty long, have you?" I say.

"What makes you say that?"

"The way Lee spoke to you the other night. He talked to you like you were an outsider."

"He's envious of my position with his father. But yes, I'm relatively new. And I rose fast."

"You're new, but you call this place your home?"

"Home is a choice," he says. "We're home when we decide we're home."

I hear a click behind me. I look back and see that Francisco has unclipped his end of the rope from his belt. That means I'm alone on the edge, untethered.

The wind whips up, strong enough that I have to lean back to steady myself.

Francisco drops the end of the rope on the ground and without a word, he turns and heads back up the trail into the forest.

Just before he disappears, he motions for me to follow him.

I unclip the rope and coil it around my arm.

Then I follow.

FRANCISCO LEADS ME DEEPER INTO THE FOREST.

We walk for ten minutes or so in silence, when suddenly he stops.

"Where are we?" I say.

"Someplace we can talk," he says simply.

The area is deep shadow, the foliage blocking out all but individual beams of sunlight. I look around us, but I see no markings, nothing to distinguish this place from any other.

"It's a long way to come for a conversation."

"I wanted to talk to you outside of Liberty, away from the electronics, the distractions, everything."

Francisco squats and picks up a pinecone. He peels it with a fingernail.

He says, "Someone sent you to Camp Liberty."

He says it simply, like it's a fact he already knows.

"I was invited," I say.

"I don't think so."

I subtly edge backward, working to create enough distance to maximize my options.

"You're right," I say, going with him rather than resisting. "My father sent me. He wanted me to have the experience."

"Not your father."

"Who, then?"

Francisco drops his hands to his sides. The gesture might appear casual to the outside observer—a relaxing of the shoulders, a lowering of the arms with palms open and turned out toward me—but it's more than it seems.

Because as he does it, his energy changes entirely.

"You were sent here by the same people who sent me," he says.

I see his power, his training. I see what he's capable of, and what he's been hiding.

Francisco is a Program soldier.

He is the dead soldier, very much alive.

I look at him, standing across from me, unblinking, revealing his true self.

"It was about four months ago that I came to Liberty," he says. "I was sent as an assassin. Just like you."

There are four meters between us. I can cover that distance in a second and a half if need be.

"If what you're saying is true, Francisco, why did you let me into camp?"

"I knew they would send another assassin after I disappeared. The only question was how he would come...."

He steps forward. Four meters becomes three and a half.

"And whether I would know who he was before it was too late. With Moore's permission, I staged the recruiting event in the community center."

"Staged it?"

"I wanted to provide an opening outside the compound where it would be easier for someone to get to Moore, and for us to get to whoever that was."

"What about the woman who tried to kill Moore?"

"The English teacher? That was my idea, too," Francisco says. "A test of sorts. I knew the scenario would be too tempting for a potential Program assassin. He could do nothing and see if she succeeded—"

"Or he could act like a hero and try to use that to get in with Moore."

He smiles. "And flush himself out in the process."

The English teacher was a trap. That's why she was coming into camp in the van the other night. She is one of them, following orders.

I feel anger flooding my chest, along with shame at having made a mistake. I should have let the woman shoot if she was going to. I should have kept my cover, even if it meant losing Moore.

"Don't be too hard on yourself," Francisco says, like he knows what I'm feeling. "Even after it happened, I couldn't be sure you were the one. You might have been some brave, crazy kid off the street."

"So you brought me closer. And you watched me."

"That's right."

"Quite a risk."

"I had my reasons," he says.

He's not showing any aggressive intent, but I don't trust what I'm seeing. As a Program operative, he should be able to control his surface emotions, misleading me and getting me to drop my guard.

I don't yet know what Francisco's trying to achieve, but I remind myself to stay sharp until I understand him better. I take long, slow, deep breaths, keeping my tired muscles oxygenated and at maximum readiness.

"When did you know?" I say.

"For sure? Not until this morning during the defense drill."

"Who else knows?"

"Only Moore and I were in on the plan. We warned Lee about you in a general way, but he is easily swayed. He believed in you."

"What about Miranda?" I say.

His eyes widen slightly.

"Does that matter to you?" he asks.

I think of her in my room the other night, standing naked in front of me. Was it all a trick to confuse me and get me to reveal myself? The idea is upsetting to me, much more than it should be.

"It doesn't matter," I say. "And she doesn't matter."

He knows I'm lying. I can see it on his face.

"We left her out of it," he says gently.

I feel relief inside. The feeling surprises me.

"You're the only one who knows, then. You and Moore."

"That's right."

"Did you bring me out here to kill me?"

"I brought you here to talk to you. Because as I got to know you, Daniel, I saw something in you that I didn't expect."

"What's that?"

"Potential."

He drops the pinecone at his feet. I keep my attention on his center mass, ready to defend myself against a strike.

But he doesn't strike.

Instead he tells me a story.

"MY NAME IS FRANCISCO GONZALEZ," HE SAYS.

"I am the son of a Mexican tycoon. My father made his fortune in banking. I had a blessed life because of the family I was born into and the natural talent God gave me. I was a soccer player, recruited to the Cruz Azul Youth Academy before the sixth grade. I was away and training when the accident happened. My parents died in a private plane crash. Pilot error, the authorities called it."

Pilot error. He says the phrase like it's an insult.

"You don't believe it was an accident?" I ask.

"I lost my parents, and then The Program came for me. Would you believe it?"

"It's hard to know what to believe when The Program is involved."

"True," he says. "The Program told me they were offering me a new life. I was lost after my parents died, and so I agreed. I chose to go with them, but I didn't know what I was signing up for. None of us do."

I remember Mother in a room of the training house after my parents died. I remember her talking to me for the first time, giving me a choice between life and death.

"How old were you when they came for you?" Francisco asks.

"Twelve."

"Do you think a twelve-year-old should be asked to make a choice like that?"

Life or death. Not much of a choice.

"What does it matter now?" I say. "It's over and done."

"I'm not blaming you," he says. "We all made the same choice in the same situation."

"*We?* You mean there are more of us?" I say.

"There are a few."

"Before this mission, I only knew about two. Me and the one who brought me in."

"Who was that?" he says.

"He has many names. But I know him as Mike."

"Mike," Francisco says. His face goes pale. "I thought he would be the one they'd send for me."

"You know him?"

He nods.

"If you know him, then you would have seen him coming," I say.

"Maybe. You never know with Mike."

"You're afraid of him," I say, surprised.

"Aren't you?"

"I'm not afraid of anyone."

"That's what you believe," he says.

"Because it's true."

He smiles and shakes his head. I don't like the look on his face.

"I'm afraid of Mike for good reasons," Francisco says. "I'm afraid because he is Alpha."

"Alpha?"

"The first. The Program began with him."

"How do you know that?"

"Because I'm Beta."

I can't believe what I'm hearing. The Program has been cloaked in mystery to me, revealing only what they felt I needed to know.

The curiosity inside me is overwhelming.

"What am I?" I say, my voice barely a whisper.

"You don't know, do you?"

I shake my head.

"I can't say for sure," he says. "But looking at you, I'd say you're Epsilon."

Epsilon. The fifth letter of the Greek alphabet.

I sort the information Francisco is giving me. I see the schematic in my head:

Mike	Alpha
Francisco	Beta
?	Gamma
?	Delta
Me	Epsilon

"There are five of us," I say.

"Maybe more," he says, "but five that I know about."

"Mike is the oldest."

"And you're the youngest."

"What happens to us after?" I say.

"You've thought about it, too," he says.

I have avoided these questions and the dangerous places they can take me in my mind, but talking with Francisco, the questions come rushing to the surface:

What happens when we reach an age where we no longer fit in? What happens when we can't pass for kids anymore?

What happens to a teen assassin who is no longer a teen?

Francisco says, "I don't know what happens, because nobody has aged out yet. Mike is the closest, but he's found a niche for himself."

"A niche?"

"Recruiter. I'm next in line, but I wasn't going to wait around to find out what happens. Not when there are better options."

Camp Liberty. Francisco's last assignment turned into his way out.

"I have a question for you," Francisco says. "What was your exact assignment here?"

"Moore," I say.

He swallows hard. "What about me?" he says.

I shake my head. "They thought you were dead. They didn't send me for you; they sent me *because* of you. Because you lost the mission."

An expression of pain crosses his face. He stands and rubs his forehead, pressing at the sides of his temples.

He is emotional, much more than I would expect for someone with his training. It makes me wonder about him, gives me some clue into his strengths and weaknesses.

"So you're my replacement?" he says.

"That's right."

He laughs, a loud laugh that echoes through the forest.

"That's fucking great," he says. "I went off the grid and they couldn't figure out how or why, so they told you I was dead, right?"

"They had to assume you were dead," I say. "What else could you be?"

He laughs again.

"Don't you see? I confused the hell out of them," he says. "Their soldier turned against them. It's so inconceivable they could only assume I was dead. I would pay to have seen Mother's face after I dropped off the grid."

"How did you go off the grid without them knowing?" I say.

"I destroyed my phone," he says. He steps toward me, his voice dropping to an intense whisper. "And something else."

"What else?"

He looks around the woods to check that we're still alone, and then he unbuttons his shirt, slips one arm out of the long flannel. It's afternoon now, and the woods are cast in a golden glow. He runs his fingers down his arm, tracing something there.

I step closer, squinting until I see them, cut marks running up and down his arms and across his chest as if he were attacked by an animal. Some are scarred over, others are still healing.

The flannel shirt. He wears it to hide the marks.

"It took me a while, but I found it," he says.

"Found what?"

"The Program. It's inside us."

He points to one particular scar on his bicep, near the shoulder joint.

"You're implanted, too," he says.

"Implanted?"

"They put a chip inside you," he says.

I flash back to the house where I was trained. I try to remember any medical procedures, surgeries, something invasive enough to have been an implantation surgery.

I don't remember anything like that.

"What kind of a chip?" I say, not believing, but wanting to keep him talking.

"It's a neurosuppressor," he says. "You already know what it does."

"How would I know?"

"Because you've felt it," he says. "It takes away your fear."

I look at Francisco standing without his shirt on, a ghostly glow around him.

I am alone on a mountain with someone trained just like me, someone who is my enemy, miles from help or support.

I should be afraid, but I am not.

I'm never afraid.

Mission after mission, through dangerous, near-death situations, I do not get afraid. I only have moments of fear that fade as soon as they arise.

"Let's say you actually found a chip. How would you know what it did? Did they tell you?"

"Never," he says. "They're not going to tell us we're the subjects of an experiment. I know what the chip does because I took it out. Then everything became clear. It's like an emotional throttle. You start to feel fear, and it clamps down, sends a signal to your brain that takes the edge off. This is why I could go into any situation, no matter how dangerous, and still function. I could think clearly no matter what was going on around me."

He's describing my own skill set. Characteristics I thought were a part of my personality and training.

"The part they don't understand..." he says. "If you don't feel fear, you don't feel joy or love. Not in any real way. Without the fear, the risk is gone. And without risk, rewards don't matter. You're left with nothing much at all. You're numb."

He watches me, gauging my reaction.

"I know what you're thinking," he says. "I would be thinking the same if someone had told me this four months ago."

"What am I thinking?"

"You're thinking I'm insane."

I look at Francisco sweating in the cool forest air, his flesh marked by a hundred cuts, his eyes wild.

"That's right," I say.

"You're also measuring what I say against your own experience. So you know it's true."

I smile, trying to placate him.

"I know you believe it."

"You still don't understand, do you?" he says. "I'm telling you these things because I want you to know. So you can save yourself."

My smile fades.

"I don't need saving."

"Do you know the easiest way to die, Daniel?"

"I know several ways."

"Not the easiest way to kill. The easiest way to die."

"In your sleep."

"Very good. And why is that?"

"If you're asleep, you don't know that you're dying," I say.

He nods. "That's you. You're dying right now and you don't know it. You are asleep and dying. I'm trying to wake you up."

He steps toward me. I look at the marks up and down his arms.

He says, "Find the joint where your humerus meets your elbow. Check an inch interior from there."

I can't listen to this anymore. It's a distraction. He's trying to trick me, get my arms out of position so he can strike.

"Check," he says, his voice urgent.

"There's nothing to check," I say firmly, and I step away from him.

He looks at me, astonished.

"They own you," he says in a whisper.

"It's not ownership," I say. "It's loyalty. I'm a soldier."

He shakes his head.

"That's what *I* thought. They taught me to forget my old life and replace it with loyalty to them. But they didn't finish the job. Because the memories came back. It took years for me, but they did. The chip only works on fear. Everything else is still there, suppressed by your training. Until it isn't anymore."

I think about the way my memories come back between missions. The way I still see my father when I close my eyes, the way he sometimes visits me in my dreams.

Francisco says, "These people you work for, they're not good people."

"They defend this country," I say. "They're patriots."

"They are not," he says. "When you remember, everything changes."

There's only one thing I must remember. My training. The things I've been taught to do, the way I've been taught to do them.

"You'll look for the chip later," he says.

He traces the cuts that crisscross his chest, some healed, some still pink and raw.

"I had to look for a while," he says. "But eventually I found it. You'll find it, too. Then you'll know I've told you the truth, and you'll get out."

"I'm not looking for a way out," I say.

"You're still asleep," he says. "I feel sorry for you."

There's something about the way he says it, what I perceive as a sneer on his lips, his tone of voice.

"And what are you?" I say, my anger flaring. "You're at Liberty training to poison the water supply, blow up nuclear power plants, or whatever the hell you're doing, and you call that being awake? You're a terrorist."

His face goes rigid. He holds up a finger in warning.

"Don't you dare use that word," he says.

"Does Moore have a different word for it?"

"I don't agree with everything Moore does," he says, "but the end justifies the means."

"What end? You're a soldier like me, Francisco. You were trained to protect the country, not dismantle it."

"I'm still a soldier," he says. "But I have a different mission now."

"What mission?"

"To wake up this country."

"They're already awake. Nine-eleven. The *Cole* bombing. The war in Iraq. The attacks in Syria. They are wide awake, and they don't need your help."

"What about us?" he says.

"Us?"

"The Program," he says. "The things their country is doing behind their backs. Are they awake to that?"

I can see now that I am the only patriot here. Francisco has become something else.

A traitor.

He is a traitor, and I cannot allow it.

So I attack.

I cover the ten feet between us in an instant, opening with a lightning-fast strike to the center of his chest that stuns him. Then I quickly turn to the side, grab his arm, and spin him hard, slamming him against a tree.

There is no reaction time before he is coming back at me. In an instant his energy shifts from attacked to attacker, so fluid it would be easy to miss.

Miss and die.

That's how well trained he is.

He aims a strike toward my head, but I sidestep and take the force of his blow to the shoulder instead. Even this is enough to send a shock wave through me.

We separate in the woods, and I look at him, shirtless, muscles rippling.

His body, his style, his reaction time—they're all too familiar to me. It's almost like I'm fighting myself.

"It doesn't have to be like this," he says.

"How else can it be?"

"You asked me why I let you into camp when I could have killed you. It's because I knew you had doubts about The Program. Just like I did when I came here."

"You're wrong about me," I say.

But it's not the truth.

I doubted during my last mission. And I doubt now. My purpose for being here, the reason I was sent in the first place.

"Look at me, Daniel. I've gotten my life back. You could have yours back, too."

"I already have a life," I say.

I come at him, indicating a high attack while I strike low at his feet.

He does not take the bait but kicks out at me, his style suddenly switching to Muay Thai. I instantly match him, our legs flying, shins crashing together, a spin kick to my head that I dodge, a return kick toward his chest that only just misses contact.

But it sends me off balance, and he pounces.

He is as fast as me and as smart. Yet he is not my equal. Not quite.

Because in surrendering his mission, he has not gotten stronger. He's gotten weaker. Something is broken inside him. I sense it like an animal senses weakness in another animal. Beneath the hard exterior, the training, the calculation, the intelligence—

He

is

damaged.

An operative who has stopped operating. Such a thing cannot be allowed to exist.

Suddenly my phone buzzes in my pocket, the single vibration that indicates a text message coming in.

Francisco senses my distraction and takes advantage of the moment, coming at me with a side swipe, then a full-on kick to my chest that sends me careening against a tree trunk.

The force of the kick is such that it takes my breath away, and a shiver passes through my body.

Francisco has the strength and training to kill with one kick.

A heart blow. A heel to the chest, a twist at the last moment to sharpen the angle, shatter the ribs over the pericardium, puncture the fluid sac, and cause heart failure.

I was out of position and the kick hit me dead center. That means he could have killed me, and he didn't.

Francisco intentionally pulled his kick, sparing my life.

Why?

He must see the confusion on my face, because he answers the unvoiced question:

"Imagine you and me, with our training...the things we could accomplish if we put our skills together."

"Accomplish where? With Moore? You traded The Program for a madman," I say.

"I'll admit he's got his issues. But there's room to shape his beliefs. We could do it together, build this into something special."

He lowers his voice.

"The Program wouldn't stand a chance with us together. Think about it."

I consider teaming with Francisco. There's something nice about the idea of being together, soldiers united rather than isolated in the world.

"You've only been here three days," Francisco says. "I understand if you're not ready to make a decision yet, but give yourself time to get to know Moore. Give us time to talk this out together."

I hesitate, the tiniest seed of doubt creeping into my mind.

"I don't *have* time," I say.

I have a mission. I can't allow myself to be confused.

"Listen to me," he says. "I'm trying to throw you a lifeline."

"I don't need your lifeline. You betrayed The Program," I say. "You betrayed your training, everything you believed in."

"I never believed," he says. He stares at me, his eyes piercing through the dimness of the forest. "Did you?"

That's when I hit him. A roundhouse to the side of his head.

He's startled by the speed of my attack. I go from stillness to a rapid strike in less than a second.

He reaches up to defend himself, and I hit him again.

He tries to grab a length of branch from the ground, but I'm too fast. I hit him a third time.

He tries to speak, but I don't wait to hear what he's going to say.

I've heard enough.

I'm trained to kill without leaving a trace.

I know two dozen ways to do it. When I don't have a weaponized implement, I know how to do it with my hands or with items in the environment. I can always kill in a manner that is undetectable if I choose to do so.

Not now.

Now I take his head in my hands, and I bash it against a tree.

He goes limp in my arms, the fight drained out of him.

I push him up against the tree, my palm pressing into his throat, choking him out slowly.

"You said you recognized me earlier," I say.

He groans, and I slap his face, snapping him to attention.

"Listen to me," I say. "Earlier you said you knew I was Epsilon by looking at me. What did you mean?"

"Your face," he says through bloody lips. "It's familiar."

"How is it familiar if you've never seen me before?"

"You look like your father."

My hand comes away from his throat. I stand before him, undefended.

"You know my father?" I say.

He stares at me, surprise showing through swollen eyes.

"You don't know, do you?" he says.

"Know what?"

"How you got to The Program. Who you really are."

"Mike brought me in."

"But why? You must have thought about it."

I have thought about it. Nobody is innocent, nobody who The Program targets. They've all done something to bring it on.

My father did something to bring it on.

But what?

Francisco strikes at me then, a wild swing as a last-ditch effort to save himself. But his timing is off, his body injured beyond repair. I sidestep, the punch narrowly missing me but glancing off the side of my skull hard enough to start a ringing in my ears.

He is like an animal, injured but dangerous until the end.

"Who am I?" I say.

"I can't tell you that," he says.

"You won't," I say.

"I *can't*," he says.

I leap on top of him, kneeling on his chest, my hands closing around his throat.

"You can't tell me who I am because you don't know," I say.

The color drains from his face, a sign that he is bleeding internally. He struggles beneath me, a sticky line of blood dropping from the corner of one lip and making contact with the ground.

His voice is hoarse as he speaks.

"I can't tell you," he says, "because you have to find out for yourself."

I squeeze his throat.

He gasps, looking up at me.

I meet his gaze, and I squeeze tighter.

My focus is singular. I must crush this boy.

I imagine him telling Moore about The Program before turning against us.

I think of him at the water treatment plant, holding Lee back, not because he was morally opposed to acting, but because he was awaiting instructions from Moore.

He fights for breath, but I do not allow him any.

This traitor. This boy who was one of us and is no longer.

I will protect The Program from the damage he has done. I will protect the country from the terrorist acts he might carry out if he is not stopped.

The phone in my pocket buzzes again and again. Someone is trying to reach me urgently, but the buzzing is like a fly far away on the edge of my thoughts.

Time seems to stop. There is nothing but this moment, and my mission.

Protect The Program.

I will destroy the voice that tells lies about my father.

The traitor's hand that reached out to me with a lifeline.

The soldier willing to poison innocent people for an insane cause.

The mind that plots The Program's downfall.

I squeeze until they are gone, and there is nothing left.

Until all is silence, and The Program is safe.

WHEN I'M SURE FRANCISCO IS DEAD, I DRAG HIS BODY DEEPER INTO THE WOODS.

A section so dense that he will never be found.

The heat and moisture will start the process. The animals and their hunger will finish it.

I reach down and take the device that turns off the laser perimeter from his pocket. I'll use it to get back into camp.

I stop and listen in the darkness.

No movement, no footsteps.

I am alone.

I hear the call of a night bird and the distant gurgle of running water.

I follow that sound, tracing it back through the woods until I arrive at the river, and I plunge my hands into cold water.

I sit on the riverbank. I take off my shirt and rinse it in the river. I twist the fabric and watch water and blood pour from it. I do the same with my pants. I wash the blood from the boots Francisco lent me.

When I'm finished, I put the cold shirt back on. It shocks me back to the present moment.

The phone vibrations earlier.

I take out my Program iPhone, but that's not where the messages are. They are on my other phone, the one I've been using to contact Howard.

Howard has sent half a dozen texts asking me to call him.

Howard.

I made a mistake asking him to come up here. I see that now.

Francisco crossed the line into treason and went insane. I will not make the same mistake.

After I am done with my mission, after I have killed Moore, I will get Howard out of here safely. I'll cover our tracks. I'll send him home, and I'll never contact him again under any circumstances.

Then I'll reconnect with The Program. Things like this will not happen again. Breaks in protocol. Questions.

Doubts.

I sit down in the woods. I feel the cool air on my skin.

I've gotten confused during my last two missions. My job is not to understand the big picture of my life.

My job is the small picture of the mission. Acquiring targets, getting close, finishing.

That's what I have to do now.

Finish.

I should stand up, but I don't. Not right away.

I am tired. My body. My mind.

Time passes.

When I look up again, the moon is out.

When did it become nighttime?

I drag myself up off the forest floor. I am lost here in the darkness. I do not know where I am.

That's when I remember the river.

Miranda told me that one side flows down to Moore, to camp, to my mission.

The other goes someplace else, someplace I do not know.

I only have to make the right choice, and I will be fine.

I follow the river south toward Camp Liberty.

I have work to do.

I HIKE OUT OF THE WOODS.

I use Francisco's device to turn off the laser perimeter and walk back into the encampment unseen and unchallenged. I go directly to my room and lock the door behind me.

I must sanitize this space. It will be my next-to-last act here.

I move through the room, erasing evidence of my presence, cleaning surfaces with tissue, then flushing them to erase genetic evidence.

My thoughts are racing below the surface, threatening to bubble up and confuse me, but I keep them down below where they cannot interfere with my tasks.

I stand in the center of the room, looking around one final time to make sure it has been properly prepared. Normally I call in a cleaning crew after I have finished, contact Father and have him send a team while I get a safe distance away. But I do not have access to those resources now.

I must act alone. I must prove myself.

Something happens to me now. I fuzz out, losing track of time.

When I come to, I'm standing in the center of the room. My hand is on my opposite arm, pressing at the bones of my elbow, searching for something there beneath the skin.

I am looking for the chip, just as Francisco said I would.

I put my hand down.

Francisco lost his mind and betrayed The Program. His words are lies, his actions suspect. I cannot allow myself to get confused at a time like this.

I have a job. I have to finish what I came here to do.

I SLIP INTO THE MAIN HOUSE.

I hear the chatter of people eating dinner on the first floor. I bypass them, and I move deeper into the house, mounting the first-floor staircase and moving on to the second.

I have done this once before. That's all it takes for the layout to be committed to memory.

I pass a few people in the hall, nodding to them as I go. There is no reason to hide, no need to mask my movement in any way. I project authority and people yield, allowing me to pass.

I take the corner stairs up to the third floor, and I arrive without incident.

The war room.

I pause for a moment, steadying my body and mind.

I feel certainty deep inside, the laser focus that has always allowed me to accomplish my missions.

It's a relief to feel it. The old me. The me without doubts.

The soldier.

I assume Moore knew about Francisco's plan this morning.

Francisco would take me up the mountain, ostensibly to repair a satellite uplink, but really to test my allegiance.

A make-or-break scenario.

I would turn against The Program, or I would be killed.

Because I am still alive, he will assume I turned. But Moore will want to know the details of what happened on the mountain.

I will make my certainty feel like the certainty of a boy who believes he has seen the truth. A boy who has made a new choice for his life.

This is the boy I will show to Moore.

I step into the room.

HE IS NOT ALONE.

Aaron is with him.

No matter.

I stand in the doorway waiting for them to notice me.

Moore looks up, takes in my appearance, registers the fact that I am by myself.

He nods to me, and I step inside.

"Where's Francisco?" Aaron says.

"In his room," I say simply.

"I thought you two were together," he says.

I note him looking at my forehead. I wipe there with my fingers. The skin is raw from a scrape. I feel the stickiness of clotted blood.

"We were together," I say. "We took a hike, talked about some things. As you can see, we had a few issues to settle between us."

"Were things settled satisfactorily?" Moore says.

I dab at my forehead. "Let's just say we understand each other a lot better now."

"Boys will be boys," Moore says.

"And men will be men," I say. I look at the blood on my fingers and smile. "You think I look bad? You should see Francisco. He's cleaning himself up, and then he'll join us."

Aaron looks at me, distrust pouring off him. But he is not the important player in the room.

I check Moore's eyes, searching for evidence of doubt.

I do not detect any.

"Francisco explained everything to me," I say.

I glance at Aaron as if I'm unsure if I should say more with him in the room.

Moore takes the cue.

"Why don't you grab a bite downstairs," he says to Aaron.

"I don't think that's a good idea," Aaron says.

"Do as I tell you," Moore says.

Aaron looks from Moore to me. His weight shifts from leg to leg, his uncertainty manifesting in his body. Aaron so badly wants to be a tough guy. He is brave but unskilled. I see that now.

"I'll pick something up and be back in a few minutes," Aaron says to Moore.

"Take your time," Moore says. "Daniel and I have much to discuss."

Aaron looks at me with narrowed eyes, then he leaves the room.

Six to eight minutes, that is my time frame. That is my estimate of how long it will take Aaron to get back here. It depends on what they're serving downstairs, the length of the line in the dining hall, and how fearful Aaron is about my time with Moore.

But the important thing is that he is gone now.

I say, "I wasn't sure how much Aaron knew."

Moore shakes his head. "We thought it was better to keep him out of it for the time being."

"You knew about me all along," I say.

"I suspected. I didn't know," Moore says.

I take a step toward him. He allows it.

He says, "Francisco warned me there would be others, that The Program would not let this stand."

Hearing him say the name of my organization causes Francisco's betrayal to hit me full force. Francisco told this stranger about us, breaking a fundamental code of our work.

Then I think of Howard waiting for me back at the hotel. I broke the same code.

Am I any different from Francisco?

I can't think about this now. I push it to the side and focus all my attention on Moore.

I say, "Francisco warned you about me, but you decided to let me in."

"I decided the opposite. It's Francisco who persuaded me to give you a chance that night at the community center. He thought you were a Program soldier, but he also thought you could be something more."

"A permanent."

"A new kind of soldier," Moore says, correcting me. "And he was right, wasn't he?"

I think of Francisco on the forest floor, his eyes bulging as I squeeze his throat.

Three minutes gone. Three remain.

"He was right," I say. I touch the bruise on my head. "It took a little convincing, but I'm a stubborn guy."

"The best ones are," Moore says. "But if you stay with us, you stay by choice. Not by force."

"Choice," I say. "That's exactly what it is."

Moore smiles.

"I'm glad to hear that," he says. "You're going to be an important part of things moving forward."

"I know how Francisco convinced me, but I'm curious to know how you convinced him."

"In the beginning?"

"That's right."

"I didn't have to convince him."

"What do you mean?"

"I don't have that power, Daniel, not really. Francisco had already turned against The Program when he met me. He just needed someone to show him a different way to live. He needed a new mission."

"*Your* mission."

Moore nods. "Which brings us to you," he says. "You were already beginning to doubt the people you work for and the things they ask you to do. I saw it that night at the community center."

I take another step toward Moore. I remove my glasses and swing them by my side.

Moore turns his back to me, looking out the window at the camp below.

"Now you're here to stay," he says. "I have plans for us."

"I want to hear about them."

"Of course," Moore says. "As soon as Francisco gets back."

He looks out across the encampment, his back still to me.

"Where *is* Francisco?" Moore says.

"He went to his room, but he should be here momentarily."

"I see," Moore says.

I step toward him, closing in on striking range. He continues to look out the window, his posture relaxed.

This is going to be easy.

Or so I think until Moore turns back to me with a pistol in his hand.

"Don't come any closer," he says.

I look at the pistol.

It's a black Beretta M9. Standard-issue U.S. military pistol. Its 9mm bullets have questionable lethality from a distance, but we're not at a distance. We are in the same room, a few feet away from each other.

"You're here and Francisco is not," Moore says. "I'm going to err on the side of caution and ask you to keep your distance until Francisco returns."

He holds the pistol steady, like a soldier does.

Two minutes until Aaron returns, perhaps five minutes before Moore becomes convinced something is wrong and sends someone to find Francisco. By then there will be eyes on the situation and multiple people between me and Moore.

I cannot let that happen.

"Francisco won't be back," I say.

"Why is that?"

"He's dead."

"Is that right?" Moore says unflinchingly. "How did he die?"

"I killed him and left his body in the woods."

Moore is silent for a moment, watching me.

"Why?" he says.

He aims his weapon at my chest. From this distance, he will not miss.

"Because he was a traitor," I say.

"To your Program?"

"Yes. And also to you."

His eyes narrow. The first real reaction I've gotten out of him. I continue quickly.

"He was plotting against you. He disagreed with your political ideas, and he wanted us to take over the camp together."

Moore looks at me, the aim in his gun hand unyielding.

"You disagreed with that approach?"

"Obviously," I say.

Moore pauses for a moment, and then he laughs. A deep belly laugh that causes him to fold at the waist.

"Would you like to tell me why you disagreed?" Moore says.

"Lee and Miranda," I say.

"What about them?"

"I like them. I trust them. And they believe in you. I thought I might just try it myself."

"You really did kill Francisco," he says.

"I saved you the trouble."

Moore lowers the gun to his side.

"I trusted him," Moore says, his face going slack.

"That was a mistake," I say, and in one motion I step forward, detaching the temple arm from my glasses. I arc them through the air, pressing the point into the side of his neck and depressing the plunger.

He doesn't flinch, only looks at me with a confused expression on his face.

He stumbles as the poison hits him. He drops to one knee.

I step toward him, removing the pistol from his hand and helping him to balance. I don't want him falling in a way that will create a blood splatter that will look strange to his people.

"You—" he whispers.

Our faces are close, too close.

I lay him back on the floor. I replace the pistol in its holster at his waist.

He gasps for air. Two more seconds—

"You're the traitor," he says.

"I'm a patriot," I say, and I watch him die.

Twenty seconds have gone by, long enough for Moore to pass beyond hope of resuscitation. I hear footsteps in the hall outside, coming toward the room.

I'm out of time.

"Help!" I shout.

The footsteps speed up. Aaron rushes into the room.

"We were talking and he collapsed," I say, making my voice shake.

Aaron scans the room, checking for a weapon, checking for any sign of foul play. I can see him looking and finding nothing. His attention quickly returns to Moore.

"I think he's having a heart attack," I say.

"Where is Francisco?" Aaron says.

"I don't know," I say.

Aaron leaps onto the floor next to Moore, checks his vital signs, then begins CPR. He's not skilled enough to know that it's too late.

"There's a walkie on my belt," he says. "Tell them we have an emergency. We need medical up here immediately."

I USE THE CONFUSION OF RUSHING BODIES TO GET OUT OF THE HOUSE.

A light rain is falling outside. The news spreads quickly. By the time I make it across the camp, teens are already rushing out of their houses, their faces panicked as they run toward the main house with umbrellas or plastic bags over their heads.

A few people look in my direction as they notice me moving away from the main house rather than toward it, but no one challenges me. I keep my head down, not allowing anyone to engage with me.

I sense the fear and confusion coursing through the crowd, along with a growing panic. Moore is the glue that binds this group together. Without him, that glue will begin to dissolve. The kids will wander away, returning to their homes and families on the outside, looking for some semblance of the life they once knew.

I will be the first to leave, but I won't be the last.

I move toward the parking area. I turn the corner, and I see Francisco's black truck is there. The keys will be in the ignition, as they are with all the vehicles here.

Suddenly Sergeant Burch steps out of the woods behind the

parking area. I notice something in his hands that he quickly slips into a pocket when he sees me.

It's an iPhone.

What was he doing with a phone in the forest?

He walks slowly across the lot, his eyes weary.

Choices:

I can engage him, try to talk my way out of the situation.

Or I can neutralize him. I'm younger and stronger than him, but there's no doubt he knows how to fight, and he will not give up willingly. I'll have to kill him.

Another soldier, another death. Burch is a good man. I'd like to avoid this if I can.

He comes closer. We stare at each other.

He nods to me, just the slightest shift of his head. Some glimmer of understanding passes between us, and I know not to stop or ask questions.

Whatever he was doing with the phone is none of my business.

I keep moving and so does he.

Neither of us says a word.

I DRIVE THROUGH THE RAIN.

The truck's tires fight for grip on the steep mountain road that leads up and out of Camp Liberty.

I made it out of camp, but I'm not free. Not yet.

The roadblock is up ahead.

I speed up to it, hoping they will open the gate without question, but that's not how it goes. I have to skid to a stop at the last moment. I roll my window down as one of the guards runs toward me with his gun drawn.

"Jesus, you scared me," he says when he recognizes my face.

"You heard?" I say.

"How is he?" the boy says.

"Bad," I say. "I'm going for meds."

"I can't open the roadblock until I call it in," he says.

"Do whatever the hell you want," I say, "but hurry. If he dies, it's on you."

His eyes roll back into his head for a second as he takes that in.

"Open!" he shouts to his partner. They yank the tire strip out of the road, and I race away.

The second I know my brake lights are beyond the view of the compound below, I pull to the side and snatch my iPhone from my pocket.

I put it in secure mode and dial Father's number.

This is standard procedure after a mission: Call Father, report the successful conclusion of the mission, and receive follow-up instructions.

The Program has been offline since the night at the community center, but maybe that was a test, some kind of challenge designed to measure my ability to act independently. If so, Moore's death will be the test's logical conclusion. Father will answer now, The Program will be back online, and everything will return to normal.

The line rings on the phone, but nobody picks up.

Father is not there.

My hope fades.

I feel foolish now, but I dial Mother's number.

The line does not connect.

It was stupid of me to use this phone again, even dangerous. If The Program has suffered a security breach, then I may have just telegraphed my location to whoever is responsible for the breach.

I slam the phone down sharply, the front right corner impacting with the dashboard of the truck. This is a fail-safe action built into the software of my phone. The accelerometer measures the angle and force of the blow and sends a signal to the battery that causes it to overheat. The battery burns through the interior of the phone, destroying it.

I roll down the window and fling the neutralized phone into the woods. It will never be used again.

I have completed the mission, but what now?

That's when I think of Howard and the multiple text messages he sent me.

I'M EXPECTING SILENCE.

That's what I realize as I knock on the hotel room door in Manchester. I'm expecting silence or worse, a strange face appearing in the door, asking me what I want.

Nothing has been right this mission. Nobody I can trust.

I knock and move away from the door, bracing myself for whatever may come. I move into a strategic position from which I can strike most effectively.

Mother has taught me to react to situations as they arise, preparing ahead of time, then improvising based on the facts on the ground.

So when the door opens, I am ready for anything.

Anything except what I find.

Howard, blinking as if I've awoken him from a nap.

"Thank god," he says when he sees me. "Did you get my texts?"

"Things got complicated. I couldn't respond."

"I thought something bad had happened to you."

I shake my head, but then the memory of Francisco pops into my mind.

Howard is looking at me strangely.

I don't know what he sees exactly, but his smile fades.

"You'd better come in," he says, and he steps back from the door, giving me a lot of space.

I walk past him into the hotel room. As I do, I scan him for weapons. I do it automatically, my mind registering the fabric of his shirt under the arms and around the waist, the flow of material around his ankles, the weight of objects in his pockets.

I treat him like he is a potential danger to me. And then I do the same with the room, bracing before turning corners, checking both hotel suites and their bathrooms, then inspecting window and door locks.

Howard stands back and lets me do it, watching me the whole time.

In fact I do it twice, two full passes through the space, double-checking everything.

When I'm done, I stand in the middle of the room, not knowing what to do next.

"Maybe you should sit down," Howard says.

I realize I'm rocking on my feet, unsteady.

I look at the chair. It doesn't look right to me. There's something about chairs that I do not like, something dangerous flagged in my memory.

I sit on the edge of the bed instead.

"I'll get you some water," Howard says.

"I'm okay," I say, but he goes anyway, rushing to the bathroom and coming back with a glass of water. I drink it down in one long swallow, and he gets me another. I drink that, too. I hand him back the glass.

"It's done," I say.

"Done?"

"My mission. I finished."

"Moore?"

"He's dead. That means you can go home, Howard, and I can go…"

I try to think of where I will go next, but I have no place to go. Without The Program giving me instructions, I have no direction.

"I have to tell you something," Howard says, his face growing troubled. "The reason I was texting you."

"I'm sorry I couldn't respond to you."

"Listen to me," he says. "I decoded the micro SDHC card."

I forgot about the card, the one I took off the leader of the freelance team.

"What did you find?"

"The card contains a file with information about the location of your safe house."

"Who would have access to that information?" I ask.

Howard doesn't say anything.

I think about the chip, the sophistication of the design that Howard described to me. The idea of hiding a device inside another device. It's The Program's MO.

"Of course, The Program had the information," I say without Howard asking, "but they would never share it with anyone outside our circle."

He opens his laptop and turns it toward me. "The data on the card was encoded with a digital watermark. I tracked it back to an anonymous communications control hub."

"What does that mean?" I say.

"It's the same hub that is the source of the secure numbers I got from your iPhone."

My mind is racing, trying to find a flaw in Howard's logic.

"The Program," Howard says. "It hired those men to go to the safe house."

"That's impossible," I say.

The Program is my employer, my commander, my life.

They're not good people, Francisco said.

He tried to warn me. He tried to give me an option.

"You're sure?" I ask Howard.

"I triple-checked," he says. "The Program transferred all the information to the SDHC card."

I sit there trying to think of a reason why.

"What do we do now?" Howard says.

"I don't know," I say.

Howard's face goes pale.

"But you always know," he says.

I lean back on the bed. My body feels heavy.

"Are you all right?" Howard says.

"I haven't slept," I say. "I can't think straight."

I lie down on the bed. I try to keep my eyes open, but it's a struggle.

I suddenly see my father's face in front of me. He's leaning over me, tucking in the covers around me.

I open my eyes to find Howard pulling a blanket over me.

"My father," I say. "You have to help me find him."

"You mean your commander from The Program?"

"No. My real father," I say. "Mike told me he was alive at the end of my last mission."

"Who?"

I try to make Howard understand me, but for some reason I can't communicate properly through the fog.

"Help me." That's all I can say.

"I'll help you," Howard says. "Whatever you need."

Exhaustion overtakes me, and I fall into a deep sleep.

I OPEN MY EYES NOT KNOWING WHERE I AM.

A strange room, a strange city, a mission I can't remember.

The room is lit by the laptop screens that line the desk. I hear snoring across from me.

I sit up in the bed, and I remember.

I am in a hotel room in Manchester. Howard is sleeping in a chair across the room from me, his face glowing blue from the computer open on his lap.

Then I remember other things. Things that I have done in the last day. Things that have been done to me.

I slip out of bed, looking for some way to judge the time. I peek out between the blinds and see it's nighttime. The position of the moon tells me there are a few hours left until dawn.

I walk quietly to the bathroom in the adjoining room. I close the door and flip on the light.

I'm still wearing my clothes from Liberty: a T-shirt and camo pants.

I lean over to turn on the water, and I wince in pain. I take off my T-shirt. There are black-and-blue marks forming along my ribs from the fight with Francisco. Damage under the skin that is only now showing.

I feel along the length of my ribs until I find the source of greatest pain. I wince as I probe there, but I determine that nothing is broken. I reverse the process, feeling along the other side. Then I run my hands up my chest, across my shoulders, performing an impromptu battlefield wound assessment on myself.

I finish without finding any serious injuries, but I keep going, probing where there is no pain, in the flesh between my elbow and humerus.

Francisco said I would search there for the chip, and he was right. I need to know.

I examine the area, but I do not find anything.

If something was implanted in me, there will likely be a scar, even a tiny one. Yet there are a thousand places to hide a chip on the human body. I see an illustration of the body in my mind, and I chart the places where the chip might be, assigning each one a percentage of likelihood. I focus first on areas of soft flesh bordered by hard structure that could keep a device anchored in place.

Next I use the schematic to search my body, feeling for gaps, probing as deeply as I am able with my fingers.

I don't find anything.

I lean across the sink to get closer to the mirror, and something hard knocks against the porcelain. Something inside the pocket of my camos.

The knife from the freelance team's truck.

I flick the button and a silver blade slides out.

I press the blade in the joint between the humerus and elbow. A half inch deep, then slightly farther. I detach myself from the pain, placing it far away from my consciousness, as I've been trained to do.

I feel flesh and skin, but no foreign bodies. I slit down, opening the wound farther toward my wrist, making sure not to nick the radial artery. I probe for a minute with the tip of the knife, but I can't find anything.

Next I check the inside of my elbow, the bony growth with an indentation in it. I push the blade in there, more gently this time. I don't cut deeply, just enough to pop through skin and the thin layer of fat beneath. Again I probe with the blade.

I find nothing.

I strip off the rest of my clothes, stand naked with the blade ready in my hand.

I glance up and catch sight of myself in the mirror—a boy with crazed eyes, blood flowing down both arms, holding a knife.

I am insane, I think. Just like Francisco.

But I can't stop thinking about the chip, where it could be, how such a device might have been implanted.

Suddenly I think of Dr. Acosta at the hospital the other day. The strange MRI scanner. The pain and heat I felt—not everywhere, just one specific location.

Under my scar.

If The Program implanted me with something in the past and wanted to cover up the scar, what would be the best way to do it?

Camouflage a scar inside a scar.

I think back to the fight years ago that ended with a knife blade inside me. I remember the way The Program brought me to a clinic afterward, how I was cleaned up, the shots I was given. The minor operation to close the wound.

How I was sutured afterward.

A scar inside a scar.

Dr. Acosta said it was an MRI that had been adapted for special use. Could it be used to adjust a chip that was already inside me?

I press my thumb against the scar, remembering the sensations I felt there, deep inside my chest.

I rinse the knife with water, and I use it to slice open the scar tissue on my chest.

Blood pools in the wound and drips down into the sink. I probe first with the knife, then I use my fingers to separate the skin, watch a pink slit open in my flesh. The pain is intense now, but I am trained to deal with pain.

I feel it, but it does not stop me. I do what I have to do.

I lean in close to the mirror and peer into the wound.

There, on the muscle of my pec, is a fistula of flesh growing out from the muscle. I prod it gently with the knife tip. It is hard inside.

Flesh grows around a foreign object in the body, forming a protective shell. I know this from my biology studies. I cut through the flesh, a nick that opens the internal scar tissue.

I see something shiny there, a faint blue glow inside it.

It's a sterile Gorilla Glass tubule, the size of a fat grain of rice.

I look again, making sure I'm not imagining it. I tap it with the edge of the knife, feel hard glass.

It's real.

I take a deep breath. Then I reach inside myself, and I pull it out.

I wash the tube in the sink, drain the blood from around it. I hold it up to the light. I see something that resembles a miniature chip with a tiny antenna coil wrapped around it. The entire device is sealed into a neat and nearly undetectable package inside the tubule.

It was glowing when it was inside me, but not anymore.

A short double wire extends from the bottom of the tube. That's the part that was inside my muscle when I pulled it out.

Francisco was telling the truth.

The Program was inside of me, hidden in the last place I would look: the scar above my heart.

I step back from the mirror. The blood runs down my body and drips onto the floor at my feet.

I don't feel any different. Maybe Francisco was wrong about the purpose of the chip.

Suddenly I hear a noise behind me, and I spin around.

Howard is standing in the doorway, watching me. His face is pale, and he's shaking.

"What are you doing to yourself?" he says, his voice quaking.

"Francisco was telling the truth," I say.

"Who is Francisco?"

I hold out a bloody palm with the tubule in it.

"He was a soldier," I say. "Like me."

HOWARD USES VODKA FROM THE MINIBAR TO STERILIZE THE CUTS.

Then he takes a roll of duct tape from his bag, and I use it as a battlefield dressing to close the wounds. It's a temporary measure, but it will stem the flow of blood and allow the body to begin to heal until I can get to a drugstore and find more appropriate dressings.

When we're done cleaning me up, we sit down in the room, and I tell Howard what I know about the chip. I tell him what Francisco said about its neurosuppressive quality, the effect it has on throttling fear.

"I've never heard of anything like that," Howard says.

"But it's possible?" I say.

"There have been a lot of experiments studying the effect of magnetic fields on the brain. But there's nothing functional at this scale. This would be a level of sophistication years beyond anything available now."

"It makes sense," I say. "If you want to create the perfect soldier, start by taking away his fear."

"How do you feel with it outside of you?"

"The same as I did before."

"So maybe it was bullshit. Or maybe he was wrong about what it does."

"Maybe so. But he wasn't wrong about the chip being there. So what else could it be?"

"Let's take a look," Howard says. He powers on his computer, then places the tubule on the lighted Plexiglas device he used to scan the SDHC card earlier.

A moment later, a magnified picture of the tubule appears on the computer screen. Howard points to it. "There's a computer chip located here. And do you see the little wire coil that surrounds half of the chip?"

"What is it?"

"It could be a power source. Or an antenna."

That's when the hotel phone rings, the noise echoing in the quiet of the room.

Howard looks at me.

"Don't touch it," I say.

The phone continues to ring.

"You have to get out of here," I tell Howard. "They're coming."

"Who's coming?"

The Program. A freelance team. Moore's people.

Whoever it is, it will be trouble.

I don't have time to explain it to him.

"Grab everything and get it into the other room," I say.

I imagine them downstairs, whoever they are, inquiring at the front desk about which room we're in. If the desk is good, they won't give out that information. But in Manchester, in the middle of the night, it's probably a young guy who wishes he weren't here. A young guy who doesn't want a hassle, who isn't above providing a little information when forty dollars is slipped across the counter.

Maybe they asked him to call to make sure I was in, or maybe he knew something was up and called after they left. Either way, it's not a coincidence. Not at five AM.

Howard starts pulling plugs from outlets, slapping his laptops closed and stacking them to carry to the other room.

"Wait until you hear the door to this room open," I tell him, "then get out as quickly and quietly as you can. Hide somewhere in the hotel, and don't come back here no matter what. Wait until there's no movement from upstairs or in the parking lot, then get yourself back home to New York. Take the train if you can, but if you need it, there's a black truck in the back of the parking lot. Keys in the front wheel well."

"What will you do?"

I shake my head, unwilling to answer.

"If something happens to me—"

"You're scaring me."

"Listen," I say calmly. "If something happens and for some reason you don't hear from me, I don't want you searching for me. Destroy any evidence of our communication. It's the only way to keep yourself safe."

"Holy shit holy shit holy shit," he says, starting to panic.

I grab him by the arms.

"You're going to be okay, Howard. I promise you."

He takes a deep breath, looks me in the eye. I see his body relax slightly.

"Be careful, Daniel."

"I will."

He rushes into the other suite, and I close the door behind him.

I spend sixty seconds fixing the room, straightening cushions, checking for anything that might give away Howard's presence.

I catch a glimpse of myself in the mirror, bare-chested with my wounds taped up.

I reach up to my chest and carefully peel back the tape there.

I press the tubule into the adhesive, then I put the tape back over the wound.

The chip is no longer inside me, but it's hidden against me, safe, until I can examine it further.

I throw on a T-shirt, realize it will not cover the cuts on my arms, and grab a hoodie from the closet and zip it to my neck, hiding the wounds.

I hear a door open and close down the hall.

Whoever they are, they came by stairs, not risking the elevator.

I turn out the lights, and I sit in a chair at a diagonal from the door.

My breathing is fast, much faster than normal. I take a moment to center myself, relaxing my shoulders and willing my breath to slow as I've done a thousand times before.

It doesn't work.

My breathing turns rapid and shallow, my chest moving in a strange way. Something is wrong with my body. It seems to be reacting without my being able to control it.

It takes enormous concentration to get calm and centered. I only have time for three deep breaths before I hear it.

IT'S NO LOUDER THAN A WHISPER.

The sound of a lubricating spray being squirted into the door lock followed by a tool being eased into the mechanism. The knob is jiggled briefly, and the door opens.

A figure enters the room, moving with the ease of a shadow.

I know the posture, the powerful way he propels himself through the world.

It's Mike.

He stares at me, and I stare back, unblinking.

He steps deeper into the room and closes the door behind him. My breath catches in my chest.

"You don't look good," he says.

I wipe sweat from my forehead.

The glow of the hotel sign comes through the blinds, illuminating Mike's profile in front of the doorway. He looks huge inside the room.

"I haven't been sleeping well," I say.

"No, it's something else," he says. He studies me curiously. "You look afraid. You're not afraid of me, are you?"

I will myself not to react to his comment. I make my face calm, breathe slowly and evenly. I touch my forehead again, and my hand comes away wet.

"Why are you here, Mike?"

"It's not a social call, if that's what you were wondering."

"That's good, because I didn't have time to buy party favors."

"You're still funny," he says. "Even under duress."

"I'm not under duress. But you obviously are. You're sneaking into a hotel room in the middle of the night."

"I didn't know what I'd find in here."

"You found me. Now why don't you tell me what you're doing here?"

Somehow he has moved closer to me without my realizing it, every step a chess move.

Francisco was right. You can know Mike yet not see him coming.

"The Program sent me," Mike says simply.

I stand up, bringing my body to a state of readiness. I want Mike to view me as an operative like him. Dangerous like him.

"The Program...has...disappeared," I say.

He looks at me strangely.

"I received my mission brief just like always. Actually, this particular brief had an 'urgent' code attached to it."

"What's urgent?"

"You. Your status here."

He glances around the room. I know he's scanning for threats, evidence of other people in the space, hidden dangers, potential weapons.

I say, "I lost communication with The Program four days ago. Even the safe house was sanitized when I got there."

I don't tell him about the freelance team. I decide to hold back that information, at least for now.

"What do you think happened?" Mike says.

"I thought The Program had been breached."

"And now?"

"Now I don't know."

He shakes his head.

"They cut you off," he says.

"What the hell—?"

I've been worried about The Program for days, confused and upset as I've tried to figure out how to move forward without their support and direction.

"Why would they cut me off?" I say. "I was on a mission."

"You already know the answer," Mike says.

"I don't."

He sighs. "They cut you off because you went into the camp."

"I had no other choice."

"That's not what it looked like. Not from their standpoint."

"What did it look like?"

"I don't know all the details," Mike says. "But I'm guessing it looked a lot like what happened before."

"You mean with the dead soldier?"

I see a flicker of tension at Mike's forehead. If what Francisco said is true, it was Mike who recruited him into The Program, and Mike who bears some responsibility for him.

Mike says, "The soldier before you was sent in and disappeared. That's why you were told not to go in, but you ignored orders."

"I didn't ignore them. It was a calculation on my part. A matter of mission dynamics."

"Calculated or not, when you went in there, you tied their hands. They had no choice but to distance themselves from you."

"It's not like I disappeared," I said. "I've been trying to contact them all along."

"How could they know it was you?"

"I was using security protocols!"

Mike squats, his hands resting on his thighs. His voice gets quiet.

"I'm not supposed to talk to you about this at any level of detail."

I don't say anything, waiting him out. There's no way to trick Mike. He'll tell me or he won't, but it will be his own decision.

"Moore is the Pied Piper," he says. "They're scared of him, scared of what he can do. One operative goes in and disappears. The next goes in against orders. They weren't taking any chances. It became a burn operation."

"Is that why you're here?" I say. "To complete the burn?"

He stands, chewing his bottom lip as he considers the question.

I make no outward change in my posture. But I am ready for him, ready for imminent attack.

I evaluate the odds. I am coming off a mission, and Mike looks fresh and well rested. That's a factor in his favor. On the other hand, we are in a small interior space, and his physical advantage is diminished by lack of maneuvering room. Besides, I'm more familiar with the space than he is. That's a factor in my favor.

But I can feel my heart beating faster than it should be before a fight. Without the chip, I have less control of my reactions.

I calculate Mike's advantage to be 60 percent to my 40.

"Let's calm down here," Mike says. "I can sense you getting overheated, and there's no need for it. It's not a burn operation. I'm here to get a status report. And deliver a message."

"What message?"

"Status first," he says.

I clear my throat. I'm not used to reporting to Mike, and I'm not comfortable with the idea. But at this point, I don't have a lot of options.

"Moore is dead," I say. "I completed the mission."

"Is that right?" Mike says, his face relaxing into a grin.

"You knew already," I say, not believing his reaction for a second.

"I knew," he says, by way of admission. "Incidentally I had no doubt that you would do it. This despite what some—uh—others may have thought."

The subtext is clear. Mother and Father doubted.

"You said you had a message for me?"

"That's where it gets interesting," Mike says. "The fact is you started the mission. You haven't finished. Not yet."

"What are you talking about?"

"You cut off the head of the serpent, but you were dealing with a Hydra."

Hydra, the multiheaded serpent of Greek mythology.

"Even as we sit here," Mike says, "things are progressing at the camp."

"Liberty is falling apart. I saw it happening before I left."

"You're wrong. You assumed it would disassemble. In fact the opposite is occurring."

I think about Lee, his anger at his father, his desperation to prove himself worthy.

"It's Lee," I say. "He's taken over."

"That's right. Along with his sister," Mike says.

I think about Miranda the first night I was at the camp. Would she be helping Lee after her father's death? Or would she use the opportunity to get free?

"I thought the camp was blacked out. How does The Program know what's happening there?"

"Someone is feeding information to the FBI. We got it on intercept," Mike says.

"An agent?" I say.

"Not likely. It's someone at the camp. He got cold feet and he's been e-mailing from the forest."

I think of Sergeant Burch slipping out of the woods after I killed Moore, the way we passed each other without a word. Burch, who served loyally by Moore's side for so long. I imagine him seeing Moore radicalize, watching the camp change into something it was never intended to be. I imagine what he went through before deciding to take action against his friend, the torture he must have put himself through.

Mike says, "We got the news, and we saw the truck leaving the encampment earlier. I was sent here to see if it was you who left—"

"And?"

"I was told to send you back in to neutralize the situation. Do you remember the first thing the U.S. government did during the Iraq War way back in 2003? It wasn't Saddam Hussein they killed."

I think back to my military history lessons when I was in training.

"It was his sons," I say.

"That's right. Because if Saddam died and his sons lived, nothing would have changed. You know where this is going, don't you?"

"Moore's children."

"You have to take care of them," Mike says. "Quickly and efficiently."

"Why don't we send the FBI in now?" I say.

"The FBI is well meaning, but it moves at the speed of bureaucracy. This has become an imminent-threat situation. By the time the FBI realizes the true nature of the threat, it will be too late."

"You're not my handler. You can't send me on assignment."

"I'm not sending you," Mike says. "The Program is sending you."

"If they're so unsure about me, why would they send me back in now?"

"I can't be certain," Mike says, "but from where I'm standing, it looks like a test."

"A test of what?"

"Your loyalty."

Sweat breaks out under my arms.

"My loyalty is intact," I say, my voice rising.

"Is that so?" he says.

I think of Francisco in the woods, his body crisscrossed in cut marks.

I killed him to protect The Program, and now I've found the same chip in me that caused him to go crazy.

I don't say any of this to Mike, but I'm unable to control the anger in my face.

Mike watches me and remains silent.

It's a classic interrogation technique. Don't incriminate the suspect. Let guilt and silence work on him until he incriminates himself.

It's not going to work on me.

I match Mike's silence with my own.

I use the time to think through the various scenarios. Is Mike simply carrying out instructions from Mother and Father?

Or does he have his own doubts about me, doubts not shared by Mother and Father?

At the end of my last mission, Mike knew I had balked when it came to killing the mayor's daughter, Samara. He treated me like a friend, saying he would withhold the information from The Program.

But maybe he lied. Maybe he told them everything, thereby creating a jigsaw puzzle of doubt with me as the center piece.

Mike sighs. Then he stands and starts to pace in the room. He moves in an unconscious pattern when he's thinking. I've seen this before from him. The only sign of weakness I can detect in him.

"Loyalty," he says, picking up the thread of the conversation. "We're taught that it's a fixed thing, a point in space that never changes. But that's not my experience. To me it's like a river. It ebbs and flows. If you're lucky, it continues to flow powerfully from the source. If you're not, the source gets choked off and the river dries up."

Mike licks his lips. He watches me.

"What's it like for you now?" he says. "The river, I mean."

"It's not a river for me," I say.

"I see," he says, like he doesn't believe me. "So what is it?"

"Why are you here, Mike?" I say.

"I told you, I'm the messenger."

"And the message is coming from the top?" I say.

"Where else would it be coming from?"

I look at Mike, trying to determine if he's telling the truth.

Truth and lies. Loyalty and deception. It's not easy to determine now. Not after doing what I did to Francisco. Not after the last three days.

"The measure of a soldier is not what you do when you're being watched," Mike says. "It's what you do when no one is looking. When you don't know where you are and your mission gets cloudy."

"The mission is everything," I say.

"The new mission," he says. "What story do you want to tell when it's all over? Is this the story of the time you had doubt and proved yourself, or is it a different story—the story of you betraying your country?"

"I know what the story will be," I say.

"That's what I like to hear," Mike says.

MIKE WALKS ME DOWNSTAIRS, THEN FOLLOWS ME AS I DRIVE AWAY IN THE TRUCK.

He tails me for miles, following several car lengths back as we head east out of Manchester. I take a left at the Nottingham Road turnoff, and I see Mike wave in my rearview mirror as he continues on in a different direction.

I think about Howard in the adjoining suite while I was talking to Mike. More than fifteen minutes passed while I was with Mike, long enough for Howard to get away.

I imagine him at the train station in Manchester, waiting to get on a train to New York.

Suddenly a voice in the truck whispers, "Is it safe?"

I jam the brakes, the truck skidding to a stop.

Howard pops up in the backseat.

"What are you doing here? You scared the crap out of me," I say. I'm breathing hard, surprised to see him.

"You don't get scared—" Howard starts to say, and then he stops in midsentence, his mouth dropping open. "The chip," he says. "It works."

I put my hand on my chest, feel my heart beating too strongly.

I take a breath, attempting to slow my heart rate, but it doesn't work.

This is why I was sweating with Mike in the room, why I had the strange feelings I was having around him.

"You're right," I say.

"I'm sorry I scared you," Howard says. "I had to find someplace to hide."

"In my truck?"

"If they thought you were inside, why would they search an empty truck? There was a blanket in the back, so I lay down and covered myself. I didn't think you'd jump in and drive away with me."

There's a certain logic to Howard's approach. I have to give him credit.

I put the truck in gear and get it back on the road.

"Are we going home?" Howard says.

"I'm not. Not yet. I have an assignment."

"From that guy?"

"You saw the guy?"

Howard nods.

"Did he see you?"

"No," Howard says. "I saw him out the window as he passed by. I'm sure he didn't see me."

I breathe out, relieved.

I'm trying to think of what I can do with Howard, how I can get him to safety. I can't leave him by the side of the road. We're out in the middle of nowhere, and Mike could be watching us remotely.

"For now, stay out of sight back there," I say.

He lies down across the backseat.

The road only narrows from this point on. I have to make a

decision about Howard. Leave him hidden in the back of the truck while I drive into Camp Liberty and hope he's not discovered, or leave him on the side of the road where I can pick him up later.

"I'm going into Camp Liberty on a mission, and I can't bring you, Howard. It's too dangerous."

"Can I pretend I'm your assistant?"

I smile. "It's not that kind of mission."

We're half a mile from the encampment now. One more bend in the road, and it will be in sight.

"I'm going to pull to the side of the road," I say. "I want you to hop out and hide in the woods until I come for you."

"How long will that be?"

"I'm not sure."

"I'm not really a woods kind of guy," he says. "I've lived in Manhattan my whole life. I don't even like Central Park."

"Do you have a phone with you?"

"I've got the iPhone," he says.

"If you don't see me by nightfall, walk back down the road until you get a signal. Call the police and tell them you were hiking and you got lost. There's only one road in and out, so they should be able to find you without a problem."

"I can do that," he says, obviously nervous about it.

I pull to the side of the road. I shut off the truck, and I sit there for a moment breathing in the fresh air and pine scent of the woods.

"I'm sorry I got you into this," I say.

"I volunteered, remember? I wanted to work with you."

"Still, it was selfish of me, and I regret it."

Howard reaches over the seat and pats me on the shoulder.

He says, "You said something before you fell asleep last night. I wanted to ask you about it."

"What did I say?"

"About your father. You said he was alive and you wanted me to help you find him."

"I said that? I don't remember."

"You said someone named Mike told you."

I exhale slowly. I've given Howard a lot of information, more even than I realized.

"The guy you saw walk by the truck earlier. That was Mike. He told me my father might be alive when I saw him in New York last month. But he could be lying."

"We should find out," Howard says.

"It will be dangerous," I say.

"I can take care of myself," Howard says. "Especially online."

"What about Goji?" I say. That's Howard's girlfriend, the Japanese girl in Osaka with whom he's been carrying on a long-distance romance.

"She doesn't know anything about what I do for you," he says.

"That's not what I'm worried about," I say. "I want you two to meet someday. I don't want you to do anything else for me that might risk your life."

"But we're friends," Howard says. "If friends don't help each other, who will?"

Howard's code of friendship. It's so simple. Unlike The Program, with its games and tests.

"If Mike said your father was alive, that means you thought he was dead?" Howard says.

"I saw him die. Or I thought I did."

"How?"

"Mike killed him. On orders from The Program," I say.

"Those orders," Howard says. "That's how we can find your father."

"I'm not following you."

"The Program lives on the Web, right?"

The Program exists online—that's what Howard discovered on my last mission. He found a network of young hackers, some as young as twelve years old, gathering data, uncovering the bytes of information that lead to the targets to which I am assigned.

"Once something is online, it can be found," Howard says. "Even after it's erased. If they gave the order, we can find that order. Or some evidence of it."

"Ghosts in the machine," I say.

"And I am a ghost hunter," Howard says.

"What do you need to know?"

"We can start with his name."

My father's name is buried inside with the rest of my past, kept out of my consciousness, where it cannot harm me. If I tell Howard, I set him on a course of investigating The Program. That is tantamount to treason.

But what is a chip inserted into me against my will? What is sending me on a mission, then withdrawing support, protecting The Program's interests at the expense of its own soldier?

I take a breath, and I pull my father's name up from the depths of my memory.

"Dr. Joseph Abram," I say.

I haven't said his name aloud in a long time. It feels strange in my mouth, like a foreign language.

"A medical doctor?" Howard says.

"No. He was a professor of psychology at the University of Rochester five years ago."

"I'll find out everything I can," Howard says.

"Thank you."

"That's assuming I get out of these woods tonight without being eaten by something."

"You're too skinny to be eaten," I say. "That's a lot of chewing with very little reward."

"You're not making me feel better."

"Be careful, buddy."

"You, too," he says. "See you soon."

He gets out of the truck and scurries into the woods clutching his blanket. I hate to leave him alone out here, but I have no choice.

A DOWNED TREE BLOCKS THE ROAD, HALF A DOZEN ARMED BOYS ON GUARD BEHIND IT.

This is not the roadblock from the other day. This is a hastily erected barricade, more substantial, more dangerous. What's worse, I don't recognize any of the boys guarding it.

There's no way to drive around the roadblock. There is a cliff on one side, dense forest on the other.

I sort through options:

I could back up, leave the truck, and set out on foot.
I could try to talk my way through.
I could abandon the mission.

Three options. Two are bad; the third is unthinkable.

I make my choice.

I slip the knife from my pocket and push it up the sleeve of my right arm, using the elastic at the hoodie's wrist to hold it in place.

Then I pull slowly forward. I'll start by talking, and I'll do what I have to do after.

Guns rise as the truck comes near. The faces behind them are grave. A taller boy steps forward, looking through the windshield. I keep both hands on the steering wheel where he can see them.

Something changes in the tall boy's expression, and he calls out to one of the boys behind him. I see a walkie-talkie pop up. A message sent, a message received.

"Turn off the truck," the tall boy says. He has a tactical-model pump-action shotgun, modified with a stock and pistol grip. He points it at me.

I look down the black shotgun barrel. Then I look at the boy behind it, staring at me, searching for a reason to pull the trigger.

I turn off the truck.

I feel the weight of the knife inside my right wrist. I can turn and snap my arm, and the motion will drop the knife into my hand. One and a half seconds to turn, a second for the knife to drop and settle, another half second for me to depress the switch that releases the blade, and two seconds to travel the distance from the window to the boy's throat.

Five seconds.

But it only takes two seconds for his mind to register the threat and depress the trigger of the shotgun.

I don't move.

I sense tightness in my chest.

This feeling. I remember it from a long time ago, a distant echo of my childhood.

It is fear.

Howard is right. The chip works.

Or rather, it doesn't work, because it's taped to the outside of my chest right now, where it can't affect me.

I will myself to look only at the steering wheel in front of me, but

I've lost impulse control. My eyes shift left to once again look down the shotgun barrel. I imagine the round chambered down below, and my mouth goes dry.

A moment later the boy with the walkie signals.

The shotgun is lowered.

"Move over," the tall boy says. "I'm driving us in."

WE DRIVE INTO LIBERTY.

I see the panel vans from the night of The Hunt, their sides modified with NORTHEAST ELECTRIC stencils.

Why have they been made to look like power company trucks?

A boy and a girl with guns stand guard by the vans. They nod to my driver as he passes.

As we come closer to the encampment, I see more teens with guns. Heads snap around when they hear the truck coming.

Everyone is armed, everyone tense.

We pass the first set of buildings, and then the main square comes into view.

I see a backhoe parked in the center of the square, its shovel raised to maximum height as if it's in the process of digging something.

There is no operator in it. The backhoe is still, parked in the upright position. As we drive closer, I see something else. A rope tied haphazardly around the shovel with a life-size doll hanging from it like a party favor.

It takes a second for my mind to register what I'm really seeing.

It's not a doll. It's a body.

Sergeant Burch's body.

His head is canted at an unnatural angle, the rope tight around his neck.

He's been hanged.

Teens walk under the body, their pace quickening slightly, eyes cast toward the ground.

I last saw Sergeant Burch sneaking out of the woods before I left the parking lot. Now I'm sure he's the one who was passing messages to the FBI. Someone found out and ordered him to be executed.

Miranda steps out of a building. She is wearing jeans and a loosely buttoned blouse, her red hair flowing free down her shoulders. Only her face betrays the seriousness of the situation.

The driver stops the truck and motions for me to get out. Miranda approaches. I note that she doesn't have a gun.

"We thought we lost you," she says.

"Lost and found," I say.

"Why did you run away?"

"I got scared after your father—"

I look at the ground, wanting her to think I'm experiencing a painful memory.

I've done this a thousand times, emulating emotions I've seen in others, feigning emotional states to make people believe what I want them to believe.

I've done this a thousand times, but now is different.

Because now I feel real pain, not for Moore or what he was trying to do before he lost his way, but for Francisco, my brother in The Program.

The brother who I killed.

Suddenly my breath is gone. My mouth opens, gasping for air, but I can't find any.

"We all got scared," she says, her voice gentle. "I'm *still* scared."

She gestures toward the backhoe in the main square.

"I saw it when we drove in," I say. "Sergeant Burch. What happened to him?"

"Lee accused him of something, and people went crazy."

The area has emptied around us. We stand alone, an arm's reach from each other.

"There are things going on that you don't know," she says.

"Can you tell me?"

"First I have to ask you something. Why did you really come back?"

"I had a feeling," I say.

She searches my face for more. "What kind of a feeling?"

"A feeling that I might be needed."

She reaches out and touches my shoulder.

"Come inside," she says. "We have to talk about some things."

I follow her through the door of a building I've never been in before. She leads the way down a long, dark hallway.

"Where are we going?" I say.

Suddenly I hear a whooshing noise behind me, followed by a propulsive bang as the twin prongs of a Taser-like device hit me from behind. My brain registers it in a second, faster even than the electricity passes down the wire into my body. I relax before it hits, knowing that fighting will only make it worse.

I've been Tased as part of my training, and I know it's possible to ride it out like a storm, coming out the other side weakened but not incapacitated. But as the electricity surges through me, I can feel that this is not a standard Taser. It's some kind of adapted, hypercharged device that takes over my body and shatters my consciousness.

I feel a stinging sensation in my neck: the sharp prick of a needle and the poisonous warmth of a chemical being injected into my carotid artery.

I try to hang on to the mission, the plan, the intent of my being here. I try to locate Miranda's face through the shadowy hallway in front of me.

But the combination of the electricity and the drug takes all of it away, spinning me down into a dark so pure it's almost peaceful.

I WAKE UP IN A CONCRETE ROOM LINED IN SHADOWS.

I try to move, but I cannot. My hands are tied behind me. I'm sitting in a chair, my body aching all over.

A stinging slap forces my head back.

It's Lee. He paces in front of me. I try to stand but find my legs are tied as well.

"Where am I?" I say.

"No matter," Lee says. "Nobody can get in, and you can't get out."

His voice has a hard edge to it. He paces back and forth, agitated.

"Where is Francisco?" Lee asks.

"How should I know?" I say.

Lee stands across from me now. His eyes have changed. There is something dark in them, an intensity and anger that is unsettling.

"You were the last one to see him," Lee says.

Lee knows I was with Francisco, but he doesn't know what happened or he wouldn't be asking the question.

And if he doesn't know what happened, he has no way of knowing the timeline. Maybe I can use this against him.

"So Francisco hasn't turned up?" I say as if I'm surprised.

"Obviously not," Lee says.

"Doesn't that make you wonder?" I say.

"Wonder what?"

"He disappeared right after your father died," I say.

"After?" Lee says, confused.

"Who cares about Francisco?" Miranda says to her brother. "Would you drop it already?"

Miranda is somewhere in the room outside my sight line. She brought me here, which means she knew this was going to happen. She set me up.

"We need Francisco!" Lee says to her. "We need his help."

"We're fine without him," she says.

"Listen," I say, trying to keep my voice steady. "I don't know what's going on exactly, but I know you're making a mistake."

"It's no mistake," Lee says. "You left the compound after my father died. Only someone guilty would do that."

"I'm not the only one who left," I say.

Lee slaps me hard across the face again.

"Lee," Miranda says, attempting to calm him.

"He's trying to confuse us," Lee says.

He whirls around and steps behind me, confronting Miranda.

"We have to kill this bastard now," he says.

"No, we don't," Miranda says.

"Dad said there could be an assassin sent into camp," Lee says.

"He's not the assassin," she says, which surprises me, because she found me in the woods making a call. She has more evidence than anyone that I might not be who I say I am. Why is she lying for me?

"We can't trust him," Lee says. "Not now, not when we have important work to do."

"Our father trusted him."

"And you saw what happened to him."

Moore said he'd warned Lee about me, but Lee was easily swayed. That means he liked me. I can play on that.

"I don't know what you're doing, but maybe I can help you," I say.

"Maybe he can," Miranda says. "You saw him during The Hunt. He did fine."

"Fine won't cut it," Lee says.

He comes around where he can see my face.

"Where did you go when you left camp?" he says.

"I panicked," I say. "I drove home to talk to my parents, but they were out. I didn't know what to do. I drove around in circles, then I went to the mall."

"He's right that he's not the only one who left camp," Miranda says.

"That's true," Lee says, thinking about it.

She walks over and joins her brother, puts an arm on his shoulder.

"Maybe we're asking the wrong question," Miranda says. "Instead of asking why he left, maybe we should be asking why he came back."

Lee looks at her. "You think he had a change of heart?"

"Maybe he's one of us," Miranda says.

Lee considers it for a moment, then shakes his head, determined.

"We can't take that risk," Lee says. "Not now. Not when we're so close."

So close to what? What is Lee planning?

Miranda lowers her head.

"We can't kill him."

"That's not your decision to make," Lee says.

He's holding the Taser-like device in his hands. When did he pick it up again?

"Your father invited me here," I say.

"I won't make the same mistake my father did," Lee says. "I don't know who you are for real, but I know I can't trust you anymore. You were kind to me and to my sister, so I'm going to spare your life."

Lee's presence is dominating now. He's changed quickly, taking on the demeanor of a military commander.

Lee says, "By the time you wake up, it will be over."

I search for Miranda, but I can't see her.

"They will find you here," Lee says. "You can be sure of that. And you will bear witness for us."

He comes toward me. I test the rope on my wrists, hoping to find a loose bond. If I can get a hand out—

Lee grabs me under my chin, pulling my face forward. His eyes are wild, his breath fetid.

"You will tell them that I was the one. Not my father. Not anyone else."

His nails dig into the flesh of my chin.

"Tell them I was the one," he says. "Do you hear me?"

"Yes," I say.

In killing Moore, I've given Lee the chance to step up and be the man his father wanted him to be. Unwittingly, I've set this all in motion.

Lee backs up quickly and aims the device at my chest.

"We all have our roles to play, Daniel. You will be the messenger. And I will be the message."

Before I can say anything, he depresses the trigger, and the surge hits me, arcing my body with wave after wave of electricity, so intense that I lose all control and the world goes black for the second time.

MY FATHER WAS IN A CHAIR IN OUR LIVING ROOM.

Mike brought me in to see him, one arm wrapped tightly around my back and under my armpit to hold me up. Mike had drugged me a moment before. By the time I got to the living room, I could barely walk.

I was twelve years old and Mike was my new best friend. Or so I thought.

Then Mike brought me into the living room so I could see what he had done to my father. And so my father could see what was going to happen to me.

This is the memory that recurs, the one that my brain clings to even when I will it to let go. It is the last time I saw my father alive five years ago.

Everything is forgotten sooner or later. Life moves on. Even terrible things grow old over time. The psychological term is *habituation*. People who live near airports no longer hear the jets. People with mansions stop feeling wealthy.

And people who lose someone eventually stop grieving.

Our minds are designed to habituate. The past is forgotten, put in its proper place. Intense stimuli become second nature. And terrible things become commonplace.

We can't hold on even if we want to.

And yet there are things that stick. Not things you choose, but things that choose you.

This memory, for example.

Mike at my side, holding me up. The feel of his arm around me. The sight of my father in front of me.

I've always thought this was a memory of Mike's betrayal, the great betrayal of a friend who is not a friend, a brother who is not a brother.

But in my unconscious state, I have a new perspective.

There are reasons I am sent on an assignment. So there must have been reasons Mike was sent on an assignment that brought him to me.

My father.

Something he did brought Mike into our lives.

This is the new understanding I have. My memory is not a memory of Mike's betrayal of my father.

It's a memory of my father's betrayal of me.

"DANIEL."

A voice calls through the haze. A hand shakes me.

"Daniel," the voice says.

Water on my forehead, pulling me up toward consciousness.

"Wake up, Daniel."

That is not my name, but it sounds familiar to me. As does the person who is saying it.

Howard.

"Wake up," he says.

I stir in my chair, moving my arms and legs. They're free. When did they get free?

Howard shakes me again.

"Easy," I say. "I'm awake."

I open my eyes. Howard stands over me, his face heavy with concern.

"Do you need mouth-to-mouth?" he says.

"Why would I need that?"

"You were passed out."

"Did I stop breathing?"

"No."

"Then keep your mouth away from my mouth. No offense."

"None taken."

I look around the room. Not a room. A bunker.

"How did you find me?" I say.

"You didn't come back by nightfall, so I hiked down into the camp."

"You got past the roadblock?"

"I went into the woods."

"You've got some skills," I say.

"Just because I'm a geek doesn't mean I can't throw down from time to time."

"Can you really throw down?"

"I don't even know what throwing down is. But it sounds cool when I say it."

I try to laugh, but it hurts too much.

"Can you help me up?" I say.

He puts an arm around me and supports me while I stand. The feeling of his arm across my back stirs up the memory of a moment ago.

My father. Something he did brought Mike into our lives for the first time.

My father betrayed me.

He was the first perhaps, but not the last.

Samara, the girl I loved, betrayed me.

Even The Program has betrayed me.

I look at Howard, suddenly unsure about him, about the faith I've placed in him.

"Can I trust you, Howard?"

He thinks about it for a moment.

"Let me put it this way: I should be at home in Manhattan relaxing, eating Cheetos, and doing AP Calculus homework. Instead I'm on a mountain in New Hampshire risking my life to save you from some kind of torture chair."

"That's a good point," I say.

"Do you still have doubts?"

"None. Let's go, buddy."

He walks me toward the door, letting me lean on him as my muscles slowly come back online.

"You really love those Cheetos, don't you?" I say.

"I like the spicy ones best," he says. "But the cheese messes up the keyboard, so I'm trying to quit."

ABOVEGROUND, LIBERTY IS A GHOST TOWN.

The entire population of the camp is gone. We walk past quiet buildings, windows half open, garbage bins waiting to be emptied.

The structures are here, but the people are gone. Wherever they went, they left in a hurry.

At first I'm careful, walking ahead of Howard while searching the ground for trip wires, laser triggers, anything that might indicate a booby trap.

But there are none.

By the time we get to the main square, my muscles have come back online and I can walk normally again. The backhoe is still in the middle of the square, but Burch's body is gone, moved to who knows where.

I lead Howard toward the main house. I open the door slowly, checking for trigger devices but finding the way clear.

I pause in the front alcove.

"Wait for me here for a couple minutes," I tell Howard.

"Where are you going?" he says, afraid.

"I have to find out where they went," I say. "I'll be right back."

I SLIP INTO FRANCISCO'S ROOM.

I'm looking for evidence of the plan that Lee was talking about.

The room is bare, hardly lived in. There's a single book facedown on the night table. A glass of water. A pillow with an indentation in it.

I look at the book. *Neuromancer* by William Gibson. I open it and flip through the pages. It's an old copy, and some of the pages are stuck together.

I search the room, the closet, the drawers.

I check every hiding place, looking for notebooks, drawings, any clues that might help, but I find only clothes and toiletries. A tool kit in a box by the door.

There's nothing here.

I take one last look around the room. Just before I go, something occurs to me.

The pages of the Gibson novel. Something didn't feel right when I flipped through it.

I reach into my pocket and remove the knife I've been carrying.

I open the book again, use the edge of the blade to separate the stuck pages. I don't find anything. But then I look inside the back cover.

It has been reglued, a bit of excess glue spilling onto the pages. I carefully slice it open.

Something flutters to the floor.

A photograph.

I pick it up.

A Hispanic man is sitting outside on a folded lawn chair. Next to him stands a pretty woman with her hand on his shoulder. On the man's knee is a young boy.

The man has his arm around the boy's stomach, holding him in place.

I recognize the boy's eyes.

It's Francisco, sitting with who I imagine are his real parents.

Francisco before he was recruited by The Program. Before he came here and betrayed everything he had been taught.

I turn and catch sight of myself in the mirror in Francisco's room. I look half crazed in my dirty hoodie.

I open Francisco's closet and find some long-sleeved flannel shirts.

I take off my shirt and ball it up. I take out one of Francisco's shirts and slide it on. I'm instantly hot, but the cuts on my arms and torso are hidden from view.

I look in the mirror again. For a second I think Francisco has come back and he's here in the room with me.

I turn away from my reflection. I close the knife and put it back in my pocket.

As I glance down, the photo of the young Francisco catches my eye.

I should burn it, then scatter it outside, let the wind carry the ashes away. This would keep The Program safe and erase the last vestige of Francisco in the world.

But I don't do that.

I reach down and pick up the photo, carefully buttoning it into the pocket of my flannel shirt.

I don't know why I take the picture with me. It's a danger to me, a piece of evidence that I should not have on my person. By all counts, it's a piece of evidence that should not exist in the world.

Still, I want to save it. I don't know why.

I jog back to the front of the house, where I left Howard. He's zipping water bottles and some snacks into a backpack when I get there.

"Just in case," he says.

"Skills," I say, tapping his forehead.

He smiles.

"Did you find any clues?" he says.

"Not yet. But I have another idea," I say.

FOR THE FIRST TIME, THE DOORS TO THE WORKSHOP ARE OPEN WIDE.

Howard and I stand there looking into an empty space. No vehicles, no people.

Long workbenches have been cleared in haste, tools pushed onto the ground, huge wire spools speared on rods along the wall, now empty of their contents. The ground is littered with sections of colored wire insulation like the red curlicue I found on the ground outside my first night here.

What look like large empty metal barrels are stacked throughout the workshop building. They have been fabricated from scratch, welded, and hammered into what look like sections of giant pipes that are open on both ends.

"What are these things?" Howard says.

"Not sure."

I look down at the concrete floor and see remnants of white beads, almost like poly foam.

"Packing material?" Howard says.

I bend down, pick up some of the particles, and examine them. I sniff. They have only the faintest odor, but I recognize it from my training.

"It's ammonium nitrate," I say.

"What is that?"

"It's a main component of fertilizer. And fuel explosives."

I look at the metal barrels, then think back to the line of panel vans waiting outside the workshop. I imagine them loaded with something like giant pipe bombs.

"Explosives?" Howard says. "What are they planning to blow up?"

My mind runs through locations in the Northeast that could be the focus of the attack, the kinds of places we went to on The Hunt earlier this week. National Guard bases, corporate headquarters, municipal facilities for water or power. A cadre of teen terrorists spreading out through the area, poised to strike.

But that was Moore's plan, and Moore is dead.

Lee is in charge now.

He will have a different approach. A bigger approach.

I think about the vans I saw as I drove in earlier. The other night they were unmarked. But now they all bear the same two words.

NORTHEAST ELECTRIC.

I remember something Lee said about the video game system the first night I came to the encampment.

It's not just a game. It's training.

He told me that he was the one who developed the scenarios for the game.

"You know your way around game systems, don't you?" I ask Howard.

"I'm taking that as a rhetorical question."

"I need you to play a game now."

"Normally I'd be thrilled, but shouldn't we be saving the country?" he says.

"The game. That's how we're going to do it."

I POWER UP THE GAMING SYSTEM BACK IN MY ROOM.

I show Howard how it works, bringing up the profile for Daniel X, my game character from the other night.

"You've got lousy stats," Howard says.

"I've got lousy *game* stats. It's life stats that count."

Howard grins. "Is that a tag line from your spy manual?"

I sigh. "I liked you better when you were a scared kid in the hallway at school."

"That's the old me. I'm an espionage guy now."

I bring up the GAME SCENARIOS prompt screen.

"This is amazing," Howard says. "They created this themselves?"

"It's like a training simulator for them."

"It's very cool," he says. "They've got some real talent here. Too bad it's wasted."

Howard scrolls through the game scenarios.

Laying Plans

Waging War

Tactical Disposition

"Where should we start?" he says. He clicks on one of the scenarios in the middle, but he's blocked from entering the game. "Actually, I asked the wrong question. We have to start at the beginning."

"Why?"

"It's an ascending level design. You can't move up to the next until you've successfully completed the previous."

"So you have to win the scenario before you can proceed?"

"Unless you have cheat codes."

"Nope."

He nods. "Then I'm going to have to win. But it's not going to be easy with your character stats. No offense."

"Enough about the stats."

"Sorry. I'll get started."

"I'm going to watch over your shoulder until I find what I'm looking for."

"What are you looking for?"

"I won't know until I see it," I say.

I'm trained to sort through enormous amounts of visual data, categorizing, sorting, and testing the data against various hypotheses. If the answer is in the game, I trust that I'll be able to see it.

"Can you play with someone watching you?" I say.

"Are you kidding? Have you ever seen a game tournament?"

"I haven't had the pleasure."

"Well, you're going to see one now," Howard says. "Time for Fro-Fro to throw down. *Fro-Fro.* That's Goji's pet name for me."

"I remember," I say.

He bites his lower lip, his face set in concentration as he clicks into the first scenario, LAYING PLANS, the one I played the first night in the camp. The schematic of the campsite comes up, and I watch as the ATF attack unwinds on the screen in front of me.

"This is awesome," Howard says.

Unlike me, he is completely comfortable with the controller, the internal commands, the ways of maneuvering the character through the game. It's like he's fluent in a second language, seamlessly adapting himself to this world with a few clicks.

"There we go," he says. "Now I'm rolling."

He races through the main square in the game, somehow gaining access to the house and making his way to safety without getting slaughtered by the ATF.

Within seconds, the first scenario is over, Howard is triumphant, and Daniel X's character stats have improved considerably.

"That wasn't too bad," Howard says. "On to the next level."

He cracks his neck once, then he's back in.

For the next twenty minutes, Howard plays as fast as he can as I watch what amounts to a gamer's tour through the philosophy underlying Camp Liberty. I see defensive strategies, offensive strategies, various means of attacking infrastructure out in the world. One of the scenarios is divided into multiple sections, part of which takes place inside an artificial World Wide Web where the Daniel X character is transformed into a digital packet that Howard has to navigate through various international servers undetected, until at last he can breach the firewall of a large commercial bank.

I watch it all with Lee in mind, comparing what I see to what I believe I know about him, his desire for attention, his need to better his father.

Eventually Howard arrives at the fifth scenario:

The Attack by Fire

Something about the name feels like it would be attractive to Lee.

Howard opens the game map. It's a series of tall buildings crowded together, a downtown cityscape of some kind.

Howard bites his lip again, studying the map as I watch over his shoulder.

"Where does this one take place?" he says. "Let's see…"

He races through the area in some kind of vehicle.

"Stop the car, Howard."

"I'm not supposed to stop," he says. "See the GPS on the dashboard?"

"Just stop it."

He screeches to a halt on the side of the road.

"Get out and walk around for a second, please."

Howard opens the door of the truck on-screen. He gets out and walks a few steps through the street. The buildings cast long shadows across the pavement from west to east.

It's sunset.

"Do me a favor. Turn around and look at the car."

His character turns. It's not a car at all. It's a white van. NORTHEAST ELECTRIC is stenciled on the side.

"This is the one," I say.

"What city is it?"

Howard uses the character to scan the area, moving to a corner where we can get a better view.

I look at the configuration of the downtown area. One of the buildings looks familiar to me. I run it through a database of buildings in my head.

"The Prudential Tower," I say.

"It's Boston," Howard says.

"What are they doing in Boston?"

Howard puts the game controller on the table. He leans back, rubbing his eyes.

"I'm trying to remember something," he says. "Something that's happening in Boston this week."

I think back to my time at the mall on Sunday. I sat in Barnes & Noble reading magazines, catching up on the news. I passed a rack of newspapers on my way out, glancing at them as I walked by.

One of them was a *Boston Globe*.

I play the scene over in my mind, trying to remember the headline that I saw.

Suddenly it clicks.

"The new JFK Federal Building," I say. "It's opening today."

IT WAS MEANT AS A SYMBOL OF STRENGTH.

A redesigned plaza built around the JFK Federal Building in Government Center downtown. A public park, a tribute to those lost, a new hope for the city.

That is where I'll find Lee.

I drive Howard back to the Manchester Holiday Inn. He remains silent on the way, lost in thought. It doesn't take long before I pull into the parking lot.

"We have to stop them," Howard says.

"*I* have to," I say.

"I want to come with you."

"You've already done your part. More than your part."

He looks at me like he's ready to argue.

"I want you to pack everything and get out of here, Howard. Don't go to New York right away. You'll have to pass through Boston and it's too dangerous. Take a train west to Albany or anywhere else you want to go. You can return home in a week or so."

"How will I know that you're safe?"

"I'll call you."

"Okay," he says. "Meanwhile I'll work on the stuff we talked about. The stuff about your father."

"Drop that for now. Just get yourself to safety. We can talk about the father stuff later. Do you understand me?"

He nods.

"Thanks, Daniel."

"Hey, you're the one who saved me from a torture chair, remember?"

He reaches across the seat and hugs me. I let him do it. Maybe I even hug him back a little.

He opens the truck door, then he pauses before getting out.

"The next time I see you, you'll have a different name," he says.

"That's right."

"But it will still be you."

"It will."

"And you'll remember me?"

"I promise."

"Be safe," he says, and he gets out of the truck.

IT'S A STRAIGHT SHOT TO BOSTON.

I take 93 south the whole way, maxing out my speed, slowing only to avoid police traps. I make good time. It's early evening when I arrive, and downtown Boston is emptying out with the last of the day's business rush.

I move in the opposite direction of most of the traffic, heading into downtown and making my way toward the new and improved JFK Building.

I'm thinking about what I might find there.

Any federal structure built since 9/11 is going to include blast-proof doors, reinforced steel, and exterior barricades. It's not as if a group of white panel vans is going to be able to drive up and park next to the building. Whatever Lee is planning, he's going to have to do it from the inside.

What's more, bombing a federal building would be news, but sadly, it wouldn't be original.

I try to get into Lee's head.

An angry boy, out to prove himself to his father and the world.

The Attack by Fire.

I can't put it together yet, but the federal building is too tempting a target. I head for it now.

Traffic is cordoned off for several blocks around the plaza, so I have to park the truck and go the rest of the way on foot. I can see the building looming in front of me, forty stories of steel and glass rising above the Boston skyline.

It is lit up for its opening, the lights burning bright to the very top, where it is capped by red, white, and blue tracer lights. From the ground, giant spotlights are aimed up the sides of the building, framing it in still more light.

As I step out of the truck, I hear an explosion far off behind me. The sound booms and rolls through the downtown area. I look toward the federal building, but there's nothing happening there. A minute later, there are multiple explosions from different parts of the city. I see a plume of smoke rising black against the sunset several blocks away.

I was wrong about the location of the attack. Maybe there was more to the video game, and I should have let Howard continue to play.

Now I can see smoke plumes rising from different corners of the skyline.

I don't know which direction I should go, which buildings are being targeted.

And then, suddenly, the street goes black.

It happens in a wave, lights blinking out from far away to near, moving up Cambridge Street and continuing past me. Cars screech to a stop as streetlights go out. I hear fender benders and horn blasts on nearby streets.

Then the buildings start going out one by one as the main power grid fails.

The vans at Liberty. They all said NORTHEAST ELECTRIC.

I imagine them parked at substations around the Boston area. Even one failing substation can cast a substantial part of the city into darkness. And several of them?

I look around and see all of downtown blacked out.

Almost all.

Because the federal building is brightly lit. It stands out from the darkness, rising like a beacon in the Boston night.

The federal building would have its own independent generators, and they'd be in operation for a big event like the one that's happening tonight.

Lee's plan takes shape in my mind.

Cast an entire city in darkness except for one building, the building that is a symbol of the government and its power.

That is the beginning, but it's not the end. Not by a long shot.

I race through the dark streets toward the federal building.

SECURITY IS BREAKING DOWN IN THE PLAZA.

The ceremony that was going on in the building has been interrupted by the explosions. Police officers in their dress uniforms rush from the area, called to their ready stations to deal with the mounting crisis. FBI agents in suits are forming around the front of the building, talking on cell phones as they look at the plumes of smoke in the sky around them.

As I approach the side door, I see a service driveway that leads under the building.

After 9/11, many new buildings moved delivery and loading areas out to satellite locations away from the main structure. Others got rid of basements altogether and even first floors, raising buildings up on reinforced pylons to increase survivability in a terrorist attack. But more security means more hassle, time delays, inconvenience. Buildings don't want to give up prime first-floor retail space and the revenue it generates, and executives don't want to wait hours while urgent packages are delayed for screening. In the ensuing years since 9/11, builders have gotten lax, trading safety for convenience.

I look toward the service entrance, where a guard is surrounded by people asking questions as they stream from the building.

It's easy enough to get by without his seeing me.

"The building is being evacuated," he's saying to someone as I pass by, pushing through a group of people and sneaking inside.

I FOLLOW THE SERVICE CORRIDOR TO THE SUBBASEMENT.

A loading dock area.

There are more than a half-dozen white vans down here. They are too heavy, their suspensions low to the ground. I look through the back window of one, and I see the same kind of barrels I saw in the Camp Liberty workshop. They are loaded into the back of the van, interspersed with spools of wire and electrical supplies. To the casual observer, this might pass for a utility van carrying needed equipment for a big event.

But I know it's carrying something else.

Explosives.

I log the locations of vans through the garage. I see the way more vans are parked toward one corner of the structure and the potential consequences of a coordinated explosion on the building above me.

This is Lee's plan. Black out the entire city, then take out the building that best represents the government. If the government can't protect itself, how can it protect its citizens?

I examine the other vans, finding no wires or hard connections between them, which means one of two things. They are on timers, or there is a detonator. If it's a detonator, it could be triggered from far away via cell phone, or it could be a device that requires the bomber to be close at hand.

I think as Lee might think. Does he see himself far away, watching the explosion and chaos from across town?

I don't believe so. My instinct tells me he's here. He's going to make this happen with his own hand, and he wants to be close enough to see it.

Now where will I find him?

I think about Lee in high-pressure situations. I remember him reaching for a brownie during the recruiting event that first night, then for a chocolate bar during The Hunt.

What would Lee do now before the biggest mission of his life?

He might eat some chocolate.

I don't see him in the subbasement, so on a hunch I ask a maintenance man where I can locate the vending machines. He looks at me like I'm crazy.

"You have to get out of here," he says.

"My brother. I need to find him," I say.

He points me toward the staircase.

"One story up on the basement level. Be quick."

I thank him and race up the stairs. I'm running down the hall toward the vending machines when I see Lee coming toward me. My hunch was right. He's biting into a chocolate snack cake, the plastic pulled back halfway to keep his fingers from getting dirty.

He stops when he sees me coming. It takes a moment for him to understand what he's seeing. I was trapped at Camp Liberty and now I am free. I am here and likely a danger to him.

His moment of confusion should be enough for me to get to him, but he recovers more quickly than I expect, dropping the cake, spinning in a 180-degree arc, and darting into the stairwell without a word.

I give chase.

The stairs lead in two directions: up to the lobby or down to the subbasement. I pause and hear footsteps echoing below me. I follow them down.

He has ten meters on me. He is fast from the physical training at the camp, but I am faster, and I make up the distance quickly. He pushes through the door into the subbasement, and I catch it a second later, right on his heels. I calculate the trajectory of a leap and tackle, but before I can accomplish it, he turns and holds his hands up in front of him.

Something glints in the light.

He holds it out so I can see it. He wants me to see it.

A cell phone. The power is on. The screen glows.

This is more than just a cell phone.

It's his detonator.

The only question is how I'm going to get it from him before he can use it.

Ten feet away. It will take me at least two seconds to get to him, plenty of time for him to press a number and complete the call that triggers the explosives.

"How did you escape from camp?" he says.

"I woke up after a few hours. I broke the chair and got myself out."

He thinks about that.

"You're good," he says. "But I don't believe you're that good."

"How do you think I got out?"

"You had help."

He looks behind me, then around the garage, checking to see if I've brought other people with me.

"If I had help, why would I risk coming here? Why not just call the police?"

"I don't know," he says, still looking around us.

I watch his hand. His finger stays in position above the button on his cell.

"Maybe I came because I wanted to be here with you," I say.

"You didn't know where we would be."

We.

That means Miranda is here.

"I figured it out," I say. "I played the game."

His eyes widen.

"Attack by Fire," I say.

"You're smart, Daniel. I always thought so. Why would someone so smart come here uninvited?"

"You're the one who showed me how to play the game. The first night at Liberty. I assumed you showed me for a reason."

He nods, conceding the fact.

"I can see how you might think that," he says. "But I almost killed you earlier."

"Aren't you glad you didn't?" I say with a smile, like all is forgiven.

I note the tiniest glimmer of doubt in his eye.

"So you came to be with me?" he says.

"Yes."

He motions around the space.

"Do you know what's going on here?" he says. "These vans are rigged with explosives, enough to destroy this building. If you played the game, then you know the plan."

"I know."

He waves his cell phone in the air.

"And this," he says, "is the detonator."

He steps back, creating more space between us.

"Do you still want to be here?" he says.

I tighten my face like I'm struggling with the decision. The most important decision of my life—that's what I want him to believe.

He says, "I'll give you a chance to leave if that's what you want."

"Why would you do that?"

"Maybe I owe you one because I shot you with the stun gun."

"You shot me twice," I say.

"So I owe you two," he says, and he smiles.

I see a hint of the Lee I met that first night. A serious kid, but a kid nonetheless.

"Some of the people up there are going to die," I say. "Is that what you want?"

"It's not what I want," he says, "but I have the guts to do what I have to do to make a point. Unlike my father."

"What about Miranda? She's up there, too."

He looks at his feet. I take the opportunity to step toward him. Now there's only seven feet between us.

"I told her not to come," he says.

"But she didn't listen to you, did she?"

"She wanted to be with me," he says. "She's my sister, and she's loyal. She said we should be together until the end."

"After The Hunt, you asked me if I had what it takes to sacrifice myself for a cause. Do you remember?"

"I remember."

"I have what it takes," I say.

He smiles.

"So it's the three of us, then," he says.

"Yes."

I move toward him a step at a time, covering the remaining distance.

At first he starts to back up, but I keep coming, raising my arms to the sides so I appear to be no threat to him.

"It'll be good to keep each other company," I say.

He tries to hide his relief, but his body betrays him. His shoulders lower slightly; the tension in his back releases.

It's not easy to die alone in a dark garage, even if it's for a cause you think is just. I'm offering company in his last moments, and he's desperate enough to want it.

I sigh and take off my glasses.

"When do we do it?" I say.

I detach the glasses from the right temple arm, and I let the frames fall to the ground.

"You dropped your glasses," he says.

The moment he looks down, I'm on him. My free hand grasps the wrist that is holding the cell phone, while my other arm swings around and presses the weaponized needle into his neck.

The same needle I used to kill his father.

The needle contains three doses of poison. I've never had to use more than one.

Until now.

Lee tries to trigger the phone, but I'm exerting all the pressure I can muster into the nerve ganglion above his wrist, preventing him from closing his hand.

I need three seconds for the drug to take full effect, maybe a little more because he's young and has some physical training. He fights me for half that time, trying with all his might to bring his thumb down on the keypad.

But I press his wrist even harder and torque backward until I feel bones being crushed.

His strength suddenly ebbs, and he slumps toward me. I grab the cell phone from him.

He falls into my arms, his face near mine.

I feel his chest expand and contract, struggling to take a final breath before paralysis makes it impossible.

His mouth moves. He's trying to say something, but he doesn't get the chance.

I shift my head to one side, feel his face slump against my shoulder, a spot of wet saliva touching my neck above my collar, as intimate as a kiss.

I don't look in his eyes.

I feel them searching for me, but I don't want to see.

I wait for the gurgling noises to stop, for the last bit of life to drain from him. I wait for the boy who was Lee to die along with his past and his future.

I take them both away from him.

Because it's my job.

At least it *was*.

I think of the tubule pressed into the tape over my chest, the Program chip contained within it. The betrayal that chip represents.

That's when I realize: I didn't kill Lee because Mike ordered me to.

I did it because he was dangerous. To himself. To me. To the world at large.

I did it, not because The Program told me to but because it was the right thing to do.

Something moves in the shadows over Lee's shoulder.

It takes my eyes a moment to adjust before I can see what it is.

Who it is.

Miranda.

She's been watching the whole time.

She turns suddenly and disappears into the darkness. I hear the echo of her footsteps and the sound of a door slamming in the stairwell.

I have to catch her. But not yet. First I must finish here.

I lay Lee's body on the concrete floor. I check for a pulse.

He's gone.

I make sure the power is off on the cell phone, and then I smash it with my heel, putting this detonator permanently out of commission.

Lee is dead, his plot thwarted.

But that is only half my mission.

The other half just ran out the door.

I pass a few remaining servers heading for the exit, and I ask if they've seen a girl. They point in the opposite direction, deeper into the building.

I grab a maintenance jacket from a door hook, keeping my head down as I weave my way through the servers, slowing my pace as I walk up a ramp into the lobby that leads to the main atrium.

There are a few agents clustered about the room, conferencing intensely about the events outside. They do not know the danger that is below them this very moment. But I need them out of the building.

"Bomb!" I shout, pointing under our feet.

That gets them going. They race through the lobby, shouting for people to get out.

I make my way along the outskirts of the room. Suddenly I see a flash of movement from across the atrium. It's Miranda, running toward the elevator banks.

I sprint across the lobby, unnoticed amid the evacuation in progress. But by the time I get to the elevators, she is gone.

I look at the floor indicators. They're all at lobby level save one. The car on the end is rising past the twenty-first floor.

I remember Miranda the night she followed me up the mountain. She's used to climbing up high, going where she can get some perspective.

Miranda should have escaped the area, but she did not. She got on an elevator.

I watch it rising ever higher. I'm guessing Miranda will not stop until she gets to the top of the building.

That's where I will go, too.

THE OBSERVATION PLATFORM.

I step out to panoramic views of Boston through glass, interrupted by a few neighboring towers of equal or greater height. I do not see Miranda, but her elevator is up here, its doors locked open, the alarm ringing continuously.

I am on the observation deck, but it is possible to go higher.

The roof.

I see the entrance to the access stairs, the door swinging open on well-greased hinges. I take the stairs two at a time, the elevator alarm fading behind me.

I open the roof door, and a gust hits me in the face. Warm night air, whipped into a frenzy by the turbulence of high-altitude winds.

Miranda is standing three-quarters of the way across the roof, steadying herself against the wind, looking away from me. I let the door close loudly behind me, hoping the sound carries.

She turns.

I want her to turn. No surprises. Not up here.

I move slowly toward her across the roof.

She waits until I'm in earshot, and then she says, "I saw what you did to my brother. He was right. You *were* sent here to stop us."

"Yes," I say.

"You're an agent of some kind."

I nod. A pained expression crosses her face.

"I should have let Lee kill you," she says.

"Why didn't you? You knew enough about me to at least be suspicious."

She doesn't answer, only glances toward the street, where the police and military vehicles are pouring into the blacked-out blocks surrounding the plaza.

"You were trying to help me from the beginning," I say. "You warned me not to come to camp, you kept my secret when you found me in the woods, and then you saved my life with your brother."

"What does it matter now?" she says, and she steps closer to the roof's edge.

"It matters to me."

"I liked you," she says. "That's why I did those things."

"*Liked*? Past tense?"

"Uh, things have gotten a little complicated, wouldn't you say, Daniel? Or whatever your real name is."

My real name.

I haven't said my real name to anyone in years.

I look at Miranda on the edge of the roof. The wind whips her hair around her shoulders.

I try to focus on my mission. Two targets, only one of which is down.

But I cannot think about that now.

Without the chip inside me, my feelings race around, intense and out of control.

"Maybe there's a case to be made," I say.

"What kind of case?"

"A legal argument. You were held against your will at camp. You didn't plan this bombing. You were forced to go along with it."

"They're still going to find me guilty."

"But there are mitigating circumstances. You'll avoid the death penalty."

"So I spend the rest of my life in prison? No, thank you. They're going to need someone to blame, Daniel. Someone to punish."

"There's still a chance for leniency," I say. "A few years in prison, and then you can go home."

"What home?" she says.

She's right.

Her father and brother are dead. Camp Liberty will be dismantled.

Her hand slips into her jacket pocket and comes out holding something.

A cell phone just like her brother's.

She looks at me across the expanse of rooftop. I step toward her, and she moves closer to the edge.

She holds up the cell phone between us like a warning.

"You know what this is?" she says.

"A backup detonator," I say.

"That's right."

A gust of wind blows hard and I have to steady myself, redistributing my weight.

I look at the way Miranda is standing. Her body is tight, resistant. She is desperate and out of options.

My mission is to kill her. At least according to Mike.

I haven't heard from Father or Mother in days. Mike showed up claiming to be some kind of messenger, but can I be sure why he really came?

For all I know, The Program has ceased to exist. Mike could be lying to me, sending me after her for his own reasons.

Maybe he was embittered by Francisco's turning against The Program. His first recruit became a traitor, so he invented a mission as payback.

If there is no real mission, I'm out here alone without a true purpose.

Which means there might be options for me. For both of us.

"Would you leave with me?" I ask Miranda.

"And go where?"

"Somewhere. Anywhere."

"You want to take me into custody."

"I'm not a cop."

"Maybe not, but the street below is filled with them. I agree to go, and you take me down and turn me over to them. Then you walk away."

"That's not what I'm talking about."

"What, then?"

She lowers the detonator.

I say, "The first night on the mountain, you told me you wanted to know what was happening in the real world. Maybe you can live there for a while, see what it's like. Maybe we both can."

Her face softens for a moment, then her eyes cloud over and her face turns to stone.

"If I left with you, what would that make me?" Miranda says.

"It would make you free," I say.

"No," she says, shaking her head. "It would make me a traitor. Like my mother."

My eyes are drawn to the motion in her hand. I look down and see her dialing a number on the cell phone.

"Don't do this," I say.

"There's no way out."

I think about four days ago, standing in a circle of soldiers with their weapons pointed at me. The riddle that Father created for me.

"That's not true," I tell her. "There's always a way."

"I'm sorry," she says, and she dials the final number on the cell and hits CALL.

I brace myself for the explosion—

A second passes, then two and three.

Nothing happens.

She looks at the cell, making sure the number is correct. She presses it again.

I'm looking at the giant antennas around us.

"We're surrounded by high-frequency radio antennas," I say. "They can block cell signals at this proximity."

Her eyes dart around the roof.

"It's done, Miranda."

She peers over the edge of the roof toward the ground.

"It's not done," she says. "You said so yourself. There's always a way. I can still get a signal. I just need to be closer to the ground."

I suddenly understand her, the insanity of what she is contemplating.

"You don't know if the vans were wired correctly. You don't know if your cell phone signal can transmit through the walls of the subbasement."

"But there's a chance, isn't there? If I were closer to the explosives. There's a chance it would work."

I hear sirens down below us, their sound carried up by the wind.

"The bomb squad may already be down there," I say. "They may have dismantled everything."

"Not everything," she says. "I don't think so. Truck bombs with fail-safes and trip wires? It's going to take them a long time."

"We don't know that."

I'm moving steadily toward her now, a step at a time.

"I think you're wrong," she says. "The bombs are still armed. They just need the right signal."

"Don't do it," I say. "Come away with me."

She smiles.

"You think you're going to save me, but you're wrong."

She looks out across the dark expanse of the city. The wind pulls at her clothing.

"I don't need to be saved. I just need to finish what we started."

"We?"

"My family. My legacy," she says, and she steps off the building.

I rush to the edge, and I see her falling back into space.

Few people could do what she's attempting. A fall like this would cause most people to flail, spinning out of control. They might pass out before they hit the ground or even have a heart attack.

But Miranda expertly adjusts her body in the air, spreading her arms and legs in the classic arch position of a skydiver. A falling object does not accelerate indefinitely. It reaches a terminal velocity and cannot fall any faster. By taking the arch position, she controls her descent, creating wind resistance and increasing the time it takes for her to reach terminal velocity.

There is no way that she will survive, but she's not trying to survive.

She's trying to complete her mission.

In the last seconds I see her pull her arms together above her head, the cell phone still clutched tightly in one hand, the other reaching to press the keys.

I turn away before she hits the ground.

A second later I feel the deep rumble of explosives detonating far below me.

The vibration travels up the steel of the building like a great shiver, and then the roof suddenly tilts to one side as a critical support lets loose in the structure far below. The angle steepens as another support gives way.

This is not a professional demolition, a neat series of explosions that will collapse one floor upon the next. It's an enormous blast in one corner of the building that sends it leaning sickeningly to one side.

There's no way for me to get out of the building in time.

The best I can do is to run in the direction of the building's fall.

My mind is racing, calculating angle and distance as it changes moment to moment.

There are perhaps thirty feet between this rooftop and the next nearest building, a smaller tower across the street.

Thirty feet away and a seventy-foot drop. An impossible jump.

But as the federal building tilts, the space between the buildings decreases.

If I can time it right, it will be like jumping from one falling domino to the next one that has not yet fallen.

If I can time it.

Metal screams and windows explode beneath me. I hear bolts snapping and people shouting from the ground below.

Terror beats in my chest. I imagine jumping into space and falling, plummeting to the ground like Miranda.

Twenty-five feet between rooftops now.

That's what my eye is telling me, but I might be wrong. Under this amount of duress, judgment can falter. I'm trained to work under pressure, to make significant and life-changing decisions under the most extraordinary circumstances.

Fifteen feet might be an acceptable risk. But twenty-five feet?

I've got seconds left to decide.

I'm too afraid to move. I'm frozen in place with the calculations racing through my mind, the distance, the possibility of making the jump, the likelihood of making a mistake.

The building tilts farther, knocking me to the rooftop. I manage to get back to my feet.

If I stay here, I'm going to die. If I jump, at least I'll have a chance.

Certain death or uncertain life.

Suddenly distance doesn't matter.

I propel myself forward, running for the edge. I wait until the last possible moment, and then I jump into space—

I'm more than halfway across when I realize I'm not going to make it.

I'm descending faster than I'm moving forward, and even though I elongate my body and reach with my arms, there's no way I will get to the other side.

I flash back to a week ago, the camp in Vermont, a beautiful summer day, a dark green lake. I was leaping from a cliff, trusting fate as I dove into the water.

It's easy to trust fate when you think it's on your side.

But sometimes fate turns against you.

The way it did me, the day I met Mike.

The way it does to the people I meet on my missions, the people who breathe their last breaths in my arms.

The way it's turning against me now.

Because now I am falling.

There is open air beneath my feet. I take a final breath, filling my lungs with oxygen, preparing myself for the terrifying drop to the pavement below.

Fate will have its way with me now in the form of a last fall.

My training doesn't matter anymore. I'm falling, and there's nothing I can do about it.

That's when I see it.

A rope.

It appears in front of me seemingly out of nowhere, bright orange knots in intervals down its length.

For a moment, I think I'm imagining it. A visual hallucination from a desperate boy who is about to die.

Illusion or not, I reach for it.

My fingers wrap around hard nylon cord. Real cord.

I grasp it and my hands slip. It takes every bit of strength I have to hang on hard enough to stop my fall.

But I am strong. I don't let go.

My hands burn down the length of the rope until I come to a stop near the very end. Suddenly I go from falling to rising into the air, the rope swinging from side to side as I'm buffeted by strong winds from above.

I look up, following the length of nylon upward, craning my neck until I find its source. The rope has been dropped from a helicopter.

I stare up at its belly as it rises slowly, the rotors catching air and pulling me away.

When I look below, I see the Federal Building collapsing onto a downtown street, a rolling dust cloud enveloping several city blocks. It is an image that is terrible and familiar at the same time.

With the building gone, the darkness in the city is complete. Boston is a black void beneath me. Above me is open air.

I climb.

I reach the skid of the helicopter, then pull myself up into the cargo hold. I recognize this helicopter. I flew one just like it in Vermont less than a week ago.

I flop onto the floor and pull the door closed behind me.

The pilot looks back at me, a concerned expression on his face.

It's Father.

"WELCOME BACK," HE SAYS.

"Where did you come from?" I say.

"What does it matter? I'm here. Dropping you a lifeline."

Lifeline.

It's the same term Francisco used.

"Why now?" I say.

"Because you needed one now, wouldn't you say?"

"And before? When I was cut off in Camp Liberty, trying to communicate with you?"

"That's a longer conversation," he says.

I watch Father, his face impassive as he scans my body, assessing my health.

"You weren't injured," he says.

More a statement than a question.

"I wasn't injured," I say.

"Then let's get you out of here."

I USE A FIELD DRESSING TO WRAP MY BLEEDING HANDS.

Then I climb into the passenger seat next to Father.

I look out through the windshield. A moment ago the sky looked like death. Now it looks like the opposite.

"I haven't been able to get ahold of you for four days," I say.

Father won't look at me. His focus is straight ahead as he monitors the helicopter's controls.

"I tried to contact you," I say angrily. "We had contingencies in place, a safe house, a plan—"

"I know," Father says.

"But you disappeared! Why?"

"I was under orders," he says. "I had no choice but to cut you off."

I take a long breath, forcing back the rage that's growing inside me.

"Tell me why," I say.

"First Francisco dropped off the radar, then you disappeared into the camp. The Program was hemorrhaging. That's what it seemed like from our perspective. We had to stop the bleeding, or we risked losing everything. Can you understand that?"

Mike told the truth. I went into camp, and The Program interpreted that as a betrayal.

"What did you think happened to me?" I ask.

"We thought you'd been recruited, that you had turned."

"You think my loyalty is that fragile?"

"As we discussed before the mission, there were questions about you."

"But you tested me. You said I was fit for duty."

"And then you disobeyed orders and went into Liberty."

"So you wrote me off."

"You can understand why we had doubts after what we've seen recently. From you and the other soldier."

Two operatives breach protocol, one after the other. From The Program's perspective it couldn't be a coincidence—they'd have to assume it was systemic. At that point everyone's allegiance is suspect until proven otherwise.

On one hand, their choice to cut me off makes sense.

On the other hand, they left me in the field to fend for myself, assuming betrayal instead of coming to get me.

I say, "If you still had doubts, you should have contacted me. We could have talked about it."

"If we had tried to contact you in the camp, Moore would have killed you. We had to assume he'd discovered our soldier and was expecting a second mission insertion. Any suspicious behavior, and he would have acted against you. So we could not contact you."

"If you were so worried about Moore killing me, why did you decide to do it yourself?"

"What are you talking about?"

"The kill order," I say.

"We never put out a kill order."

I watch Father's face to determine if he's lying. I don't see any evidence of it, but he's expert at hiding such things.

I say, "You sent a freelance team to attack me at the safe house."

"That team wasn't meant for you," he says.

"Funny, because it was me they were shooting at."

Father exhales slowly, his grip tightening on the cyclic.

"We know you left Camp Liberty to go on an operation at Lake Massabesic."

"The water treatment plant."

"That's right. We saw the photo that was transmitted from the plant. We had to assume you'd turned. If so, you had likely given us up to Moore. Maybe you'd told him about the safe house. He would send people to investigate, perhaps try to access our comms. We hired a freelance team to wait for them. Just in case."

"But you'd already sanitized the house. Even if Moore's people had come, they would have found nothing."

"It was an opportunity."

I look at Father. His face is composed again, his control of the helicopter precise.

"What kind of opportunity?" I say.

"The woman you met at the safe house is an ex–FBI agent. She was part of a team that investigated Moore a decade ago."

I think about the woman, her reaction under fire, the way she managed herself in what should have been a panicked situation.

"You put a freelance team in place so if Moore's people showed up at her house—"

"It would look like Moore was exacting revenge," Father says. "An attack in a suburban neighborhood. Civilian casualties. Moore's people on the scene."

"You were setting him up," I say, suddenly understanding.

"It would be an incontrovertible reason for the FBI to go in and break up the camp. Not the mission we had in mind, but we realized we had to take Moore out one way or another."

It's an ingenious plan, if you disregard the fact that The Program was willing to sacrifice an innocent family to achieve it.

I realize now that I made a mistake thinking the freelance team was sent for me. If The Program wanted me dead, they have other ways to do it.

Quieter ways.

Father says, "We had no way of knowing you would be the one to go to the safe house."

"But it *was* me," I say. "And I was alone."

"Regretful," Father says. "But you did what you were trained to do. Thank god you survived."

Father adjusts the helicopter, arcing to the west, away from Boston.

When I look back at him, he's watching me.

"You spent a long time inside that camp," he says.

"Barely three days all told."

"But it was enough," Father says.

"Enough to kill Moore? Yes."

"Enough to find out the truth. About our soldier."

I nod. This is what Father is interested in. I see him struggling to appear casual.

"What happened to the soldier?" he says.

"He's dead."

I watch Father's face, gauging his reaction, trying to understand what he feels, *if* he feels.

I see nothing there. No sadness. No pity.

"You're sure he's dead?" Father says.

"I'm the one who killed him."

He clears his throat.

"He turned," Father says, his voice barely a whisper.

I nod.

"How did they do it?" he says.

I remember what Moore told me. Francisco had already turned against The Program long before he got to Camp Liberty. Moore only provided the possibility of a different life, an alternative to The Program. One that was more attractive to Francisco.

I could tell this to Father, but for some reason, I don't want him to know.

It's frightening enough for him to think that The Program could be outmatched by another organization. But the idea that his soldiers are thinking autonomously would be far more damaging.

I will hang on to this information until I need it.

So I tell Father a different story.

"Moore brainwashed him. Cult induction techniques at a sophisticated level. Thought reform, complete isolation, induced dependency, paranoia of the outside world..."

"That shouldn't have worked on someone like Francisco."

"I was up there for three days and things started to get confusing. Francisco was there for almost four months."

"So he's gone?"

"I made sure of it."

"Protect The Program," Father says.

I meet his gaze.

"My prime objective," I say.

"Well done," Father says.

I buckle myself into the seat and lean back.

"Enough for now," Father says. "There's plenty of time to debrief later."

I nod and close my eyes.

My body shuts down after all it's been through, slipping into recuperative mode. After a few minutes I fall asleep.

I jerk awake only once to find Father looking at me. He gestures to a water bottle by the side of my seat. I take a chug, spit soot on the floor between my legs. Then I gulp down half the bottle, lean back, and fall into a deep sleep again.

The nightmares, whatever they might be, will come later.

Now I dream only of wind and sky, the thud of the rotors carrying me to safety, the magic of a rope appearing in front of me from out of nowhere.

I wake up when I feel the helicopter begin to descend. I'm looking down at a military base.

"Hanscom AFB," Father says. "We're about thirty miles northwest of the city."

"Won't we be seen?" I say.

"The Air Force and National Guard have been mobilized," Father says. "And there's nothing unusual about a military helicopter putting down on a military base."

Father lands the helicopter, the blades slowly winding down above us.

I look at my jeans and the bloodstained shirt. Father notes it.

"There's a bag behind the seat for you," he says.

I find a small duffel in the back. I open the bag and take out a new military jacket and camos. An ID card identifying me as a National Guardsman.

"That should get you off base easily enough. Not that you need the help," Father says.

I can't take my shirt off in front of Father or he will see my wounds. There will be questions. Instead I slip the military-issue coat over my bloodied T-shirt, then I slide on the pants.

"Reports from Boston suggest that casualties will be minimal. You triggered the evacuation early enough to save lives. Homeland Security is rounding up the squads that blew the power grid."

"They're just kids," I say.

"Dangerous kids," Father says. "But they'll be dealt with fairly. In any case, it's got nothing to do with us. Not anymore."

I pull the Guard ID out of the bag and slip it into my pocket.

"What happened on that roof?" Father says. "You couldn't stop this?"

"I misjudged the girl."

"That seems to be an issue for you."

I hold my body still, willing myself not to react to Father's statement.

"Not an issue," I say.

But I'm lying. Because I tried to save Miranda.

Would I have really left The Program in order to be with her?

I'll never know. She didn't give me the chance to find out.

"Once is an anomaly," Father says. "Twice is an issue."

He's right. Samara was one. Miranda is two. There won't be a number three. The Program won't allow it.

"I didn't know she had a backup detonator," I say.

"You couldn't get it away from her?"

Father's question makes me angry.

"She jumped before I could get to her," I say quickly. "I watched her die."

I want to say more, but I stop myself. Without the chip in place, my emotions are raw, too close to the surface. I can't trust myself to speak.

Father's expression changes at my tone. His face softens.

"You've been through a lot," he says.

He says it like it matters to him, like he's concerned for me.

"The explosion shook me up a little. I'll be okay."

The rotors whir above us. I pull my emotions inside, hardening my face to a soldier's countenance.

"I think you'll be okay, too," he says. "In fact I'm sure of it."

I grab the duffel and open the helicopter door.

"This thing we have is fragile, Zach."

Zach.

It's a shock to hear him say my name.

"The Program is fragile," he says. "It doesn't seem so, but it is. It's based on a foundation of trust."

"Of course," I say.

"We have to trust each other," Father says.

I think of the freelance team in the backyard of the safe house.

I think of the chip hidden under the tape on my chest right now. The things Francisco shared with me about The Program.

Francisco may have gone insane, but there was truth to what he said.

I look at Father.

I don't trust him. Not anymore.

I use every skill at my disposal to hide my feelings from him, masking them under layers and layers of other feelings, then capping those with a surface of calm.

Father's waiting for me to say something.

"I trust you," I say.

"Good," he says.

He nods once. We're done.

"Leave the base. Destroy your phone. There's a Stop&Shop two blocks away with an Infiniti G37 in the lot. Check your e-mail from a safe location when you get clear. We'll send you instructions."

Back to business as usual. The assignment followed by the waiting.

"Will it be a long wait this time?" I say.

"I can't be sure."

I start to climb out of the helicopter.

"Zach," Father says.

I hesitate in the doorway.

"If it gets to be too much, will you call me?"

"Too much?"

"The thoughts. I know waiting can be difficult for you."

"I'll call."

"I'd prefer it. These last few days—" He pauses, choosing his words carefully. "I had to make some choices that were difficult for me on a personal level. I'm not supposed to be telling you this, but I think it's important that you know. I'd like it if this was an anomaly, something that we move on from."

"I'd like that, too," I say.

"Call me if you have an issue. Don't let it get to this point again."

"I won't. I promise."

I step onto the tarmac. The blades rev up behind me, whipping the air into a frenzy as the helicopter takes off, banks hard, and disappears in the night.

There is an iPhone charging in the center console and a set of documents in the glove compartment. I push down the visor, open the vanity mirror, and blow hot air on it. A number appears there, the secure PIN for the phone that will serve as my code for this waiting period. I memorize it and wipe the mirror clean.

I start the car. The engine roars to life. It's the big engine that Infiniti is known for, 330 horsepower of muscle, a rare indulgence these days.

I pull out of the parking lot, the wind whipping through open windows.

The Program is back, our protocols are in place, and the elements have been arranged for my safe egress.

It's as if the last four days never happened. The Program never disappeared, never left me.

Part of me wants to accept this. I was used and I survived. This was my mission. It was more complex than the ones that preceded it, but so be it. Everything is back to normal now.

But another part of me knows this is a lie. I trusted these people once.

Never again.

A phone vibration snaps me back to the present moment.

It's not coming from the new Program iPhone in the center console. It's the iPhone I forgot I had. The one connected to Howard.

"Jets leave trails in the sky," he says when I answer the phone.

His voice is rushed and excited, Howard in fast-forward mode.

"I'm not following you," I say.

"Jets leave trails. So do digital signals. E-mails, voice messages, interagency communications. They all leave faint trails online, even the secure ones. *Especially* the secure ones, because even though they are erased, they are not overwritten by the amount of traffic that overwrites normal public communications."

"Where are you going with this, Howard?"

"I followed the trails."

"Followed them where?"

"To your father."

I've accelerated without realizing it, and when I look up, I'm bearing down on the rear bumper of the truck ahead. I swerve, narrowly missing it as I switch to an empty lane.

"Where are you now?" I say.

"I'm still in Manchester."

"I told you to get out of there."

"I just had to do one thing before I left," he says. "And one thing led to another, and the data started to come in—"

"Promise me you'll pack up as soon as we get off the phone."

"Absolutely," he says. "I triple swear it. That's what Goji makes me do when I promise to FaceTime her in Osaka, but I forget and—"

"My father. Tell me where you found him."

"Right, right," he says, getting back on task. "He was in the historical data. The Program data. Remember that twelve-year-old hacker I told you about when you were in New York?"

"The Loop kid."

"That's right. Infinite L∞P. The one who thinks he's hot shit. Well, guess what? He screwed up and left a back door open in the rear quadrant of a firewall. Not really open. More like a tunnel that looks closed from the outside when it's not. The point is I got inside and I cracked one of The Program's remote servers."

"You're telling me you found data about my father on a Program server?"

"That's right. They were communicating with him."

"You mean they made secret contact as a precursor to killing him? Like setting him up before the mission?"

"That's the weird thing," Howard says. "They were communicating openly with him."

"I don't understand."

"Like internal agency communications."

"My father was working for The Program?"

"No," Howard says. "The Program was working for your father."

"How is that possible?"

"I've got e-mail evidence, secure text messages, even some—"

Howard stops talking.

"Howard? Hello?"

The line goes dead.

I slam the brakes, skidding the car to the side of the road.

I dial Howard's number, let it ring. There's no answer.

I wait sixty seconds and do it again.

Nothing.

I wait another two minutes, and I call again. Still nothing.

I whip the car around, crossing four lanes of traffic to the protest of angry horns. I race back east, plotting a route that will avoid Boston while taking me north toward Manchester.

I call Howard five more times over the course of several hours without a response. Finally I give up, knowing I'm not going to reach him. I try to imagine a reason why that might be, a reason that does not include something terrible happening to him, but I cannot.

There's nothing left for me to do but focus on the driving, the road in front of me, the mile markers ticking off on the highway, one every thirty-seven seconds.

THE HOTEL CLERK TELLS ME HE NEVER CHECKED OUT.

I go to the suite and knock, but nobody answers.

I note light along the bottom edge of the doorway. That's when I pick the lock and slip inside.

The room is empty. A single overhead lamp has been left on in the front room, like you might do if you were leaving during the day and not coming back until evening.

There's a half-eaten bag of Cheetos spilled across the desk. Nothing else.

I find Howard's duffel on the floor of the closet. I unzip it and look through the contents.

There are multiple cords and power supplies, but his laptops are missing. At least they're not in the bag.

I check the rest of the room, then force my way into the adjoining suite.

It's empty, too.

The laptops are gone. Perhaps Howard had to leave in a rush and took them with him? For a moment, my mind is flooded with hope, the possibility that Howard is safe, that he used some of what I taught him and his natural skill set to get away.

But then my eye settles on a spot on the carpet. A single dark spot, less than the size of a dime.

It's blood.

My hope fades.

I examine the spot more closely and see that it is crusted on the surface of the carpet. No vacuum has passed over it, no footsteps have crushed it into the pile.

Which means it's fresh blood.

I told Howard to be careful. I told him his life depended on it.

Now he is gone, and there is a drop of blood.

On a hunch I take out my iPhone and dial his number. I hear buzzing coming from somewhere in the suite.

Howard's phone.

I search top to bottom. I finally find it deep under the bed, pushed all the way up against the wall at an unusual angle.

I imagine the scenario. Howard is struggling with someone. The phone falls and gets kicked under the bed during the struggle. Whoever grabs him fails to go after it. Maybe they didn't see it fall, or they were in too great of a rush and could not afford to take the time to retrieve it.

I tap through Howard's phone menu until I get to recent calls. I see nine missed calls from earlier today and a tenth call made just now.

All from my number.

Nothing else.

Perhaps there is more information to be had from the phone. I put it in my pocket to examine later.

I do a final pass of the room, looking for any clue I might have missed.

I find nothing.

I'm on my way out the door when the hotel phone rings.

I look at it on the bedside table, the red light flashing to indicate an incoming call.

Three rings, and I pick it up.

"I knew you'd come back," the voice says.

I know the voice instantly.

It's Mike.

"Listen to me carefully," Mike says. "This is an open line."

I grunt acknowledgment.

"They have your friend," Mike says.

"They?"

"You heard me correctly."

Mike is a part of The Program. If it's The Program who has Howard, Mike should have said *we*.

We have your friend.

But he didn't say *we*. He said *they*. Two possibilities:

1) Someone other than The Program has Howard.
2) The Program has Howard, but Mike is excluding
   himself from the equation.

"I have to see you," Mike says.

I've seen Mike twice since graduation. Both times have been on his terms. Both times my life has been in danger.

"Do you remember the first place we ever met?" he says.

It was the middle of seventh grade. Mike appeared in our school as a transfer student. I first saw him at school, but that's not the first place we met.

I was at Twelve Corners in Brighton, New York, a suburb of Rochester, one afternoon. I bought a pizza bagel, then walked out of the store and bumped into him.

"You're the kid in my homeroom," he said.

My life would end six weeks later because of that meeting, but I had no way of knowing it then.

"You remember, don't you?" Mike says on the phone.

"Yes."

"Meet me two days from now," he says.

And nothing more.

I hang up the phone, my head spinning.

I glance at my reflection in the mirror above the dresser. I am haggard from lack of food and sleep. I cannot think clearly or organize my thoughts.

Worst of all, I am afraid.

I take off my shirt. I peel the tape from over my scar, and I locate the chip on the back of it.

The neurosuppressor. That's what Francisco called it.

I pull it from the tape.

The wound on my chest is still fresh. I use my fingers to rip the skin apart, revealing pink-and-red flesh below.

The blood comes. I ignore it.

I put the chip on the tip of my finger, and I put it back inside me, pressing it hard against the flesh of my pectoral muscle.

The pain is incredible, but it doesn't stop me. I press until the miniature probes pierce the muscle. A faint glow emanates from within the glass tubule.

It's working again.

I close the wound and reseal it with the tape.

Already I can feel the emotional edge receding, my body coming back to stillness, my mind slowing.

I look at myself in the mirror again.

I look stronger, more capable. Maybe it's only in my imagination. No matter.

If I'm going to find Howard, I'll need every advantage I can get.

ACKNOWLEDGMENTS

I'd like to thank my publishers—Little, Brown Books for Young Readers in the U.S. and Orchard Books in the U.K.—for their continued support of the Unknown Assassin series. Special thanks to the LBYR team—my editor, Kate Sullivan; Leslie Shumate; Andrew Smith; Megan Tingley; and so many others who have been with the series from the very beginning.

Thanks to the many foreign publishers who have picked up the series and translated it for readers around the world.

Thanks to Sony Pictures and Overbrook Entertainment for their efforts in bringing the Unknown Assassin to the big screen.

Special thanks to Judy Kim for her support and encouragement throughout the writing of this second book.

And finally, an extra-special shout-out to the readers, bloggers, booksellers, and librarians who read and enjoyed the first book when it was published as *Boy Nobody*. You've shared it with friends and family, reviewed it online, and helped to spread the word in so many ways. Now the series has grown into the Unknown Assassin. I hope you're as excited by that as I am. It's a pleasure to share another book with you.